**TWO COMPLETE TALES OF
CLASSIC WESTERN ACTION
BY THE WEST'S MOST
POPULAR STORYTELLER
AL CODY**

THE OUTCASTS

The Blackfoot camp welcomed Johnny Hawkins as he fled from unfriendly tribes—until their hunters started coming back empty and their people began to go hungry. They blamed their bad luck on Johnny's presence, and the only way he could regain their faith was to capture a wild white horse, which legend said meant the end of famine.

THE RANCH AT POWDER RIVER

Montana Abbott thought he was in for an easy time when he took over the job as foreman of the ranch at Powder River. But soon he was caught in a deadly crossfire when he realized that the herd he was driving had been rustled from another ranch—and the rustlers had left no witnesses in their wake, just a bloody trail of corpses.

THE OUTCASTS

Floundering, Johnny went under, choking on water as he tried to yell; the sound came out as a smothered gurgle. Then he was caught by a quickening current, swept like a log in the depths. Frantically he tried to swim, getting his head above water, gasping, before being rolled under again. The dark waters were terror-laden . . . .

THE RANCH AT POWDER RIVER

Montana stripped his shirt and tore it into long, thin strips. Mercifully, the wounded man remained unconscious. But a groan was twisted from white lips as Montana took the protruding arrowhead in both hands and broke it with a swift motion. Then, seizing the shaft on the opposite side, he pulled swiftly and strongly to extricate the crimson rod. Its removal was followed by twin gusts of blood. After the bandaging, it would be up to the Almighty whether the man would survive or not . . .

THE OUTCASTS AND THE RANCH AT POWDER RIVER

—— AL CODY ——

LEISURE BOOKS   NEW YORK CITY

A LEISURE BOOK®

November 1989

Published by

Dorchester Publishing Co., Inc.
276 Fifth Avenue
New York, NY 10001

THE OUTCASTS

1

Somewhere, back in the darkening woods, an owl hooted.

At the eerie gabbling, Johnny Hawkins' already dragging feet anchored, as though he had stepped into wet sticky gumbo. Chills not caused by the prairie wind chased themselves up and down his spine, playing tag among the hairs crowding suddenly against his old coonskin cap. Probably that had been an owl, just as it was supposed to be; on the other hand, this rim of the Nebraska country was extremely wild and lonely, here along the upper reaches of the wide, wild Missouri—

The sun had set only moments before. It seemed as though there should have been a splash, for the effect, glimpsed through tree branches, was like a lantern dropping into the middle of the river, with the oil spilling out in a burst of flame. Now the light was gone, as though smothered by the rolling current. Among the trees, darkness was settling like a flock of crows.

As though the owl's outcry had frozen all movement, all stir and sound had ceased; the only audible noise was the pounding of his own heart. Gulping a deeper breath, Johnny forced his feet to move again. After all, he had volunteered to come ashore, along with the crew members, to load wood which had been cut and stacked a short distance back from the river, wood needed to fuel the engines of the river boat.

The *Oregon* was a stern-wheeler, long and wide and light enough in draft to run on a good dew, as her pilot liked to boast. She was moored a stone's throw away, swinging in the current from a pair of stout ropes which ran around a stunted pine near the water's edge. The paddle wheel hung poised, so that a quick thrust and dip would send the packet away from shore like an unhooked trout. Smoke drifted above it in a lazy curl, then blended with the night. To Johnny's imaginative eyes, it took on the form of a question mark.

His armful of wood, sawed into yard-long lengths, was piled as high as he could carry, forcing him to tilt his chin to see over the top. Not even Lanky Bill Dykes could carry a bigger load. But perhaps the rest of them were out of practice, whereas until a few weeks before he had kept the woodbox at home well filled. Moisture stung his eyes as he realized how empty that box would be now.

Emerging from the gloom of the trees, he boarded

the boat at a dog trot, having discovered that the trembling gangplank was less uncertain when taken at a run. Dumping his load, he hesitated, wishing that he could stay in so cosily safe a place. But there was more wood to fetch. He turned back, taking such pleasure as he could from the spongy feel of damp earth under his feet. The sound, he decided, must have come from the throat of a real owl.

Even if it had, it was still shivery back on shore, as scary as the yarn with which Sam Muldoon had regaled the crew the evening before. A Mountain Man, Sam knew the country to which he was returning, after a trip down-river to sell fur at St. Louis. If he didn't have a legend to fit an occasion, Johnny was certain that Muldoon would make one up.

"I've been listenin' to what folks have to say, and observin' as we travel, and while it's still kind of early in the season to be sure, it strikes me that this is the year of The Hungry Horse," he had pronounced. "That's the Indian term for famine—represented by a big, ghost-white horse that comes in the hunger moon. There's some that claim it's a real, sure-enough cayuse, and it can sure be real enough by next winter, 'less all the signs are wrong. Maybe the rest of you ain't took no note, but all the way up-river, game's been harder an' harder to find. Seems like it's done a vanishin' act. Yeah, next winter could be a starvin' time, right enough."

Here the scariness was real enough. Cottonwoods grew almost to the water's edge, with some cleared patches where the choppers had been at work. The stacks of fuel were almost depleted.

A second time the owl hooted.

Something was getting in the way of Johnny's breathing, even though he'd heard plenty of owls back in the Ozarks. The trouble was that there was a quality about this one that didn't seem to be associated with feathers; or if feathers were involved, they'd be stuck in a bonnet or dangling from a scalp-lock.

Grunting angrily at the foolishness of such thoughts, Johnny went on. The trouble was that, back in Missouri, he'd known for sure that there were no lurking Indians. Here, there well might be. Had he needed proof, it was provided by the fact that Captain Jenkins, who liked to stretch his legs ashore as well as any of them, was remaining on board, watchfully close to the ten-pounder with its load of shot and shrapnel. The knowledge of the cannon's readiness was reassuring.

I'm a sure-enough tenderfoot, and thinkin' like one, he adjured himself. It was almost black under the trees, though the cottonwoods were still leafless, their bare branches like ghostly arms against the lighter sky.

At most refueling stops, the axe men were careful to leave no trees standing near the water, to afford possible hiding places for enemies. Here only a few had been felled, since few river boats had ever gotten this far up the river. Only the *Chippewa* had surpassed their effort, making it as far as the mouth of the Marias the year before.

That record seemed likely to fall within the next few days. Bust-a-Boiler Jenkins was far from satisfied with the distance they'd covered so far, up through the vast reaches of the Nebraska country, across the wide Dakotas. He was determined to take the *Oregon* clear to Fort Benton, or leave her bones piled on some lonely beach.

To the east, as the sixties took shape, were rumblings of dissension and possible war. On the frontier, the new decade loomed as a time for great accomplishments, and Bust-a-Boiler was a man determined to have his part.

The fuel had been ready for them, though there was no sign of the woodcutters. No one had answered the captain's hail. That was suspicious, but they had to have the fuel. While loading the wood, they had found no clue as to why or where the cutters might have vanished.

Downstream, where the river twisted out of the east, a fresh glow betokened the rising moon. It would be close to the full tonight, so they'd probably keep shoving against the current as long as the light held.

Sound popped among the trees, breaking the fragile silence, a noise that every ear had been stretched to hear. Though it was new to his ears, Johnny had no doubts. There could be no mistaking the high, shrill crescendo of a war whoop, breaking out from all sides, swelling to a fierce cacophony.

Along with the shouting came a crackling of guns, then the rush of wood-gatherers, scurrying back along the paths. Some discarded their burdens, the better to run. Others clung to their loads, taking the risk.

Johnny's feet planted him in a deeper patch of shadows just off the path. He saw Bill Dykes coming, prancing like a Mountain Man at rendezvous. He was almost alongside when something hurtled viciously from the trees opposite. A tomahawk twisted, the blade gleaming like bared fangs in the moonlight.

Dykes was a tricky as well as a moving target. The war axe sheered the dangling tail from his coonskin cap, but it missed his skull, smashing into his armful of wood. At the impact, the blocks spilled, scattering. Dykes stumbled on a round stick and went sprawling. As he fell, the owner of the tomahawk burst from among the trees. Howling, he snatched a hunting knife from his belt and pounced.

During the long voyage up-river from St. Louis, Johnny had come to count Bill Dykes as a friend. The tall mountaineer had worked with Captain John Mullan surveying a road across part of the Oregon country. He'd enlivened the long evenings with tales of the land and its people. Also, he knew Jonathan

Wilde, who was not only a Mountain Man but also Johnny's uncle.

Johnny hoped to find his uncle somewhere in the vicinity of Fort Benton. Wilde was now the only kin he had and, aside from Bill Dykes, almost his only friend. Breathing hard, Johnny snatched up one of the fallen blocks and threw hard. The stick caught the Indian below the knees, spilling him a jump short of his intended victim.

That was sufficient for Dykes. He came up running, dashing out of sight like a rabbit with a fox on its tail. By now, the gangplank was crowded with crew members. There was furious activity as they prepared to cast off and get open water between the boat and its foes.

It was high time for him to be getting back on board. The trouble was that someone had glimpsed him when he threw the stick, and all at once this portion of the woods was swarming with Indians, most of them anxious to add him, or at least his hair, to their private collections. And some were right in the way, no matter how he tried to turn.

The *Oregon's* whistle blasted, the eerie sound overriding the war whoops. Johnny doubled and twisted, but again his path was blocked as another overly ambitious warrior got in the way. Jumping and dodging, he could fairly feel the lifting tomahawk, which in another instant would be smashing down—

A trick about which his uncle had told him popped into his head. Johnny stopped abruptly, crouching in the denser gloom cast by a big tree.

The ruse worked. His pursuer sped past and out of sight, but there were too many others, swarming like gnats on a summer night. Something, perhaps his breath, was choking him. Johnny let it out, trying to do so silently. That had been too close for comfort.

The entire attack against the *Oregon* had been a near-thing, though it appeared to be failing, not timed quite right. The Indians must have been a long way back from the river when they first sighted the ship's smoke, and they must have counted on it putting in as it had for fuel. They had tried to beat it, but even with hard riding, the supplies had been mostly loaded by the time they could attack. If they had been even ten minutes earlier—

"Bee on a thistle, but I've got to get back, fast," Johnny breathed, though again his feet were in disagreement with his mind, wanting to glue themselves where he stood. But it was now or never. Any move would be extremely risky, for the enraged, disgruntled warriors were swarming openly along the bank. While not quite as close as before, plenty of them were in the way.

Now it was no longer a matter of choice. Unless he could rejoin the boat, he'd be left alone with these Indians. What tribe they might belong to he had only the foggiest notion in his mind, but their intentions were clear. He tensed to run, then checked, feeling as though he'd stepped by mistake into deep water.

The *Oregon* was backing out, a widening gap showing between it and the shore. He was already cut off, left alone with half a hundred frenzied enemies.

2

Johnny dug his knuckles against his eyes, forlornly aware that the gesture was not solely to obtain better vision. He felt orphaned all over again, no longer big for his age and grown-up, but lost and insignificant. Sometimes at home, when he went out after dark, it had seemed that enemies might lurk behind every bush, or crouch in the deeper pools of darkness. But he had always known that it was only imagination. This time it was grimly real.

The enraged gabbling of the Indians lifted to a frantic chorus as they swarmed along the river bank, venting their disappointment in a shower of arrows toward the fast-moving *Oregon*. There were a few shots from smooth-bores, which they probably realized would be futile. But the realization only increased their rage.

Moonlight flooded the river bank, and Johnny decided that his first estimate had been on the short side. There must be more than half a hundred, a large enough force to have caused plenty of trouble, had they been able to get aboard.

Under those conditions, the skipper had lost no time in moving out as soon as the last crewman had come tumbling aboard. In the confusion, he had probably supposed that everyone was back, and there had been no chance to check or call the roll. Delay might have spoiled any chance to get away.

But understanding what had happened, and the necessity for the *Oregon's* sudden departure, didn't help much. Johnny leaned against a tree, shaking as though he'd come down with swamp fever. Bill Dykes and his uncle had both regaled him with tall tales, some of which he suspected had probably been embellished. But at the moment, he could recall no situation which they had mentioned that seemed any less promising than the one he was in. Now, in the middle of the river, the *Oregon* was reversing, starting to plow ahead, bucking the current as it moved upriver.

In the confusion, it could still be quite a while before a check was made and his absence discovered. Once that happened, it would be beyond their power to help. They would conclude that he had been killed or captured, and for their own safety, they would have to keep going.

A new idea occurred to him, and he reached as high as he could, grasping an outjutting limb of the big tree under which he stood. Pulling, he hoisted himself, got his feet on the branch which had been overhead, then climbed and crouched against the trunk.

Having vented their feelings in a final series of yells, the Indians fell silent. The shore line, white under the rising moon, seemed empty. That meant that they were once more prowling among the trees, coursing the pathways. Probably it had occurred to them that some of the boat's crew might have been cut off, and they were again eagerly on the hunt.

A pair of darker shadows took substance, converging to halt under his tree. Johnny listened tensely as they exchanged a few words. Whatever was said sounded like gibberish, which left him reasonably certain that they were not Blackfeet.

Probably it wouldn't make much difference what their tribe was, if they discovered him. It was only that he knew more about the Blackfeet than any other tribe, which made him feel a sort of kinship with them. His Uncle Jonathan had spent half his life as a trapper, and he had come to know most of the tribes of the Northwest, the Blackfeet best of all. Jonathan Wilde had become fluent in their tongue, and Johnny had gathered that, while hating and fearing them, Jonathan also rather admired the Blackfeet.

Two winters ago, Uncle Jon had returned to the Ozarks to visit his sister and other kinfolk. He had spent the winter with them, cooped up, as he'd complained, like a turkey in a hen yard. Despite his pleasure in visiting his sister and brother-in-law and becoming acquainted with a suddenly tall and gawky nephew, he had grown restless.

He'd whiled away some of the time teaching Johnny the Blackfoot language, and Johnny had proved an apt pupil. Though his mother had considered such activity a waste of time, she had raised no objections. By the time Uncle Jon had started back for the headwaters of the Missouri, they had been able to converse understandably in Blackfoot. Johnny had declared his intention of joining his uncle within a few years.

The chance had come sooner than he'd anticipated or desired. Suddenly orphaned, he had decided to work his passage on the *Oregon*, which was heading for Fort Benton, hoping once he got there to find his uncle.

He was tall for his years, and had an easy grin that widened his freckles. So Captain Jenkins had listened to his reasons for going and agreed. Until now, the adventure had been on the mild side. The worst part, short of tonight, had been in St. Louis. So large a town, spreading more extensively than the farm, was right scary.

Now Johnny had serious second thoughts. The vast reaches of the western country were beyond belief. A hill which appeared to be right at hand might turn out to be a day's ride away. It was still a long way, a

mighty far piece, to Fort Benton or any other settlement of which he'd heard.

They had passed Fort Union, squatting isolated near
the junction of the Yellowstone with the Missouri, a
couple of days before. It had been a disappointment.
There wasn't much to the fort, compared with the pattern he'd carried in his mind.

Somewhere beyond Benton, clear on the far side of
the Rockies, was Fort Owen and a mission to the
Indians. But that was so far distant that it would be of
no help. Somewhere along the Yellowstone was another fort, and that, too, might as well be on the moon
so far as he was concerned.

This wasn't like the Ozarks, where you could find
a settlement somewhere within half a day's walking or
riding. These plains Indians had never had towns, and
most whites had learned to get along without them,
too. Men like Jonathan Wilde saw no need for them.

It was a scary situation, but at least he was alive,
and both his uncle and Bill Dykes had been in equally
dangerous situations. His course of action had delayed
him and kept him from getting back to the boat, but
it had saved Bill Dykes' scalp.

The Indians were still prowling, as silent as hunting cats. The pair who had been under his tree had
gone on, not suspecting that he was hanging around.
The confusion and darkness were in his favor.

Johnny grew cramped and stiff. By then, the moon

was riding high, making a long and crooked silver
sheet of the river. There was no longer any sign of the
packet, not even a smudge of smoke against the
horizon.

A rabbit hopped along the path below, pausing to
wrinkle its nose, then running a forepaw over its head
and one ear, somewhat after the manner of a cat. Then
it went on without any particular concern. Again an
owl hooted, but the sound was not repeated. This time
it probably was a real owl. Johnny slid to the ground,
stretching cramped limbs, trying to be silent.

Every shadow appeared to jiggle or flit, and the
night sounds held unknown menace. His shiver was not
wholly because of the night's chill.

Reckon I'm just too big a coward—too scared of
everything—ever to make a Mountain Man, he thought
miserably. But I've got to keep going. There's no one
else to depend on.

He made a tour of the woods, which appeared to be
empty. Back from the river, he found where horses
had been not long before. Evidently the Indians had
ridden up, then left their horses while attacking on
foot.

Though they had withdrawn, they might be camped
somewhere close by. It would be better to wait for
daylight, to take no risks he could avoid. Daylight
might even find the *Oregon* swinging back to look for
him, though that was a slender chance.

High, dry grass from the previous year made a dense growth back from the trees. Burrowing deep, he planned to keep awake, but was soon asleep. The night was warm for so early in the season. Though warmly dressed, he'd already taken inventory of his possessions and found little that was encouraging. Most of his possibles were back on the boat.

He carried only a single trinket—a keepsake given him by his uncle. It was a piece of broken axe-head, and Jonathan Wilde had remarked that it was particularly good to use with flint, to strike sparks and to start a fire.

If he was lucky, he might find a piece of flint rock to go with it. His last thoughts were an effort to recall what he had heard about the upper river; it wasn't much. Somewhere farther west, it came swinging up from the southwest, but he doubted if there were any big turns or twists, such as had been the case far back in the Dakotas. There, the river made such devious twists that on two or three occasions parties had gone ashore, hunting; then, moving overland, they had rejoined the boat when it came along.

There was no prospect of such a reunion now. He'd have to make his way west, more or less following the river. If he was lucky, he'd eventually reach Fort Benton—provided he didn't starve or get lost or killed or captured.

He awoke to sunshine and an empty plain, which

poignantly reminded him of the empty feeling in his stomach. Food was an immediate necessity, and likely to prove an urgent and increasing problem. That talk about The Hungry Horse and famine was suddenly real.

Birds were singing, but nothing else moved. There was no more sign of the Indians than of the *Oregon*.

"Which sort of evens things," he muttered. "But I guess this puts it up to me whether I'm any good or good for nothing."

He set out, not trying to follow the river, which would be difficult if not possible. Not only were there many twists and turns, but much of its course ran among high hills or deep in canyons. He'd head west, guiding himself by the sun, trying only to keep the river in sight.

Early flowers splashed color against the lingering drabness of winter. The sun was high when he sighted an alien object. He halted, studying it, then, as there was no movement, ventured cautiously closer.

Something sprawled loosely. It was a horse, apparently dead. Then, as he came closer, a figure partly rose from behind the horse, waving and shouting. Johnny dropped flat in the grass, his heart pounding. It was an Indian, and calling for help. But was it a trick?

3

The Indian fell back behind the horse, as though hurt or sick. His voice was pitched on a note of desperation, and Johnny had no trouble recognizing that he was calling in Blackfoot. But it could still be a ruse, despite the dead animal, to lure him within striking distance. As he hesitated, the Indian spoke again, and his words were startling.

"Begorra, man, and 'tis help I'm needin', and no mistake!"

The words were English, with an unmistakable Irish accent. Even if this was a trick, which seemed unlikely, Johnny knew that he could hardly be worse off. Also, if it was a trick, pursuit would be swift should he try to run.

He walked ahead with no show of hesitation, making sure that the horse was dead. In falling, it had caught and pinned its rider. He was held by his right ankle. Now he waited, torn between hope and doubt, his face tense. He appeared to be about Johnny's age, not quite a man or a warrior, but no longer a boy.

The poor devil's just as scared as I am, Johnny decided, and trying just as hard not to show it! And why shouldn't he be? He's trapped, and I'm his only chance—but I could as easily be an enemy as a friend.

Remembering what his uncle had told him, Johnny held up a hand in the sign of peace. Then he tried his own rusty Blackfoot, uttering a few words of greeting.

"What has happened? Is my brother in trouble?"

A look of astonishment crossed the Indian's face at being addressed in his own tongue. Relieved, he volleyed an answer, the words tumbling so fast that Johnny could make out only an occasional one. He held up a hand.

"Bug on a beanstalk!" he protested. "You're going too fast for me. Let's try a little of the Irish, along with the rest."

The Indian looked bewildered. "Irish?" he repeated. "I speak the English, but sure and that's all."

"That's good enough," Johnny granted. "We should make out fine. I can savvy Blackfoot if you go slow. What happened?"

The answer came in Blackfoot, this time more measured. "Enemies, riders of the Sioux from the land of the Dakotas, surprised me during the night," he explained. "Myself and my two friends. What happened to them, I do not know. My horse was shot, through it ran for a while, so that I lost them in the darkness. All at once my pony stumbled and went down. Being careless, I was caught."

Johnny saw where an arrow protruded from the horse's side. Unable to free himself, the Blackfoot had lain throughout the night and most of the day, with only a remote chance that any help might come. Even if someone did, the odds were that they would be enemies.

"I have tried to be courageous, to face death, if I must, as a Blackfoot warrior," the boy confessed miserably. "But at times I have been afraid, very close to being a coward. There are those who would taunt me that that is my father's blood, but Seamus O'Casey was no coward! But you cannot know how glad I am to see you!"

"Root hog or starve, I reckon I'm just as tickled to see you as you are to see me," Johnny returned. Looking more closely, he could see traces of white ancestry in the Indian. There was a glint of red in the black of his hair, and—just as surprising—his eyes were blue. "That must be mighty uncomfortable, the way you're pinned down. But we'll get you loose."

A coulee gashed the flatness just at the side, and at its edge he found a pole. Using it as a lever, he managed to lift the dead horse enough for the Indian to pull his foot free. Lying back, panting, his face wet with sweat, he stared up gratefully.

"Ottertail, nephew of a chief, will not forget," he promised, then sat up, grimacing as the blood worked back into his foot and ankle. "For a while, I feared that I must perish miserably. My friends, who rode with me, I hope escaped our enemies in the darkness, but if they did, they would never find me. You too are alone, with a lonely look," he suggested.

"And I've been feeling more that way than the needle lost in a haystack," Johnny granted. He gave his name, explaining what had happened at the river. Ottertail nodded his understanding. Each of them had apparently been surprised by the same band of raiding Sioux.

Ottertail's leg was swollen, but apparently no bones were broken. Thirst was his most pressing problem. With Johnny's help, he managed to walk to the coulee. Near its head, a tiny spring trickled from beneath a shelf of rock.

"There is wood for a fire, and we have meat," Ottertail observed. "A small fire should be safe enough, if only we can manage one—although, if we must, we can eat it raw. I have a striking flint, but my iron has been lost."

"In that case, we're all right. I have an iron," Johnny said, and held out the broken axe-head. Ottertail's face warmed.

"Ai, but it is a fine one, with the look of having been much used," he exclaimed. "If you will gather dry sticks for the fire, I will secure the meat." Hobbling back to the horse, he picked up a knife, also a bow and quiver of arrows which had fallen nearby. Then he set about carving a steak.

Johnny gathered dry brush along the fringes of the coulee. Dining on horse meat would be a little outside the range of his experience, but he could not afford to be squeamish, having missed his supper as well as today's meals. Companionship, someone who knew the country and how to live off it, made a big difference.

Ottertail quickly had a fire going in the deepest part of the draw, using only a few sticks of wood at a time. The blaze was virtually smokeless.

Because of his ankle, Ottertail would not be able to do much walking for a few days, but it might have been worse. The season was spring, and summer was ahead. To him, survival, at least for the immediate future, presented no problems.

Ottertail was intensely interested in Johnny's knowledge of the Blackfoot language, and how he had become familiar with it. He nodded at the mention of Jonathan Wilde.

"Hah, the old one!" he exclaimed, to Johnny's surprise, for he had never thought of his uncle as old. Apparently that was a term of respect. Everyone knew about the old one. If he was not exactly a friend of the Blackfeet, at least he was admired for his prowess. But Ottertail shook his head at the suggestion that

Wilde might perhaps be found in or around Fort Benton.

"Often the old one has been there in the past," he admitted. "But I doubt if he is there now. I heard mention of him in the last moon of summer. The report was that he journeyed with a couple of companions to the land of the setting sun, to the Great Waters."

The news was disappointing, but not very surprising. That might well be, for his uncle had mentioned his hope of making such a journey, to have a look at some new country. If he had gone on to the Pacific, it would be hopeless to try to find him this summer.

Ottertail noticed his face. With one hand he extended a steaming piece of meat, laid out on a chunk of dry wood. Impulsively he threw his other arm across Johnny's shoulders.

"Begorra, man, ye look like ye'd lost your last friend," he exclaimed, then reverted to Blackfoot. "Here, eat. Then you will feel better. And do not allow yourself to be bothered that he is gone. Some day, sooner or later, be sure that he will return to the land of the Blackfeet, for it is country which he loves above all others. Meanwhile, I owe my life to you, and a Blackfoot does not forget! When the old one returns, you will be able to greet him, knowing the country even as he does!"

Johnny had refused to admit, even to himself, how

desperate was his plight. Now things were better.

Gradually he learned more of his companion. Running Wolf, Ottertail's uncle, was a chief among the Blackfeet, and it was in Running Wolf's lodge that Ottertail and his sister lived. They belonged to the Piegan nation, one of several divisions in an associated confederacy. The Blackfeet counted themselves as Lords of the Plain, one of the strongest tribes in the northwest.

He gathered almost as much from what Ottertail did not say as from what he told. Ottertail had been proud of his father, Seamus O'Casey, who had been, if not a great warrior, at least a mighty hunter. Unlike the average "blanket white man" who had chosen to live with Indians as an Indian, Seamus had never forgotten his Irish heritage or pride. He had taught his son and daughter to speak English, and while they thought of themselves as Indians, they too shared some of that pride.

Apparently it had been a hindrance to O'Casey and was somewhat of a stumbling block to his children, despite the favor of their uncle the chief. Others of the Piegans regarded them with suspicion, as not quite loyal Blackfeet. Life was not too easy, Johnny gathered, and that had perhaps helped influence Ottertail to set out on a hunt and an exploratory trip, a chance to get away and at the same time to prove himself.

The primary reason had been to search for game.

Here, as along the river, there was a disturbing absence of game, even in spring. By fall, if there was no improvement, The Hungry Horse might roam the prairies, thrusting his head, camel-like, into the lodges of the people. . . .

Again, Ottertail made no mention of it, but Johnny could see that he was troubled by the loss of his two friends, who had chosen, in spite of the disapproval of some of the others, to accompany him on this journey. If they failed to return, and Ottertail did, that would be one more count against him among his own people. Through no fault of his own, he was half an alien, almost an outcast.

That, too, might be partly his fault. Seamus O'Casey had refused to become wholly an Indian, retaining the pride of the Irish. Ottertail counted himself a Blackfoot, but clung stubbornly to that same pride. . . .

They rested while Ottertail's ankle improved. There was no sign of anyone, but that was no guarantee that Sioux, Crow, Cheyenne or Arapaho might not be on the prowl. This was a disputed range, claimed by representatives from many tribes.

Bumblebee on a thistle, Johnny thought. Back East folks are arguin' about secession and war—and here it's the same thing, when you come right down to it. Always something to squabble about.

Ottertail insisted on slicing and cooking as much meat as they could conveniently carry. On the third day they set out on what would be a long and arduous journey. The necessity of traveling on foot, and the possible perils, did not worry Ottertail. What irked him was that as a Blackfoot he was forced to walk instead of riding through his own land.

"But we may not walk all the way," he said. "We will see."

Johnny did not mind the walking, did not care how long it took. The summer was before them, and with Jonathan Wilde off on a journey, there was no reason to hurry. Food was no longer a problem. Edible roots were easy to dig, and Ottertail knew each one. But there were other troubles.

Tormented by thirst through most of an afternoon, they approached a promised water hole, and there was water. But as he took a better look. Johnny stopped in dismay.

Animals, perhaps buffalo, had been ahead of them, slaking their own thirst. In the process they had fouled the water hole, trampling and rolling like horses just free of the saddle.

"That's too filthy to drink," Johnny said. "Is there no other?"

"None within a day's walk," Ottertail assured him. "But we will drink, and water will be good. At least here is favorable sign, the first in a long while."

"What's good about it?"

"Game has been here. So at least there is some

game left in the country. Where the big herds have
gone, I do not understand. We should see many herds
of buffalo, numbers to darken the plain. But where are
they?"

It was a recurring question, which became more
troublesome as the season wore on. They scooped out
a hole for the water to gather in, clearing away the
muck, though it appeared almost hopeless. Since this
was not running water, it would not clear itself.
Despite his thirst, Johnny shuddered at thought of such
filthiness.

Ottertail gathered several of the prickly pear, split-
ting the cacti open and dropping them in the pool.
By the time their meal was ready, Johnny was astonished to find the water was clear. The spongy fibers
had absorbed the dirt.

The next day, Ottertail put the cactus to a new use.
Now there was plenty of fresh water, but they had
been unable to take game or find roots. This time he
peeled off the spiny outer layer of the cactus, placing
the pulp on a flat, hot stone by the fire. Fried, it was
both nourishing and edible.

Ottertail spent hours instructing Johnny in the proper use of the bow and arrow. That had been a hobby
of his back in the Ozarks, and he was pleased with the
aptitude which Johnny showed.

"Ai and begorra, soon you will be as skilled as your
uncle, the old one," he commended Johnny. "He can

live like an Indian." To a son of the land, there could be no higher compliment.

Rains soaked them; there were long days and nights when storm rolled across the land, and travel, slipping and sliding, was miserable. On other days the sun was warm. The wind kept up a steady, unending thrust. They moved, but everything else appeared to stand still, the distant haze of the mountains coming no closer, taking on form only to lose it like a drift of cloud.

The prairie turned to a vast carpet of green, decorated with wild flowers. Prairie chickens and sage hens were abundant now, and Ottertail killed several with his arrows. Even Johnny succeeded in knocking one over.

"We live well, you and I," Ottertail said, but he viewed the empty plain with increasingly troubled eyes.

"This is a strange time," he added. "Ordinarily, journeying as we are doing, two small ones who create no disturbance, we should see game everywhere, herds of the buffalo to darken the plain. Sometimes they are a peril to one who journeys on foot, a danger even to men on horses. But where are they? Not since I set out, a moon ago, have I beheld even one of the great ones, and there is no sign of a herd! And buffalo are life for the Blackfeet!"

"But we are finding other game," Johnny pointed out.

"A few deer, a running coyote, prairie dogs—and the birds which fly. Even they are too few. Without the buffalo, they are not enough. My people eat fresh meat. When a hunt is good, the surplus is dried or made into pemmican for the long trail or the lean days of winter. From hides we make tepees, rugs, coats. Sinews and bone are our tools. A buffalo hide makes a boat for the river. Without them, we perish."

They were south of the river. When they occasionally glimpsed it, the current was awesome. There had been much snow in the mountains during the winter, and it was still melting. The river rolled, a sullen, relentless flood.

They crossed smaller streams, sometimes forced to swim, managing by drifting with the current until they could work across. On the big river, that might not be so easy. And cross they must, for the camp of the Blackfeet lay beyond the far shore, in a secluded valley among the Little Rockies. This isolated range was not impressive in comparison with the greater hills farther to the west, but they were a favorite hunting ground.

It was still night. Johnny awakened to a whisper, felt his friend's hand on his shoulder. Excitement quivered in Ottertail's voice.

"Be very quiet. Enemies are close!"

4

Bug on a—Johnny thought dazedly, and bit off the thought as he came fully awake. This was like being back in the trees while the *Oregon* backed away and left him stranded, but at least he should be getting used to such things.

They had made camp on top of a small butte, burrowing back among the high grass. Plenty remained from the previous summer, but this season's growth was tall and rank. Such grass showed that no buffalo, and not much else in the way of game, had come that way for a long while.

Ottertail always picked the high ground when he could, not liking the seclusion of a coulee. From such a spot, they could see or hear anyone who might approach.

Eyes accustomed to the gloom, Johnny made out where shadowy figures moved rather too close for comfort. A tired voice seemed to ask a question; another replied briefly. They were not Blackfeet. Apparently they were debating whether to make use of this same high ground for a stopping place.

Could make things kind of crowded, Johnny reflected, and was surprised to find that he was no longer disturbed at the prospect. It could be quite a surprise party.

After a short discussion, the others went on, swallowed by the gloom. Ottertail came to his feet.

"Crows," he explained. "Soon they will stop to sleep. They have been traveling steadily, hurrying, because they are afraid, being in Blackfoot country. Begorra, and they've a right to be! I thought they might want this place!"

Johnny was fully awake. Something which had puzzled him about the others, showing like dim ghosts, was suddenly clear.

"But they were riding!" he exclaimed.

"And that is our luck, not theirs!" Ottertail agreed excitedly. "They will soon stop and, being very tired, will sleep heavily! Tomorrow we will ride!"

He was already gathering up their few possessions and setting off in pursuit. The night was very still, and faint sounds guided them. Johnny shared his friend's excitement. If they could obtain horses—

Setting the Crows afoot would be no worse than what the Crows would do to them under similar circumstances. Horse stealing among the tribes was not considered thievery, but a game, high adventure and an exercise of skill. The coming of horses to the plains had almost completely altered the Indians' way of life.

Sounds had ceased, but something bulked larger against the starshine—the horses, hungrily cropping a few last bites of grass before they were ready to rest.

Circling carefully, they counted four horses. Johnny had figured on only two. The cayuses were hobbled, but no one seemed to be on watch.

"They are tired and careless," Ottertail whispered. "Already they are asleep. They are in need of a good lesson—such as losing their hair! But being left on foot will perhaps do as well. It is too bad to miss so fine an opportunity, but they might be too many for us."

Having located where the others were asleep, they returned to the horses. Ottertail moved among them, creating no disturbance. Presently he led a horse to where Johnny was keeping watch. It was a raw-boned, hammer-headed cayuse, the color of buckskin and the most ungainly, homely-looking animal he had ever seen. A length of rawhide was looped around its nose, up over its ears, then twisted back into a combination bridle and halter. With this, the horse could be controlled or guided with only a slight pressure.

"This looks like a good animal," Ottertail observed. "Are you a good rider, John Hawk?"

Johnny felt a new queasiness, a sense of apprehension. It would certainly be a lot pleasanter to ride than to plod endlessly. But he hadn't stopped to think how it would be on an Indian pony, without a saddle. He had done quite a lot of riding, but never under such conditions.

"I guess I can manage," he admitted.

Ottertail passed him the end of the thong.

"When I come with another horse, jump on his back, then ride and yell as loud as you can, to start the other horses," he directed. "We will scare them and leave the Crows afoot. But we will not try to take the extra horses. Two of them are very poor animals, not worth the trouble. One is lame; the other has a sore back."

He slipped away to get a horse for himself. He was bending over, removing its hobbles, when Johnny saw something, like a shadow which moved, creeping up behind his friend. Johnny's breath choked as an arm lifted, and starlight reflected the sheen of a tomahawk.

For a moment he was almost paralyzed, trying to understand. None of the sleepers had stirred. Actually, they had posted a guard after all. But, close to exhaustion, he must have gone to sleep, then been awakened by the movements of Ottertail or the horses. Ashamed at this late moment to rouse the others, he was counting on redeeming himself and the situation.

Johnny's own voice seemed to clog his throat, so

that he could not shout a warning. He hurled himself forward, jerking his pony along, coming from behind, using his only available weapon—head lowered, butting like a goat. It wasn't the sort of combat that could be boasted of around the campfire, but it was effective. Caught by surprise, the Crow whooshed like a tired cow, then was sent staggering, tumbling.

Ottertail spun about, startled, but was quick to understand. With a leap he was on his pony, shouting, forcing it to a run as the sleepers came awake and joined in the clamor. Since he had already freed the poorer animals of their hobbles, he had them running before the Crows could reach them. With a frantic jump and kick, Johnny managed, to his own surprise, to land across the neck and back of his own cayuse, clinging desperately. Luckily, it was following the lead of Ottertail's horse, so he was able to give his attention to getting straightened out. By then, they were swallowed by the night. If any arrows followed, they were very much at random.

Ottertail swung his pony alongside Johnny.

"Again you have saved me," he exclaimed. "Begorra, man, but it was a warrior's deed! I was so sure of myself that I grew careless."

"Bear in a bee-tree, I guess we didn't do too badly," Johnny agreed. Not only were they riding, but, better still in Ottertail's view, on spoils taken from enemies. To an Indian, only the taking of a scalp in battle ranked higher than stealing horses from rivals. That matched hunting as a means of survival, a test of merit.

After being so long on foot, it was a relief to ride. By sunup they sighted the river, still flowing wide and sullen, but Ottertail showed no sign of nervousness.

"We will cross, then camp on the far side," he decided. "Once it is between us, we will be beyond the reach of the Crows, even should they be so lucky as to join with friends. Tomorrow we should reach the camp of my people."

He urged his horse into the current, and Johnny followed. Within moments, both horses were swimming.

All his life, Johnny had heard the Missouri extolled in song and story; it was the wide, wild river, the great barrier between the settled East and the unknown West. Traveling on the *Oregon*, he had been impressed not alone by its power but by its crankiness and unpredictability.

Ottertail made no attempt to cross straight over. He turned his horse's nose downstream, so that they moved with the current, gradually working toward the center of the river. The water was a muddy yellow with no suggestion of the golden, still very cold despite the warmth of the sun. Considerable debris was swept on the current, anything from sticks and logs to uprooted trees.

As his horse began to swim, Ottertail slipped off on the downstream side, clutching its tail with one hand. It looked easy, so Johnny followed his example, shivering as the water closed over him, leaving only his head and arm free. For an instant he knew panic as his fingers almost missed their hold on the tail.

Then he was being towed along, and the water felt more comfortable. He was partly sheltered as well as supported. As the far shore came in sight and the water grew shallow, Ottertail swung back on his horse.

Johnny, about to try to do the same, found his horse no longer in place, but swallowed from sight. Floundering, taken as much by surprise by the sudden deep hole as his pony, Johnny lost his hold. He went under, swallowing water as he tried to yell; the sound came out as a smothered gurgle. Then he was caught by a quickening current, swept like a log in the depths. Frantically he tried to swim, getting his head above water, gasping, before being rolled under again. The dark waters were terror-laden.

Something closed on his arm, tugging upward, and his head came free as his floundering feet found a hold. Ottertail was alongside, still on his pony, holding fast to his arm. Then they were splashing out through shallow water onto the shore. Johnny's cayuse was already there, shaking itself with an air of surprise.

"But—bug on a bonnet," Johnny gasped. "I don't

know what happened. But if it hadn't been for you—"

"Your horse went into a deep hole," Ottertail explained. "At least I was able to help you as you have done for me."

They stretched on the grass in the sun, resting and drying before going on. Johnny had figured himself to be a good swimmer, but the sudden terror of dark waters and dragging current had confused and dazed him.

"Reckon I might as well tell you," he confessed "You'll find it out anyway. When something happens I'm always scared, just plain scared. I'm afraid I'c never make a warrior—or amount to anything as a Mountain Man."

"Sure and begorra, man, I noticed that." Ottertail grinned. "I saw how you were so scared that you ran right into that big Crow last night. And I'll bet *he* was scared almost out of his moccasins."

Beyond the river they surprised a badger, digging for gophers. Throwing up dirt at a great rate, powerful paws like scoops, it was nearly out of sight in the hole, so did not see them until Ottertail rode alongside. Then it reared up, snarling, only to take an arrow which flattened it in a loose sprawl. Ottertail sprang down, elated. They had had no fresh meat for several days, and both were hungry.

As he stooped, the badger revived, snarling, leaping for his throat. Surprised, Ottertail lost his knife, then was in a wild tangle with the enraged animal. A fighting badger could be a nasty antagonist.

Johnny slipped from his own horse and snatched up the dropped knife. Seeing an opening, he stabbed hard. Still growling and clawing, the badger fell back, then lay still.

Ottertail's arms and hands were scratched and bloody, and he was breathing hard. He eyed the badger ruefully; then his grin returned. However much Indian he might be, that grin was pure Irish.

"That's another time you were scared, I suppose," he observed. "And do you know, so was I!"

They cooked the meat, spending the rest of the day eating and resting. By now the mountains were showing above the prairie. By noon of the next day they came upon the camp of the Blackfeet, still pitched in the same spot as it had been when Ottertail had set out on his journey weeks before. From a distance, everything looked neat and orderly, but as they drew nearer, Johnny could sense there was something wrong. The feel of it was like smoke in the air.

Children were in sight, but they were not playing, nor did they come running at the approach of the newcomers. A few squaws were at work, moving slowly. There were also a few men, and someone recognized Ottertail and set up a shout. But along with the welcome there was a question, an almost desperate eagerness.

"The strange one returns—but not with the companions he set out with," a small boy muttered to a companion.

"And they bring no meat," the other returned. His large, wide eyes fixed on Johnny in doubt and fear. "His skin is white," he added, and scuttled for the shelter of his mother's skirts.

"Have you seen game?" others questioned eagerly. Another added, half in question, half on a note of reproach, "What has happened to your companions—those with whom you set out?"

Running Wolf appeared, a man of poise and dignity. He was not only the chief, but Ottertail's uncle, in whose lodge Ottertail had been raised. His greeting to Johnny was courteous, but even he could not hide the eagerness which the others had shown.

"You have found no buffalo—no game?" he asked.

"We have seen no buffalo," Ottertail confessed. "There were many birds far toward the sunrise, but these became fewer and fewer with each day. Other game is equally hard to find."

"No buffalo?" Running Wolf repeated incredulously.

"The buffalo have vanished."

There was a sound between a groan and a sob from the onlookers. Johnny knew that his feeling had been right. There was desperate trouble here. Not actual hunger, since this was summer rather than the long cold

of winter. But if there was no game in summer, what
would winter bring?

"And your companions?" the chief questioned.
"Where are they?"

Ottertail explained how they had become separated
at night when the Sioux had surprised them; told about
his own accident, and how Johnny had come the next
day and saved him from a lingering death pinned
down by his dead horse. Mink Woman, Ottertail's aunt,
placed a hand on her nephew's shoulder, then, as she
listened, put the other arm about Johnny. She was a
strong, good-looking woman, her smile warm, but he
sensed that this did not extend to the others of the
tribe.

There was scarcely veiled hostility in the faces of
many. Johnny could understand. Having always dis-
trusted whites, they would not find it easy to change.
Ottertail was the son of a white man, and although he
had lived as an Indian, neither he nor Seamus O'Casey
had ever become as wholly Indian as was counted
proper.

Ottertail had ridden away on a hunt with friends—
and they had not returned. In their place he had
brought another white. Not only that, this man was kin
to Jonathan Wilde. Everyone knew the Mountain Man
and respected his prowess—

They fear and hate him, he added, a feeling that he
returns.

"Everyone hoped that we would bring good news rather than evil," Ottertail explained soberly, once he and Johnny were alone. "But they believe that my companions are lost, and I fear it must be so. I have clung until now to the hope that they had gotten away, that I would find them here when we returned. No one has seen or heard of them. Probably they have fallen to the Dakotas, and that is cause for grief."

Remembering the war-like Sioux, his own and Ottertail's narrow escapes, Johnny understood.

"Some are disappointed that you did not turn out to be one of them. That is why their greeting was cool. Many have never seen a white man aside from my father, who for many years was more Indian than white. For the most part, the Blackfeet distrust all whites."

He was far more sober than when they had been on the trail. Conditions at the camp were far worse than he had expected.

"Not only have you and I found little game, but the hunters, who have been ranging widely, have returned day after day all but empty-handed," he went on. "The old ones are beginning to whisper of The Hungry Horse—"

Here it was again, no idle tale of a Mountain Man. Hunger, like the sun, could cast a long shadow ahead.

"The Hungry Horse is a great white animal which comes during the long cold winters," Ottertail went on.

"It is famine—death. And already, while it is still summer, there is a lack of enough to eat."

Johnny had another flash of understanding.

"And since you went away with others and returned with me—and because my skin is white—some of your people wonder if I am not an omen of bad luck?"

Ottertail's nod was somber.

"You are a man of perception. I'm afraid that some of them do. It is foolish—but all this season our luck has been bad, and with each moon it grows worse." His grin flashed. "But sure and begorra, don't let that worry your head, Johnny. You are my friend."

Fawn Who Runs, Ottertail's sister, Johnny found shy but friendly. She was her father's daughter, as Ottertail was his son, torn now by the distrust and trouble which had come upon their people.

Johnny was made to feel welcome and at home in the lodge of the chief. They would not fail in hospitality. Weary from the long journey, now finally ended, Johnny slept late the next morning. He awakened to find that Ottertail had gone hunting by himself, heading for the highest mountain in the vicinity. Fawn Who Runs explained that the others had scoffed at the notion that he might find game so close to camp, but he had decided to try.

"Probably he figured that he had to get away from me, to think things through," Johnny decided. "And who can blame him?"

5

"Cat in a woodbox," Johnny muttered, "but I've had about enough of this!"

There was sanctuary and friendliness in the lodge of Running Wolf, but he could not spend all his time cooped up inside. Otherwise the camp was derisive if not openly unfriendly. Coyote Man, who was clearly jealous of Ottertail, seemed to lead the opposition. Like Ottertail, he was not yet quite a brave or an accepted warrior, but ambitious to build himself up at the expense of anyone he could tear down.

I'd like to take him down a few pegs—and I reckon I could do it, Johnny reflected. But that wouldn't add any to my popularity. I'd better get out before I have to let off steam.

Getting his horse, he set out, riding aimlessly. Time enough to head back when Ottertail returned. A few miles from the village, he dismounted and stretched in the sun.

He awoke with a start, realizing guiltily that he hadn't intended to sleep. His horse was running, though he had hobbled it as a matter of course. As he came angrily to his feet, he saw that a shower of stones, flung by several Indian boys, was the reason. More derisive laughter followed him as he ran after the horse.

Finally, beyond sight and sound of their tormentors, the pony allowed him to come up. Johnny stroked the glossy neck, raging, knowing that he could do nothing by way of retaliation. Whatever he did would probably only make things worse.

Ottertail and I get along fine—but the rest of them don't understand, he reflected. Likely I'd be the same way, if I was in their place.

The afternoon sun was bright on the slopes of the mountain. He could see a long way, but there was no sign of Ottertail. He should have been back before this—

Something was moving high above, a huge shaggy beast. Johnny's hunch was strong.

Bug on a burr! He's after game, and there it is— maybe after him. I'd better have a look.

In climbing those steep slopes, a horse would be more of a hindrance than a help. Tying his cayuse in a sheltered spot, Johnny set out.

Ottertail came awake, carefully immobile. He had been dreaming, but what part was dream, what belonged to reality? A painful twinge furnished the answer. He had been climbing, then had slipped and fallen into darkness. From the ache and the lump on his head, he must have hit it, knocking himself out—

How long he had lain, how much he might be injured, was uncertain. Now there was a prickling sense of danger, like the little winds which played around the crags; that had probably roused him in a desperate warning. His eyes jerked open; then he stared disbelievingly, wondering if this was dream or nightmare. He had been dreaming, and there had been a mighty herd of buffalo sweeping across the prairie, the sounds of thousands of hoofs like the roll of thunder.

That thunder was an ominous growl, rumbling from the throat of a grizzly bear. The big fellow was poised a few feet away, surveying him out of reddened eyes.

Ottertail's back was against a wall of rock, part of a small, natural enclosure high on the mountain. With what he was sure had been a dream still vivid, it was hard to sort out the reality.

The grizzly was huge and shaggy, easily the biggest of his kind that Ottertail had ever seen, staring down, hungry and bad-tempered. The mood of a grizzly at such a time was always unpredictable, and he was probably having the same problems as other hunters in this season of scant game. There was reason for the bear's ill-temper.

Its right foreleg spraddled outward, as the grizzly favored it because of a not quite healed injury to its shoulder. The torment of that hurt probably plagued the bear with every step.

Ottertail could guess how it might have happened. Some other hunter, most likely one of his tribe, had been at equally close quarters with this big fellow not many weeks before. Both because he was eager to return to camp with meat and to protect his own life, he had discharged an arrow, sending it deep into the shoulder of the grizzly.

What had happened then was a matter for grim speculation. Tearing at the tormenting barb, the bear had broken the arrow, leaving part of the shaft embedded. There it remained, the jagged end showing through the hair. The wound continued as a festering reminder of the two-legged creature who had caused the hurt.

Ottertail shrank back against the rocky wall, his heart sounding like a war drum in his ears. In falling, he had lost his bow and arrows, as a desperate glance about him confirmed. Weaponless, he was face to face with a grizzly which probably equated him with that other troublesome hunter. If he tried to get away, it would be upon him with a rush.

Restless, always hungry, troubled by the arrow in its shoulder, the grizzly had prowled the mountain, and a vagrant breeze must have brought the hated man-scent to its nose. That smell was always coupled with fear for any creature of the wild, but today pain and rage left only disdain for lesser emotions.

Its senses quivering with eagerness, the bear had followed its nose, ranging back and forth until it tracked the scent to its source. Now it was close enough so that its nearsighted eyes could assist its nostrils. Here was the creature which had dared offer battle— or another of the same sort. The bear made no distinction.

The hairs on Ottertail's scalp were emulating the great ruff on the grizzly's shoulders. Aside from the rap on the skull, he hadn't been much hurt by his tumble, so as far as condition went, he might try a dash down the mountain. That would entail the risk of stumbling and falling. What spoiled the whole notion was that, in such a race, the grizzly, disregarding its lame leg, could travel at almost the speed of a rolling stone. Flight would bring instant pursuit.

Ottertail held his breath, staring back. A bear was usually of uncertain temper, especially a grizzly; its moods were unpredictable. If he did not move, there was a chance that it might not attack. Slender though that chance was, it seemed his only hope.

Even with bow and arrows or a stout hunting knife, a contest with a grizzly would be hopelessly one-sided. The unknown warrior had driven his arrow deep, but it had hardly given pause to the bear.

The growl rumbled louder in the grizzly's throat. A cloud drifted across the peaks, the shadow like a foretaste of darkness.

Ottertail started at a shout from close at hand. The bear's attention shifted. Ottertail recognized Johnny's voice and turned his head in time to see an arrow slip from the bow. Then it was quivering in the grizzly's neck.

There it hung as the bear reared, howling, tearing at this new thorn with wildly slashing paws. Since its raking claws slid hopelessly off the shaft and did nothing to abate the pain, the grizzly swung, with a roar which dwarfed its previous efforts, and charged its new tormentor.

Ottertail was up and running, shouting wildly, both in encouragement and in the hope of distracting the bear. He had breathed a prayer for help, and the answer had been Johnny's arrow. What he was doing was worthy of a warrior, but foolhardy. In attracting the grizzly's attention, inducing it to turn upon him, John Hawk was risking death.

Johnny had climbed, mindful of the risk but apprehensive as he'd glimpsed the slumped body of his friend, then had seen him stir at the worst possible time. Today, at least, he was as well-armed as an Indian. Running Wolf, after listening gravely to the tale of their adventures, had shown his appreciation by presenting Johnny with a bow and arrows.

Whirling, he discharged a second shaft at point-blank range. In the long weeks on the trail, Ottertail had given him many lessons until he had attained a reasonable skill.

The arrow seemed to lose itself in the wide-open, crimson gullet of the bear without appreciable effect. The grizzly was almost upon him. Johnny jumped to the side, and the momentum of the charging monster carried it past, the sharpness of the slope helping.

The infuriated beast roared on for half a hundred feet before it could stop and turn, claws rasping off smooth rock, tearing loose smaller stones and sending a small avalanche ahead. Clashing as it tried to brake, it checked its plunge, then started to climb again.

Now the fury of its initial rush was lost. Those arrows had found its vitals, and though the grizzly's tremendous strength drove it a few further desperately scrambling steps, the slope of the hill was against it. Halfway to Johnny it sprawled, then made a last desperate effort, hunching crab-like. All at once it lay glaring upward, no longer stirring.

Reaching Johnny's side, Ottertail placed an arm about the shoulder of his friend. It was reassuring, but Johnny felt a trembling which matched his own reaction.

"Ai and begorra, but never have I seen anything to match what you have just done, either for boldness or skill," Ottertail breathed. "With only a bow and arrow, you have killed a grizzly! Again, my friend, I owe my life to you."

The words seemed like the buzzing of bees on a summer day, coming from a long way off. Johnny sat down suddenly, sure that his legs would let him down. Now that it was over he was more scared than when the *Oregon* had backed out into the current, leaving him behind.

"I was lucky," he managed. "I happened to see him up here and sort of had a hunch; then I saw that he was stalking you. You seemed to be asleep."

"I was dreaming," Ottertail conceded, and explained his own mishap and unpleasant awakening. "He would surely have avenged that old arrow which troubled him had it not been for you." Descending to where the bear sprawled, he examined it cautiously, making sure that it was really dead.

"It was my destiny to travel toward the rising sun, as I did, and to meet you," he said soberly. "Together, my friend, we will do great things. Let us return to camp with this meat, which will be most welcome. Now those who have been doubtful must realize that you are one of us."

If it worked out that way, it would be worth the bad moments they'd both endured. Ottertail was bursting with a new thought, new ambitions. While he had lain unconscious, he had dreamed, and the remembered dream was wonderful.

Johnny knew that Indians placed great stress on dreams, especially when something about the time or place made them unusual or outstanding. A dream could reveal or foretell a warrior's medicine, reveal what was to come. What they adopted as their own particular medicine was often the result of such dreams.

Most of that might be superstition, but he was in no mood to argue any of it. If Ottertail had dreamed a good dream, that was fine.

"Your dreams were good, then?" he asked politely.

"They were very good," Ottertail agreed eagerly. Normally he would have been reticent, even secretive, on such a matter, but this was a special occasion, as his next words confirmed.

"There were two parts to my dream, and you are in it, John Hawk. We shall go upon a long journey again, once more head toward the rising sun. With you helping, I will find a great horse, as pale as the winter!"

He paused, awed by a new thought, then went on soberly.

"A pale horse in winter! Why, that—it must mean The Hungry Horse! And one who tames and rides that great beast will be a savior of his people! But in the dream—it is only by finding and taming it that famine and death can be averted. The Hungry Horse, tamed, will bring prosperity for my tribe! It will be my medicine, this ghost horse. With it, we will find the vanished buffalo."

Johnny was inclined to be skeptical, but he was careful not to show it. In any case, he'd be glad to journey with Ottertail again through the warm days of summer. That would be more pleasant than remaining in or around the camp.

"That sounds good," he agreed. "You say that I am to go along?"

"After what has happened on the plain and here on the mountain, would I venture on such a trail without you? Sure and that would be a fool way for a man to behave! You are a part of my medicine. Without you, I would surely fail.

"In my dream there was the sound of thunder, the pounding feet of many buffalo. Only when I awoke, it was the growl of the grizzly—and from that you saved me!"

His eyes changed, suddenly grew sharp.

"But something is wrong. I know that you were guided here, where I needed you. But why? Tell me."

"It's nothing," Johnny protested. "As for my taking a ride, there was nothing to do, and you know how I like to ride."

Ottertail would not be put off.

"It is lonely to ride far alone, and it may be dangerous—as it was," he reminded Johnny. "Were some of the others unfriendly, so that you were not well treated in the camp of my people?"

"Your sister, your uncle the chief and his woman treated me as though I were indeed your brother." Johnny assured him. "But as for the others—I think that some are jealous that you, the chief's nephew, should take a white man as a friend. I overheard what some of them were muttering. Some are sure that anyone with a white skin must surely be bad medicine and bring evil upon the tribe—and think it has already touched them. Since the day when you set out upon that trip during which we met, they say that bad luck has dogged them."

"Such talk sounds like Coyote Man." Ottertail shrugged. "He is well named, a vain one with a jealous heart. They who speak jealously speak foolishly. With your help, good will come to my people. Now we will return with meat for all."

They dragged the grizzly down the mountain, no great task due to the steep slope. When it would slide no farther, they skinned it, wrapping part of the meat in the hide, hoisting the remainder off the ground, suspending it from the limb of a big pine. It would be safe there from predators until they could return for it.

"Of course, it will be a long and tiresome journey to find and capture The Hungry Horse," Ottertail observed. "You do not mind?"

Johnny was almost beginning to believe in the dream. In any case, so long as Ottertail did, that was enough. By hunting far enough, instead of sitting despondently in the tents, as some were doing, they might find the food that was required.

He was also intrigued by the prophecy about The Hungry Horse, the great White One. Most wild horses, like the Indian ponies, were red or brown, spotted, gray or dun. Not since leaving the Ozarks had he seen a white horse. One must indeed be a ghost animal, as well as a rarity. White was the color of the winter snows, the hunger moon. The Hungry Horse might turn out to be more than a symbol.

"The old men are saying that never, since even the most ancient among them can remember, has there been so great a dearth of buffalo," Ottertail added. "As we know, the herds have vanished from all their usual feeding grounds. Everyone fears the starving time."

"Who can blame them?"

"Ai, who, indeed? Even in my dream, I beheld a storm spreading from the mountains, enveloping the prairie; a storm of deep snows, of long cold."

Johnny's horse objected to carrying a burden of bear hide and meat, but Ottertail talked to the pony, rubbing its nose and ears. Then, though the cayuse trembled, it submitted to being loaded. Ottertail had a way with horses.

Back at the village, there was awe and amazement at what Johnny had accomplished. It was a feat such as few, even among the older warriors, could boast of. Others hurried to bring in the rest of the meat. Then, with fresh fires kindled and meat in every cooking pot, much of the antagonism which had been apparent that morning seemed to disappear, though some, it was clear, were still mistrustful.

The feast was joyous, but one good meal, after a succession of lean days, would have a very temporary effect, be soon forgotten. Again there was a grim report as another party of scouts returned from a long search, bringing no word of buffalo. It was time to set out in quest of The Hungry Horse.

6

Fawn Who Runs shyly presented Johnny with a pair of moccasins for the journey.

"May they carry you swiftly and safely," she said. "So much depends on you."

Johnny was deeply appreciative. Even if Ottertail had not slyly pointed it out, he would have realized the careful bead work was a mark of her friendship. He asked Ottertail about his sister.

"Fawn Who Runs is a pretty name," he said. "But she's like you, part Irish. Did your father give her no other name?"

"Sure and he did," Ottertail grinned. "Kathleen, no less."

"And that's Irish, and mighty pretty—as she is," Johnny observed.

Not many of the tribe approved of this new journey by the two of them, one white man and a half-white

Indian, who seemed to become more white and less Indian under his influence. They were too young, and Johnny was alien. Of course, there was Ottertail's dream. What he had revealed of it was impressive. Still, to go in search of the ghost animal, the fabled Hungry Horse—

The slaying of the bear and the eating of its meat was a good sign. But there were many portents of evil, to weigh against the favorable omens. Even the summer wind held a wail like that of mid-winter.

Night still brooded over the land as they prepared to set out. The rest of the camp was asleep. Mink Woman had a warm pot of meat and berries ready for their breakfast. Fawn Who Runs watched gravely while they ate. The chief made a ceremony of shaking hands.

Johnny climbed on his hammerhead, while Ottertail proudly bestrode a sorrel with three white feet, the gift of his uncle. It had been captured not long before in a raid against the Crows.

"Among them, this animal was counted as strong medicine," Running Wolf pointed out. "So shall it be strong for you. On such a journey, you will have need of all possible good medicine."

They rode into the eye of the rising sun. It did not matter that to the southeast lay the wild country of the Dakotas. When a brave followed a medicine trail, there could be no turning aside.

Spring lay across the land, as though to blot out memories of cold and suffering. The trees were a bright green, the new leaves as glossily waxed as a teal's wing. The grass, long untouched by grazing herds, stood tall and rich. Johnny drew a deep breath. The sheer bigness was a challenge.

Only one thing was wrong. Across a plain so rich with grass, there should have been countless antelope and buffalo, along with swarms of wild fowl. But nothing was changed. On the first day, they sighted a skulking coyote.

They camped near a small creek, catching fish and roasting them over a tiny blaze. As darkness settled, they followed the now familiar pattern, moving back from the dying embers, going for nearly a mile before settling for the night.

"We are in our own country," Ottertail explained. "Probably no enemies would venture here, but it is better always to act as though a war party might be lurking behind stones or creeping in the grass."

A long downpour soaked them, but there was sun the next day. They recrossed the river, and here the streams ran strongly. Among the foothills, creeks were numerous, their course marked by cottonwoods and willows. There were deep pools filled with beaver, trout and muskrat, then stretches where the water coursed above mossy stones. Smart weed vied with reeds, giving a heady pungency to the air.

As the prairie widened, the streams grew few, were almost hidden in sunken beds. Trees became rare. The water slid silently, as though fearful of attracting attention to itself in so lonely a land.

"It may soon be necessary for us to sleep by day and travel at night," Ottertail observed. "But not yet. This is still Blackfoot country."

Johnny understood. He had a feeling that they should skulk by night now, but Ottertail could not bring himself to do so while still in the Blackfoot range. The Lords of the Plain rode boldly, as befitted a proud people.

Johnny came awake with a sense of wrongness, the feel of danger in the air. The moon had vanished, leaving the stars remote and lost. A fine tracery of frost covered the grass.

The gloom was beginning to thin, like a skin too tightly stretched. Johnny sat up and looked around, then stared, apprehension gripping him like cruel claws. He could see no darker humps against the dull flatness of the land, nothing to break the pattern of the horizon.

Lacking any draw or coulee in which to conceal their horses, they had picketed them close. Even if the horses had lain down to sleep, they should loom up.

Ottertail was beside him now, exclaiming under his breath. They moved in a widening circle, but even the brightening dawn made no difference. Their horses were gone.

Ottertail studied the sign, then shook his head in mingled exasperation and resignation.

"Sure and I am the foolish one!" he mourned. "They have been stolen—and what makes it worse, taken by a single man—someone who must have been afoot, as we now are. He was probably a Crow, a venturesome one who risked coming into our country to try and steal back their medicine horse. Now he has it! He did not risk disturbing us, counting the horses as more important. And while he robbed us, we slept!"

"Is there any chance of getting them back?"

Ottertail swept an arm in a wide circle. They could see for miles, but nothing moved. Having the horses. the triumphant brave would lose no time returning to his own people.

Johnny felt sick. To be afoot again, in so vast a land—if that was not disaster, it was teetering on the brink. They might be able to make their way back to the village, as they had done before, but doing so would be a confession of failure.

Yet without horses, how could they hope to complete their quest? Stealing a horse from an enemy was one thing, but to find and capture wild horses, particularly The Hungry Horse, while they themselves were on foot, threatened to be virtually impossible.

What made it worse was that he had heard something in the night, some disturbing sound. Undoubtedly it had been the raider. Had he been properly alert, he would have roused himself and investigated instead of going back to sleep.

7

"Skunk in a hen-house!" Johnny observed disgustedly. "I should have known. I was half-awake, enough to know that something was going on. But I just went back to sleep."

"Whatever you heard, I should have heard it, too," Ottertail protested. "We both failed—and what makes it so bad is the shame that a Crow should fool a Blackfoot in such a way!"

Then he grew cheerful again, shrugging off the misfortune.

"But sure and begorra, we're not licked yet! We were careless; we slept so soundly. But were we not on foot before, and did we not return in triumph? What we have done we can do again."

"Sure," Johnny agreed. "And we'll find The Hungry Horse." But his words sounded hollow.

Now on foot, in enemy country, it was necessary to move with increasing caution. Should they be discovered, it would be impossible to escape enemies by outrunning them.

Though claimed by the Blackfeet, this was really open land, where hunters from many tribes ventured. The flatness had given way to easy rolling hills, and as they topped a crest, Ottertail threw himself flat. Johnny was only an instant behind him. There were mounted men not far off. Had they been seen in turn?

Plain enough now to count, six horsemen moved along the skyline. Ottertail drew a deep breath.

"They saw us," he observed grimly, "or they think they did. So of course they will investigate."

All at once it was hard to breathe. Here it was again, and he had not felt so scared even when facing the big grizzly. Then he had been thinking of his friend, taking no time to consider his own peril. Now they were far from any sort of help, on foot, with mounted enemies closing in. In such open country there were few hiding places.

There had been no rain here for days, so the ground was dry. The grass was not very high, so they left little sign in moving through it. But there was not enough to hide in, and there would be enough of a trail for enemies to read.

Off at the foot of the slope was a creek. Ottertail led the way. It was their best, probably their only chance. They would have to circle, taking advantage of every sort of cover, to reach it.

As they came close, Johnny viewed it dubiously. It

would serve for drinking, but he could see no hiding places. Here there was no brush, lining the banks. Even the banks were low, with the water creeping along, mostly quite shallow. And their enemies would be sure that they had taken to the water.

At this point there was motion to the current, while the creek bed showed rocky. Reeds grew along one shore, and there were tracks in the mud, mink sign. Scratchy imprints suggested muskrats.

"The puma hides by stretching flat along the limb of a tree, while the rabbit makes himself part of a clump of grass," Ottertail whispered. "Step carefully, so that no stone is disturbed," he added, and entered the water. Midway across, he plucked a reed, breaking it off beneath the surface.

"Lie down and stretch flat on your back," he instructed, "close to the reeds, but *not* among them. Let the water flow over you. Breathe through the reed, holding the tip just above the surface. Do not stir, no matter what, until I signal you. It may be a long ordeal, but it is our only chance."

Johnny lowered himself into the water, allowing it to flow over his face; his bow and arrow were under him, ready to grasp. Breathing with the hollow reed was fairly easy; the hard part was fighting a groundless but real fear, that of being totally submerged. It took all his will power to resist the impulse to move, to thresh about. But one careless movement might dislodge a mossy stone, making sign for sharp eyes.

Once he was settled, it was not too bad. He could breathe normally again, though he wondered about Ottertail's instructions to lie near but not among the clumps of reeds. Then he realized that his body would flatten them, a sure betrayal to the scouts.

Since the creek was shallow, the water was comfortably warm. He ventured to open his eyes, something he had never tried under water. Objects appeared distorted, swaying and unreal. For a moment he was startled, for someone was standing looking down at him. Then he saw that it was Ottertail and relaxed.

Apparently Ottertail was satisfied, for he nodded and left to stretch out somewhere near by but not too close. Johnny remembered to tip his feet so as to disturb the flow of the current as little as possible.

He was covered, blanketed, but at best the water was a shallow, transparent shield. Keen eyes would search the stream. Could their enemies fail to see them? They had to trust to the same sort of camouflage that wild creatures depended upon.

But unless the hunters were observant enough to discover where they had entered the water, they could have no sure way of judging where the two they sought might be, within a range of a mile or so. That left a lot of water to search. Unless a man looked closely, at exactly the right spot, it would be difficult to notice anything. The ripple of moving water was deceptive.

There was always the chance that they might see something, yet that risk had to be taken. Johnny found himself rigid, holding his breath, and started to breathe again. The water was cold, now that he'd been submerged awhile. It was a temptation to change position. Stones, which had seemed flat and smooth at first, had a way of gouging into his back and hips.

He managed to remain still, resisting the impulse, but unable not to shiver. By now those six riders must have reached the creek. They might be passing along either shore at this very moment—

Something was in the water, churning it, close to his nose. Johnny breathed again as he realized that the commotion was made by a big fish, heading upstream. But almost at once there was a greater confusion which he could see and feel. A huge creature loomed monstrously; then the hoofs of a horse splashed past, close alongside him. If the searchers were suspicious enough of this particular stretch of water, or clever enough to ride, all abreast, up and down it, they could hardly fail to find them.

Now the impulse to move, to jump and run, was almost irresistible. Desperately he held himself rigid, watching the shaky line of horsemen through the water. He counted five more crossing just above him. Now their nearness was a piece of good luck. The splashing water from the hoofs of their horses rained on the smooth current, blurring it, helping to distort their vision.

Then the horses were gone, the thudding hoofs no longer like echoes. Johnny relaxed, though he found it no easier to remain quiet, with all the former aggravations multiplied. The water was icy.

But Ottertail had warned him not to move until he gave a signal, and if Ottertail could stand it, so could Johnny. The realization that the horsemen might have left the water, then halted to watch, hoping for such a telltale movement, was a timely aid.

The softly pliant moccasins which Fawn Who Runs had given him would be stiff once they dried out from this soaking. So far they had been very comfortable. And her name was Kathleen! She'd worry until Ottertail returned—maybe about him, too. That helped, somehow.

There was a touch on his arm, and he turned his head to see Ottertail. It was a relief to move, to emerge into the sun. Never had the world looked so bright and pleasant.

As he was about to speak, Ottertail gestured for silence, then led the way, keeping to the middle of the stream, until a rocky bank offered a safe place to step from the water. There the wetness would soon dry, leaving no sign.

"I think they have gone on," Ottertail said softly. "They crossed back and forth several times, up one side of the creek and down the other. Now I think they must be unsure whether they really saw anyone or not. Still, we will hide for the rest of the day."

They chose a knoll back from the water, where the grass was a cover. It was pleasant to lie with the sun beating down. Ottertail spread the bows and arrows to dry, so that they would again be effective. A soaked bowstring would be useless.

As night closed down, Ottertail tested his bow, knocking over a sage hen for their supper. Here there were increasing signs of game, but still no trace of the vanished buffalo.

The country was changing, the hills becoming more ragged and more rugged. In the distance shone the blue of evergreens. The hills were higher, though the timber was small in contrast to the trees of the western mountains.

"This is the country of my dream," Ottertail declared confidently. "Somewhere among these hills we will find The Hungry Horse."

"I hope it's soon," Johnny said fervently. "My moccasins are almost worn out. We've come a long way—on shank's mare."

"But we have fared well," Ottertail reminded him. "True, we lost our horses, but we have escaped such enemies as we encountered. What more could we ask, except to find the buffalo? Do you see something?"

"There is something which moves off there," Johnny

agreed. "Men on horseback."

His own vision had become at least the equal of Ottertail's. The men they glimpsed were a long way off, moving between two hills. Selecting a hiding place, they watched them dip from sight, then presently reappear much closer. There were three horses and three men.

"They follow a course, not us." Ottertail pronounced. "They will pass well to the side—"

He sprang suddenly into the open, waving and shouting to attract attention.

"They are Blackfeet. And I think they are from our own tribe."

The trio hesitated, surprised, wary of a trick. Then, reassured, they approached. But the elation at finding other Blackfeet was tempered as Johnny and Ottertail recognized them. Coyote Man was in the lead, and the two who rode with him were his friends, not Ottertail's.

"Nonetheless they are Blackfeet, and they left the camp after we did," Ottertail pointed out. "For all we know, they may have been looking for us."

"If they were, they're sure good at hiding the fact." Johnny shrugged. "Only part they're going to like is getting a chance to laugh at us."

Ottertail shrugged ruefully, watching the faces of the three as they discovered that he and Johnny, who had set out boldly to do great things, had allowed themselves to be set afoot.

"Sure and begorra, and it's right you are," he admitted. "But the dog which barks at dawn fills a cooking pot at noon."

Their guess confirmed, Coyote Men laughed loudly, his companions following his lead.

"You are the one who boasted how he would ride high on The Hungry Horse," he taunted. "Instead, you run like a dog."

They explained that they were on a mission for the chief, hoping to find a neighboring tribe which was allied to the Blackfeet. These were the Gros Ventres, or Big Bellies. Their camp was believed to lie somewhere to the south.

"It may be that they can help us," Coyote Man added. "They may know where to find game. We had hoped to encounter you and receive a good report— but all that you have to report after so long and foolish a quest is that you are hungry already!"

8

Coyote Man and his companions spent the night with them, implying condescendingly that they bestowed a favor, since it might be risky to travel with such inept warriors. Yet despite their superior attitude, companionship was welcome after so lonely a journey. When the trio rode on the next morning, soon becoming only specks against the horizon, a greater sense of loneliness closed in.

"At least they are your people," Johnny pointed out. "I'm not, that's the trouble. I'm a white man, which is bad enough, and I'm Jonathan Wilde's nephew, which is a lot worse. They blame me for the bad luck which seemed to come with me. If I hadn't been along, they might have offered you a horse."

"They could not spare us an animal, having no extras," Ottertail returned. "As for distrusting you, they are foolish. But it is not you alone they distrust. They do not forget that I am the son of my father, not quite an Indian. Besides, they are jealous of us, of my dream. They would almost rather that our people starve than that we should be the ones to help."

They set out again, their course almost opposite the one taken by the three. Here the horizons were closer, and did not require such an endless time to reach a goal. But each stone or clump of cactus seemed rougher.

Leading the way through brushy country, Ottertail reached hastily for his bow, fitting an arrow to the string. Though Johnny could see no sign of game, he did the same.

Ottertail kept moving, but his pace was barely a crawl. He was watching something not far off but close at hand, almost at their feet. Johnny saw that the ground seemed to wiggle or move. There were small huddled specks, motionless again, which were almost invisible as they crouched.

These were prairie chicks, a half-grown flock, blending so well with their surroundings that they believed themselves unnoticed. Usually they took to their wings at any sign of danger, but sometimes a ruse such as this was even more effective.

Ottertail kept moving, since to halt would send them into the air like a whirlwind. "Now!" Ottertail breathed the signal, and loosed an arrow. Johnny's was gone in the same instant. There was a burst of flight, and the flock was gone like a dream, but both arrows had found targets.

"We will have a good meal today," Ottertail said jubilantly. "And what is much better, we are finding game again. My medicine is good. It has led us truly. When we do our part, all else is right."

Johnny was gaining a new insight into Indian philosophy. On the whole, it made good sense.

"We used to have a neighbor, back when I was a boy," he observed. "He spent most of his time in a rocking chair on the porch when the weather was good, in front of the kitchen stove when it was not. He was always whittling—but was too busy to split wood to keep the fire going. His wife had to do that. He was always saying that the Lord would provide, but it didn't seem to me that He did. Now I understand why."

"The Great Spirit gives us game, but it is there only if we make use of it. We have eyes to see with, feet to travel with, arms to draw a bow. Meat does not come; it must be taken."

Johnny nodded, but his gaze was fixed across the valley. He pointed, and Ottertail followed his signal, then lowered his voice to a whisper, though they were miles away from the objects of their gaze.

"Now your eyes are sharper than mine!" he breathed. "At last we have found them, the wild bunch." He gazed, noting how they spread over a wide section, grazing, looking like toys from that distance. "What a mighty band."

Johnny was just as excited. Their first objective, the band of wild horses, was at last in sight. Ottertail had no doubt that The Hungry Horse would be the leader of such a band. There were hundreds of ponies, grazing along the slopes and down in the meadows. From a distance they looked no different from Indian ponies, no wilder.

They moved eagerly but carefully, crossing the valley, keeping well hidden. From a nearer vantage point they saw many colts running and playing. Then Ottertail sucked in his breath sharply. Among the many, one animal was coming into sight, moving to the hilltop. He was a great white stallion, and the regal manner of its progress denoted that it was clearly the leader, the king. From the highest point he turned, surveying his domain, keeping watch for possible danger.

Johnny's heart pounded against his ribs. Until now he had never been quite certain what to expect, or even if he believed that Ottertail's dream could become a reality. But here, beyond any doubt, just as the legend had pictured it, was The Hungry Horse.

"Is he not magnificent, a true king?" Ottertail breathed. "Ai and begorra, but to think that I shall own him!" His first excitement was giving way to complacency. "Now we have but to capture him, and another for you," he added, then grinned.

"If Coyote Man and his companions had suspected that the wild band was so near at hand—But ours is the luck, for they turned the other way and saw nothing of them. Which is well, for they would have chased after them as wildly as young pups and have made our task almost impossible."

Johnny did not say so, but it seemed to him that it must verge on that in any case. They had journeyed for weeks to find the wild horses, and whether it was Ottertail's medicine, perseverance or pure luck, they had found a band. That, after all, was not very unusual. But how would they make any of the wild band captive?

As a boy, he had watched riders round up domesticated but half-wild ponies; fearful and suspicious, they would often make a wild break for freedom just short of field or corral. And more often than not, they would succeed.

Even if Ottertail and himself had been well mounted, as when they had left the camp in the Little Rockies, catching one of the wild ones would not have been easy. To manage such a feat while they were on foot seemed out of the question.

Having anticipated such a situation, Ottertail seemed not at all worried. In the gathering darkness they moved closer to the band, testing the air, swinging to approach them from down-wind. At this stage, they did not want the horses to take alarm at an alien scent.

But the wild ones would be suspicious when they came in sight, being wary of two-legged creatures. Johnny expected them to take to their heels at the first sight of Ottertail and himself and probably run for miles. Once they caught up again, would not the same pattern be repeated?

"Of course they will run from us, many times," Ottertail conceded. "For us, that will mean more days spent following them. That cannot be helped. Each time that they see us, they will grow more used to us, taking note that we are slow and clumsy creatures, unable to harm them. Soon they will view us with as much disdain as Coyote Man does. Then they will lose all fear and allow us to come closer. All that is needed is to keep following, with much patience."

They each carried a necessary tool, a lariat rope made from braided rawhide. They had held onto these despite all their troubles on the trail and, working the rawhide as they walked, had restored the softness and pliability after they had been soaked. Ottertail was working his again, and despite the quietness with which he spoke, Johnny knew that he was excited.

The horses were now clustering along the far slope of a long, wide valley, shrouded on three sides by mountains. A creek, lined with willows, wound where they grazed. This was Crow country, range where the Blackfeet would be unwelcome. But the fact that the wild band were summering here was proof that no one had discovered or disturbed them.

"Only my medicine was strong enough to find them," Ottertail said seriously, "though many must have sought them. Such a band is a rich prize, doubly so in such a year as this. Crow, Sioux, Arapaho, Cree—any would be happy to find them."

Taking shelter behind trees and brush, they worked closer, finally making camp a couple of miles distant. The next morning, they climbed a short, brush-lined slope to see where the horses might have drifted during the night. Ottertail, in the lead, stopped suddenly, a look of amazement on his face.

Holding his breath, Johnny moved to a spot where he could see, then caught his breath. During the night the herd had drifted, but toward them. Now they were spread out along the slope below, scores of horses, some almost within reach of a long rope.

Viewed at close range, they were different from the Indian ponies that Johnny had seen, with shaggier manes, yet an over-all effect of well-fed sleekness. The scarcity of other game had resulted in rich grass, and they were in perfect condition.

Some raised their heads, ears pricked forward, and Johnny started to duck back, then remained motionless. They had to be seen not just once, but many

times, and this was as good a time to begin their educa-
tion as any. The horses eyed them, uncertain whether
or not to be afraid. Then, like a wave, the knowledge
of an alien presence seemed to flow through the
herd.

There was a tension in the atmosphere, as though
a thunderstorm were about to break, though the
morning sky was cloudless. Johnny understood his
feeling as the white king trotted into sight a short distance away. He stopped, looked at them, tossed his
head, and a look of rapture spread over Ottertail's
face.

The wild leader was a magnificent animal, bigger
than any of the others, long in the barrel, with a look
of fleetness. He deserved the position he held from
almost any point of view. Pale as the snow, he might
indeed be The Hungry Horse of legend, but he was
also fat and saucy, his coat like sun glinting on
frost.

Johnny shared Ottertail's excitement. If a man owned such a horse, it seemed as though it would be
easy to accomplish anything, even to find the vanished
buffalo.

But there was a vast difference between seeing such
a horse, even at close range, and taking it captive. As
though reading their thoughts and growing angry at
so brash a notion, the big white reared, pawing the
air, sounding a shrill neigh of challenge and defiance.

Dropping back on all fours, he lowered his head and charged straight at them. The others who were near enough, taking their cue, swept along at his heels.

Terror prickled along Johnny's spine. This was even worse than being surrounded by Dakotas, as bad as being face to face with an angry grizzly. Johnny managed to resist the impulse to run, knowing that to do so would be the worst thing possible. They would be able to take only a few steps before being overtaken and trampled.

A horse, especially a wild one, was not like other creatures of the mountain or plain. Descendants of ancestors first brought over by the Spanish, they had learned, through many generations, to cope with every challenge of nature, heat or cold, snow or drought, as well as natural enemies. Fleetness of foot, and occasionally massed defiance, had made them the real Lords of the Plain.

A wolf or panther, faced with danger, especially the new or unknown, would hesitate, snarling, and prudently draw back. But the horses, particularly the white king, had only disdain for danger which they could see. Now they were expressing their contempt in an open challenge.

When the grizzly had charged him on the mountain, Johnny had expected it and had had a plan of campaign, a chance to dodge the rush by taking a quick step aside, a certain advantage in the steepness of the slope. Here there was nothing like that, no place either to run or hide.

Ottertail stood until the horses had halved the distance. Then he yelled, not loudly, but rather a derisive sort of hoot. *Hoh-hoh!* The unexpectedness of such a thing brought the ghost animal to a sliding stop only feet away. Nostrils flaring, he stared wonderingly, defiantly. He was superb, his silver mane as shaggy as a lion's, his eyes glaring.

He stood a moment, then leaped high, all four feet together, twisting around, coming down and facing the two-legged creatures again. A second time he snorted, then spun about and raced away, the others following obediently.

Johnny's legs felt like cornstalks in a high wind. If he had been worried, Ottertail had hidden it well. Now he was jubilant.

"The Hungry Horse!" he breathed. "Only he was not hungry, not at all. He was warning us to get out, away from his range, telling us that he is not afraid of us! What an animal! From now on he will ignore us as creatures of no account."

"I didn't feel of much account for a minute there," Johnny confessed. "What if he had kept coming?"

Ottertail nodded gravely.

"He is a great king, of a high spirit," he admitted. "Had we shown fear, he would surely have killed us. Never have I seen one like him. But what could be better? What horse, save The Hungry Horse, could do what must be done in this time when the hunger moon coasts even the summer skies?"

"He's a great horse, all right," Johnny agreed. "Really magnificent."

"Such a meeting with them, with him, was good luck," Ottertail added. "Now they have viewed us at close range and decided that we are harmless. That will save us many days."

The horses, as they expected, ran for miles before halting to graze. Ottertail was certain that the king would not go far or try to lead his band to a new territory. He was too confident, contemptuous of them. Like Coyote Man, he found it necessary to show his disdain. Also, this was a long, rich valley, well secluded. The wild band would not readily desert such a haven.

Here, for the first time, they found an abundance of game, after the dearth of the open prairie. More then once they had been reduced to digging roots to avoid going hungry. Now, on every hand was sign of deer and elk, along with smaller game.

But nowhere, even here, was there any sign of the buffalo.

"Well, no matter about the big ones; we will find them in good time," Ottertail asserted confidently. "We will take a few days now to hunt and feast, to prepare skins and make new moccasins and whatever

we need. We will stay within sight of the horses, so
that they will grow used to us."

The days were long and hot, but among the hills the
nights were cool. Hunting, working skins and taking
care of chores was restful after the long journey. They
stayed near the wild band, so that the horses could
see them whenever they looked up.

Each day they ventured closer. True to prediction,
the wild bunch, having shown their defiance and contempt, largely ignored them. Only when the two-
legged creatures came too close would they edge
away.

They moved boldly, not hurrying, doing nothing
which might startle the horses. They called *hoh-hoh* at
frequent intervals, a sound which the horses came to
associate with them and ignore.

Johnny was surprised at how well these tactics worked. Within a few days they were able to walk among
the herd, approaching fairly close to almost any
pony.

Ottertail proved surprisingly adept at fashioning
new moccasins, and since Johnny was clumsy at that,
he watched awhile, then climbed the tallest convenient
peak. The view, spread out on all sides, was breath-
taking.

To the north, a storm played through the hills,
thunder growling in a manner reminiscent of the
grizzly. Far off to the south he picked out a river,

which he guessed would be the Yellowstone. Beyond it, the country was different. It took him a minute to understand. As far below the river as he could see the land was black, as though newly plowed. But such virgin sod had never known the nudge of a plowshare.

There's been a fire, he thought, startled at the magnitude of the holocaust. A prairie fire. With high dry grass from last summer, it must have been something!

Its northward progress had been checked by the river, but below that it had made a wide sweep. The new grass had not yet fully covered the scars.

He reported the burn to Ottertail, and also posed a question. "It looks like a big one. Do you suppose that it could have something to do with the buffalo not showing up north of the Yellowstone? They might come that far, then swing away for lack of grass; maybe drift east instead of north."

"It is an idea," Ottertail agreed. "Something happened to them. Well, now comes the real work. It is time to go after our horses—one for you, The Hungry Horse for me. Which horse do you want? There are many to choose from."

"Why, I hadn't thought about it," Johnny admitted. "Almost any one, just so long as it is a good animal."

"That will make it easier, since we must catch yours at the same time that we rope The Hungry Horse.

Once we have taken them captive, including their leader, the others of the band will take fright and run. So when we make our try, we must not fail."

With the capture in mind, Johnny had spent a lot of time practicing with the rope. To use a lariat skillfully was a high art. The Spanish riders of the Southwest, and some of the Texans, were trained in roping, but few plainsmen of the north country had such skill or any need for it. Only the Indians, who were horsemen both by liking and necessity, had trained themselves.

"I will try and rope The Hungry Horse, then tie my end of the rope to a tree, and catch a second animal with your rope before they can run," Ottertail outlined his plan. "To manage, we must come upon them in a good place, some small meadow which has only one way out. If I have trouble, you must be ready to try and rope a horse for yourself."

It would not be too serious a failure should they catch only one. One pony, as soon as it was trained, would make a big difference. Ottertail could ride among the herd and use it to cut out or rope another. But even such a partial success would mean a delay of several days, and the long days of summer were speeding by. All at once they begrudged the waste of even one.

The sun was blazing in glory along the tops of the mountains when Johnny awoke; the valley bottoms were still in deep gloom. Slinging his bow and arrows across his shoulder, rope in hand, he climbed to the crest. He always liked to see where the wild bunch might be.

At the top he stopped with a sudden catch of breath. Here was the sort of luck for which they had hoped, almost a repetition of their first sudden encounter with the horses. A dozen head had drifted into a meadow below. Several were grazing, the others stirring from sleep.

One of them, and as usual the most alert, was The Hungry Horse.

This was a chance of a lifetime, now that some of them had drifted so close to where the boys camped. For they would pay no attention to man-scent, even if they caught it. Johnny stared, fascinated, as the possibilities dawned on him. Then he stepped back out of sight.

Ottertail was still asleep. Johnny tossed a small stone, and as it fell near his head, Ottertail awoke. Johnny gestured for silence, with further motions to indicate that the wild bunch was close at hand. Ottertail caught up his own rope and started to climb.

Cautiously, Johnny looked again. Not only were the horses right at hand, including The Hungry Horse, but this was the sort of place that Ottertail had had in mind. They had drifted down the little valley, along whose far side a small stream flowed under a high bank. Above the bank the hill rose steeply, dark with evergreens.

Where the creek twisted out of sight, the shoulder of the hill jutted, leaving only a narrow gorge, occupied by the water. The natural way out was up the slope, then past the spot where Johnny stood. The route was wide enough for a road, though to follow it a wagon would be forced to wind and twist among the pines.

The horses must have drifted there the afternoon before, then spent the night. Johnny and Ottertail had chosen the place for their night's camp equally by chance.

Seeking escape, a frightened horse might race up the slope through the trees, or make a long jump from the bank down to the creek. Barring those expedients, they had to come past the spot where Johnny stood. Knowing the lack of fear in the leader, Johnny had no doubt as to what he would do.

Now the king's snort warned that the horse had seen him. Fearful of a trap, he broke instantly into a run, heading straight toward Johnny. The others followed.

This time they would neither slow nor halt until they were past the danger point.

9

Johnny's heartbeats seemed to be trying to match the hoofbeats of the big white horse. There was not so much danger as when some of the wild band had first charged them, for here there were trees to dodge among or climb. The trouble was that they had been presented with a perfect opportunity, and now that the ponies had taken alarm, the chance would be lost. If they escaped, it was certain that The Hungry Horse would never again allow himself to be caught in a similar situation.

Hearing the sound of driving hoofs and guessing what they meant, Ottertail was coming as fast as he could, but he would arrive too late. It was now or never, and Johnny was excited, yet cool and ready. Things seemed to work that way at a moment of crisis.

His rope was open in a wide loop, as he had learned to manipulate it. Desperately he flung it as the white streak flashed alongside; then there was a satisfying jerk as the noose settled.

He had his father's training to thank for his next move, having watched him work half-wild animals on the farm and remembering his word of caution.

"When you rope a horse or cow, be ready to snub your end of the rope around a saddle-horn or post—and fast! Otherwise, don't be crazy enough to dab a loop in the first place. If you ain't prepared, it's worse than tyin' onto a runaway locomotive."

Jumping back, Johnny made a quick twist of the rope around a tree, while some slack remained. Holding desperately, he braced himself for the shock.

Sensing danger as the noose settled over his ears, The Hungry Horse increased his speed to a frenzied rush. As the rope became taut, he was jerked and twisted, turning over. The force of his rush upended him; his hoops threshed wildly.

Despite the half-hitch and the purchase which it afforded, the violence of the jerk almost tore the rope from Johnny's grasp. Working feverishly as the rope slackened, he knotted the end to the tree. Shaken and enraged, the king surged to his feet. He screamed defiance, mouth wide and ears flattened, and charged his tormentor.

Johnny dodged to safety among the trees, and again the taut rope brought the white king up, twisting him about. This time he managed to keep to his feet.

The other horses were streaming past, escaping

from the trap—all but one. Ottertail rushed up in time to swing his rope and settle the noose over the head of a big bay, which promptly began fighting back.

Ottertail also tied his end of the rope, jumping out of harm's way. The drum of hoofs receded and vanished as the other horses disappeared, but the frantic struggle continued as the wild ones fought enemies of a sort wholly beyond their experience. The result at times seemed in doubt. Ottertail and Johnny watched, elated with their success, apprehensive lest their captives escape or injure themselves as they fought the ropes.

The bay had been last in line, so the two horses were far enough apart not to interfere with each other as they struggled. They continued to fight the terrifying strands, jumping, kicking, until it seemed to Johnny that they would either break the ropes or their necks.

Ottertail circled through the trees and came up beside Johnny, grinning widely.

"Ai and begorra, but the luck of the Irish is with us this day," he breathed, "and the strong medicine which came to me when you arrived! Think of it, that we should capture *two* such horses, one The Hungry Horse! You, John Hawk, are mighty in action."

"I knew you wanted him, and he is yours," Johnny gasped. "But, bee on a bonnet, they'll break their necks or choke to death."

Ottertail was not much worried. "Some animals

kill themselves before they learn," he admitted. "But a horse is a wise one, and he learns fast. See, already they are starting to think about what has happened, to take time to figure it out."

Though still straining against the ropes, both horses were easing enough so that they could breathe. Ottertail viewed them with mingled pride and sympathy.

"Hoh, but this is hard on such proud ones—to find that something is stronger than they are, and that such puny creatures as we are to be feared, after all! They are imprisoned by the web of the spider, when before they could outrace the wind! But hard times come to all the proud ones, a time of testing. The moon of hunger lurks in the northern sky, and you, Ghost Animal, are the only one who can outrace it! So this is necessary. And since you are wise as well as proud, you will survive."

The Hungry Horse was slightly bigger than the bay, though the beast that Ottertail had roped matched him in grace and build, and had the same look of speed. Johnny was elated at the thought of riding such a horse, and apprehensive at the same time. These were of the wild bunch, not at all like the plodding farm animals he had known, or even the hammerhead which had been stolen from him.

"I could never have managed without you, John Hawk," Ottertail said gratefully. "Not only have you saved my life repeatedly, but now you have made captive the medicine animal. By rights, he is and should be yours."

Johnny shook his head. "Seems to me I remember something about you savin' me," he returned. "Anyhow, we work together, and he is yours, as your dream showed. I will be well pleased with the one you roped for me. I would be too scared to try and ride The Hungry Horse."

"You could ride him as well as I," Ottertail insisted. "But as you say, we work together for the good of all. The only part that I regret is that some of my people do not understand or accept you."

The captives still struggled, especially when Ottertail or Johnny ventured near, but they were learning. The Hungry Horse, showing the qualities which made him a leader, was the first to quit fighting the noose. Deciding that what he was doing was useless, he eased up until the rope hung slack, then waited, still proud, almost disdainful.

The glossy sides of both animals glistened with sweat. It was still early, and hunger reminded the two men that they had had no breakfast. Hooking trout from the creek, they made a meal; then Ottertail prepared for work.

"We will start their training now," he explained. "With the weather so hot, we must tame them enough to lead them to water before the day ends."

Johnny's task was to assist, doing the same with the

bay as Ottertail did with The Hungry Horse. Nervous
though he was, Johnny was elated and eager to try.
After all, his cast of the noose had been accurate, and
he had played a real part in the capture.

Having eaten, they approached slowly, murmuring
soothingly, an endless monologue. Both horses drew
back, straining at the ropes. But when Ottertail reached out and touched the head of the white horse, he
neither jerked nor reared. A proud king, he quivered
from head to foot, but stood sweating. The bay responded to Johnny's ministrations, too.

Taking plenty of time, they gradually rubbed their
hands over each part of the heads and noses, next
fondling the sensitive ears, talking all the while.
Ottertail slipped his fingers beneath the taut noose
under the throat, slightly loosening the rope, enabling
the horse to breathe more easily. Again, Johnny followed his lead. He was sweating just as much as the
captives, his own heart thudding. These were still wild
horses, and if one should rear suddenly, lashing out
with forehoofs, or spin and kick, there might be no
chance to escape.

The Indian method with a horse was to win its
confidence rather than force it to obey. Gradually,
they moved their hands to necks and shoulders, talking, rubbing. When finally they sat down in the shade,
Johnny felt as tired as though he had been struggling
against the rope. The horses also rested, no longer

trying to pull loose. When the lessons resumed, they accepted them almost meekly.

Now Ottertail untied the rope which held the Hungry Horse and, working together, they led him to water by easy stages. Trees grew at convenient intervals all the way to the creek, so they were ready to take a quick snub of the rope and anchor it quickly, if the need arose. But the ghost horse gave them no trouble, not trying to break or run.

Reaching the water, he drank, then lifted his head and eyed them, as if trying to adjust to these strange happenings.

Johnny's horse was not so docile. Finding that he was partially loose, he tried to run, but Ottertail swiftly snubbed the loose end of the rope, and the noose again jerked him back. After that, he seemed to have learned his lesson.

Resigned now to this new existence, the horses cropped the grass, no longer struggling. Ottertail set about preparing supper.

Johnny climbed the slope merely to look around. There seemed no real need for extra precautions; still—

Ottertail turned swiftly as Johnny came beside him again, breathing hard, gesturing toward the hilltop.

"Someone—many riders—off there," he whispered, as though the riders might be close enough to overhear. "Perhaps a war party."

10

Ottertail stared, shaken. Then he jumped up, snatching for his bow and arrows, and followed Johnny back up the hill. Lulled by the peace of the remote valley, they had relaxed, feeling secure. Both realized how misleading the feeling had been. Others, like themselves, could find this place, whether it be a hunting or war party. Should they be discovered, the difference would not mean much.

Even if they escaped detection, another party could ruin all their hopes. Once they discovered the band of wild horses. they would be determined to capture them. In the process, they would at the very least run them out of the country.

There was no need for whispering, for the horsemen were still a couple of miles away, outlined against the setting sun. Standing behind a tree, Johnny counted nineteen. He breathed easier as they pulled up, evidently ready to camp.

"Our luck still holds," Ottertail breathed. "You

have the eye of a hawk, John Hawk; otherwise they might have been upon us before we knew it. Clearly they have not found our sign or that of the horses—yet. So for the moment, we are safe."

"But tomorrow they probably will," Johnny suggested.

"Unless our medicine is stronger than theirs."

"Who are they? Can you tell their tribe?"

"It is a little far to be certain, but they are probably Crows, possibly Dakotas. It makes little difference."

"Reckon you're right. It'd take some heavy thinkin' on my part to decide whether I'd prefer to have my topknot decoratin' a Crow lodge or danglin' from a Dakota's belt."

In the mountains, even these summer days cooled quickly as soon as the sun went down, but that accounted only in part for the chill which Johnny felt. This was a worse crisis than when the six horsemen had hunted them and they had taken refuge in a creek. On that occasion, the enemy had only been suspicious, probably not really certain if they had seen someone or not.

This was a far larger party, and if they continued on the course which they had been following, they would come upon sign, both of the wild band and the boys. Still worse, The Hungry Horse and the big bay presented an almost impossible problem.

Moments before, the success of their quest had seemed almost assured. The horses had been captured and partly tamed, and all was going well. Once the horses were broken and they were mounted on them, they could laugh at enemies, running away from even the fleetest Indian ponies.

But the horses were not yet at that stage. They could neither ride, lead, nor drive them to safety, nor hope to hide them where eager searchers would not find them. They might turn them loose, to prevent The Hungry Horse from falling into rival hands, but that would be almost as bad.

If they waited here, they risked being hunted down. By abandoning the wild ones, setting out at once and traveling all night, using all possible guile, they might avoid capture. But they would be hunted, with nowhere to go, nothing to return to. To trudge again into the village, as failures, in a camp gripped by despair, threatened by hunger, no longer able even to hope—

"If that is the best we can do, then we had better not return at all," Ottertail said heavily, showing that his thoughts followed the same line. "Ai, but this must not be! Sure and begorra, there's got to be a way, and who says we can't find it? We haven't come this far, making such great ones captive, to fail!"

Feeling a sudden excitement, Johnny clenched his fists, almost frightened by the notion which had popped into his head. It was a wild idea, but so was their situation. The possibilities were staggering, though he was not at all sure if such a scheme would be workable. At best, it would be hard and risky, but with the danger which already menaced them, what difference did it make?

"You're right. There may be a way," he said slowly. "I've got an idea, one which just might work."

Ottertail's grin came back. "If you were not a part of my medicine, it would not amount to much," he admitted. It was the Irish in him which admitted a sort of heresy which probably accounted for the distrust with which the others of the tribe viewed him. "I am eager to hear," he added.

"I was just thinking," Johnny explained, trying to put his thoughts in logical order. "Since that war party is making camp now, they can't have found any sign or be suspicious of us, or guess that the wild bunch is anywhere around. They are probably on a hunt for game, with no particular plan in mind."

"I agree. They have probably come a long way and are tired. But after so long, any sign—either of men or horses—would make them wildly excited. They would follow it as long as the light lasted."

"Is it not a shame to disappoint them?" Johnny grinned. "Suppose, when they awake tomorrow morning, they should see a small steamer of smoke rising as if from a cooking fire, far off to the north, back in the hills, in the far reaches of the valley—" His

gesture indicated a direction opposite the course followed by the wild bunch in their flight. "Would they
not be excited, and head for it to have a look, hoping
at least to take a scalp or so?"

Quick to understand and grasp the possibilities of
the plan, Ottertail nodded.

"Almost surely they would," he agreed. "In so
empty a land as we and they have found this summer,
almost anything new, especially the prospect of a
scalp, would be a welcome change. And if they headed
that way, then they might keep going in the same
direction, not bothering to come around here, missing
any chance to stumble upon the wild band—"

He broke off on a note of doubt.

"It is a good plan, John Hawk," he admitted, "but
dangerous. One of us would have to travel all night
to make the smoke in the morning. Then they would
be after him as quickly as possible, and on fresh
horses, it would not take them long to catch up. Whoever goes would still be on foot, tired, hunted. For
one of us must remain here to care for our horses—"

"I've thought of that," Johnny agreed. "You will
have to stay, since you can handle the horses so much
better. I'll go and make the smoke—and try to lead
them farther away. As soon as I can, or when it seems
safe, I'll circle back."

Soberly, Ottertail nodded agreement.

"It will be hard," he agreed, "but perhaps no more

so than to do nothing, which would lead to ruin. You have become as skilled a trailer and hunter as anyone of your age among the Blackfeet; better than most. Your uncle would be proud of you. But you must use great care, John Hawk. I—" He swallowed, then thrust out his hand. "You know what I mean, Johnny."

"Of course," Johnny agreed. "But since we saw them first, and have this advantage, we can't afford to waste it."

Ottertail prepared a small pack· of food; then Johnny set off, into the settling night. For a moment he thought wistfully of the rest and sleep to which he had looked forward, tired from a long hard day. There would be little sleep this night, perhaps not much for the next several days. The days to follow, with enemies on his trail, could be pretty rough. He had to lead them away from this valley, this section of the country. It was imperative not merely to lure them off-course for a day or so, but also to make sure that they would not turn back.

Something more than a single smoke, glimpsed in the dawn, would be needed. It would be a game of fox and hounds, with himself the dog. This would be a real test as to whether or not he was able to take care of himself. To fail would be to die.

Setting off alone, without Ottertail, was the worst part. He felt almost as lost as on the morning after the departure of the *Oregon*. With the son of Seamus

O'Casey he had traveled a long trail. Ottertail always knew what to do. Now he was on his own.

Still, he was not too helpless or inept. Ottertail had given him high praise, and he had escaped from the Sioux at the river. He'd faced a charging grizzly, had roped The Hungry Horse. Those were deeds which even a warrior would boast of.

It was tiring to push through the hills at night, and somewhat scary. Every sound—the rustling of leaves, the skulking of night creatures, limbs which cast strange shadows in the moonlight—presented a new and unpleasant possibility. The vastness of the land seemed doubled.

He ate some cooked meat when he stopped to rest some time after midnight. When his feet dragged and his legs ached, he stretched out and slept.

When he awoke, he knew a moment of panic, was uncertain as to how well he might have done. It was as necessary to awake at the proper time as it was to rest. If he had overslept—

Studying the stars, listening to the twittering chorus of birds beginning to tune for their welcome to the new day, he decided that he had awakened as he had planned. The stars were growing pale, but it would be another half-hour till dawn. Time enough for what he had to do.

He had traveled most the night, but men on horses would be able to reach this spot by the middle of the forenoon.

In his first enthusiasm, he realized that he had overlooked one important detail. That war or hunting party was undoubtedly made up of trained scouts, who would almost certainly pick up his trail once they found the ashes of the campfire. And they had to do that to hold and quicken their interest. Finding his trail would be useful, in that he could lead them still farther away from Ottertail.

But they might catch up with him by midday. In that case, could he elude them during a long afternoon or in the days to follow? On that would depend success or failure.

Gathering wood, he chose a likely location, sufficiently in the open so that the smoke could be seen from a long way off. He had become adept at striking fire and igniting the wood. The smoke ascended, rising well in the still air. If the hunting party were alert, they would be able to see it.

Going on, he used all his skill to hide his trail, as any lone traveler would. Trained scouts could follow ordinary sign as fast as a horse could run. They did not need a line of footprints. A broken twig, a crushed blade of grass, a disturbed stone, a partial print in mud or soft soil—all were meaningful to such men as would be after him.

An hour later, he had a piece of luck. He came unexpectedly upon a small creek and stepped carefully into it. Looking back, he doubted if even an Indian could tell where he had entered. Even if they did, they would be puzzled as to which direction he might have taken.

He turned upstream, following it for a quarter of a mile, keeping to the center, careful not to splash or disturb any stone, to avoid mud. Rounding a bend, he saw game—a fat muskrat, perched on a small hummock near the bank, lunching on a root.

It would be an easy bow-shot, but he dared not take it. The victim would flop, leaving blood and sign, spoiling all he had done until now to hide his trail. He kept on, watching the muskrat dive.

Soon afterward, he was thankful he had resisted the temptation. A big fir tree was on the bank, its limbs overhanging the water. He drew himself up, climbing, then stepped from the tree to a rocky strip of ground.

It might be clever, even safe, to do what the hunters probably would not expect—to hide, instead of trying to keep ahead, and let them waste time searching. This was excellent country for the hunted.

11

Not far back from the creek, Johnny found what he sought. Here were thickets of dense brush, with occasional trees and scattered boulders. He burrowed deep among brush and grass and lay quietly. Warmth and peace, together with weariness, overcame watchfulness, and he slept.

He came awake with nerves strung like a bowstring and the impulse to jump and run. Instead, his training during long weeks on the trail held him motionless, like a young fawn. From somewhere, much too near for comfort, came a guttural voice, then the soft thump of horses' hoofs. The hunters were close.

Had they picked up his trail, or were they merely following the stream, searching, working a reasonable distance back from either shore? Much depended on the answer.

The sounds assured him that they were getting closer, but there was a quality to their progress which suggested calmness and routine rather than eagerness

—not the excitement of being about to close in on their prey. If they kept on, they should pass not far to one side.

Suddenly there was a new sound, a swift crashing, contrasting with the progress of the horsemen. A deer burst into sight, a blacktail buck with a fine set of antlers. Surprised by the invaders, he was fleeing.

The buck stopped abruptly, doing a turn-about almost in mid-jump as it sighted more men ahead. So terrified that it plunged heedlessly, it headed back, almost within sight of those who were still coming, before it disappeared.

Voices cried out, and Johnny had no need to understand the language to know what was being said. If they were not sure, at least the hunters guessed the reason for the deer's change of route. The probable cause was that it had come upon the fugitive, catching the dreaded man-scent from an unexpected direction. Wasting no time, they were changing course to follow this unexpected clue.

His hiding place had been secure. Now, unless he could outwit them, he'd never ride the big bay.

After their first exclamations, the Indians grew silent. Johnny wriggled from under the grass, moving fast, trying to leave no betraying sign. Such broken terrain as this would be difficult to comb very thoroughly.

Another odor assailed his nostrils, growing stronger.

It reminded Johnny of the farm back in the Ozarks, of prowlers about the hen-house at night. A skunk was somewhere about.

Neither the deer, the Indians, nor himself were afraid of the little striped animal with the big tail. All would treat it with respect if they came upon it, but its presence would not cause the hunters to alter their plans.

Judging by the sounds, though the brush still screened him, some of them were getting close. Johnny picked another thicket, dropping to hands and knees, crawling. The odor grew heavier.

It was hard not to panic with enemies almost at his heels. Past experience was no particular help. If they kept coming, they would soon find him.

Ahead was a darker opening, instead of a lighter one as was usual where brush ended. He saw that the growth covered the side of a hill, and there was a sort of small cave. Back in that, he might be safe.

He advanced a few additional feet, then paused at the entrance. Just inside was the skunk.

Its white stripes showed clearly; the head, bright beady eyes and inquisitive nose all pointed his way. The bushy tail curled warningly over its back, and Johnny knew what that meant. If he came any closer, there would be trouble of the sort which even its most formidable enemies respected.

Should he crowd his way in, the sudden vastly

stronger scent would lead the Indians straight to him. They would have a good idea of the cause. If he didn't go on, they'd find him anyhow.

Johnny drew a deep breath, almost choking, moving carefully, slowly, as Ottertail had approached The Hungry Horse after it was roped. He crowded as far as possible to the side, leaving room for the skunk to depart if it wanted to.

It did not appear to have any such desire. It watched him sharply, half-turning. The cave, it seemed to intimate, belonged to it by right of discovery.

This was a test which he would gladly have foregone, but Johnny kept on, with a careful pause between each advance. The skunk hesitated, disturbed by the sounds of the approaching hunters, clearly bewildered by such lack of fear or respect.

Then, abruptly, it scuttled past and out, and the Indians, moving eagerly, came upon the skunk before they realized it. Apparently it felt hemmed in and lost patience. Johnny could not see what happened, but the powerful odor, so strong that he could taste it, told its own story.

Some of the eagerly crowding warriors cried out in anguish; then there were the sounds of hasty retreat, receding and dying away. The skunk had been strong medicine, as potent in its way as Ottertail's.

From a vantage point, Johnny presently saw the Indians, riding fast, heading on a course which would take them back to more friendly country. Apparently the wild horses were in no danger of discovery by them.

Probably they figured that the skunk had frightened the buck.

It was the evening of the second day when Johnny approached the spot where he and Ottertail had camped. Skilled at looking for sign, he glimpsed a tiny smoke, lost before it cleared the tree-tops. Ottertail crouched above the fire, tending to his cooking with a listless air.

At Johnny's call he sprang up, then came running, his grin returning.

"John Hawk!" he exclaimed. "Ai and begorra, you are back! I have been worried about you."

Talking eagerly, they returned to the fire to eat. Ottertail's pride matched his delight in The Hungry Horse when Johnny explained how he had lured the hunters on a false trail, finally sending them from the hills in disgust.

Undisturbed, Ottertail had made good use of his time. Almost casually he commented that both horses were now tamed and broken, ready to be ridden.

The ponies did not greet them with welcoming nickers the next morning, but they showed no sign of fright. The choking ropes had long since been removed and replaced by hobbles. They had even learned to obey a lead strap.

This was done with a combined halter and bridle, which differed from either the halters or bridles with which Johnny had been familiar. It was a long, thin loop of rawhide which encircled the nose, going up behind the ears, then down on the far side, under the nose loop. A sudden pull could tighten it painfully against the sensitive nose, should the horse struggle or pull against it. Quick to learn, by now the beasts understood what was expected of them and responded almost to a touch.

"But how did you do it?" Johnny asked. In comparison, his own accomplishments seemed small. These were wild horses, and they had been far from tamed when he had left.

"Everything depends on gaining their confidence," Ottertail explained. He had continued to run his hands not only over their heads and noses, but had gradually extended his touch to every part of their bodies, even the legs. Johnny could guess how much courage that required on the part of the trainer. He decided that he'd sooner face the skunk.

Ottertail had continued to murmur reassuringly as he worked, and gradually both horses had lost their fear. Through it all, they neither jumped nor kicked.

He had induced them to accept a skin blanket on their back. All that remained was actually to ride them.

Ottertail adjusted the bridles and removed the

hobbles. The Hungry Horse quivered as the blanket was dropped in place, then stood quietly. Resting his arms and elbows, then more of his weight on its back, Ottertail drew himself up, avoiding any sudden movement. He threw a leg across and sat upright.

Observing carefully, Johnny followed each move with the bay, with similar results. Both wild ones were uncertain, but they did not try to jump or run. Encouraged with words and a few soft pats on the neck, they walked away, bewildered and almost bemused, as though trying out their feet for the first time. It was easy to guide them in a wide circle, and finally down to the creek to drink.

"Remember to be deliberate, and always to speak, so that your horse knows you and what you want," Ottertail emphasized. "Soon they will accept this life as a matter of course."

No longer frightened, the hobbled horses grazed, fast regaining their sleekness. The first few days of their ordeal had rendered them as gaunt as The Hungry Horse was supposed to be.

"It was hard on them, but they did not go hungry for long," Ottertail observed. "So smart an animal seldom does. Even when the snow lies deep, horses will paw aside the cover to reach the grass, while other animals shiver and starve. In the morning," he added, "we will start back for the camp of my people."

He was envisioning his triumph when he returned

with the wild horses which they had caught and trained, one of these, as he had promised, being The
Hungry Horse. Coyote Man and his friends would
probably have reported that their horses had been
stolen and they had been set on foot, so this feat would
be even greater. To come mounted on the medicine
animal of his dreams would be something which even
scoffers could not brush aside.

By training, Ottertail was all Indian, and like all
braves, he savored the limelight. Johnny kept his
doubts to himself, along with questions which still had
no answers. Certainly they had accomplished a lot,
making such a journey deep into enemy country,
finding and capturing The Hungry One. But they had
been riding good horses when they had set out, and
despite the long journey, they had found no buffalo,
no sign of the big herds.

Ottertail had no such doubts. His medicine had led
him to The Hungry Horse. Its strength had been
proven, and in due course that would take care of
other problems.

And that might well be the case, Johnny reflected.
By now, other wide-ranging scouts might have located
the meat herds. White men were inclined to worry.
Indians, save where every sign pointed to hunger and
disaster, were ready to live one day at a time.

The camp would have been moved during the weeks
they had been away, so their first task was to find it

again. Because Indians seldom planned far ahead, there was no way of knowing where they might be now. They could have trekked north, south, east or west, according to the whim of the chief, or as reports of game made a particular course seem best. The new camp might be only a few hours' ride from where the old had stood, or many days distant.

Finding it should pose no serious problem. Tepees and household goods were loaded on travois, sometimes utilizing the same poles which held the skin coverings of the tepees. These pseudo-sleds would be pulled by the horses, the ends of the poles digging into the ground as they were dragged. The method was workable but crude. Anyone as sharp-eyed as Ottertail could follow such sign as fast as a horse could run.

The horses were eager to run. Once they understood what was expected of them, they were easy to control. A slight pressure of the rein, or of knees and voice, was enough to turn, start or stop them. It required adjustments for riders as well as animals, but as they became accustomed to each other, Johnny was delighted. His hammerhead had been a good horse, but the bay was very nearly the equal of the white both in speed and stamina. He had never imagined such a mount.

From the crest of a hill they glimpsed the band of wild ones farther down the big valley. They were grazing, apparently having adjusted to the change. By now some new leader would have assumed command.

If The Hungry Horse noticed his erstwhile subjects in the distance, or felt any regret about what had happened, he gave no sign.

After the long miles of plodding on foot, and the foray to lead the hunting party astray, this was like moving with the wind. By the evening of the second day, they found sign, already old, made when the camp had been moved. The direction was toward the south.

"I think I know where to find them," Ottertail said. "There is a favorite spot at this time of year. We should find them tomorrow."

The shadows were lengthening when they came upon a small band of deer grazing in a secluded glade. Johnny discharged a couple of arrows, and to his chagrin as well as surprise, missed. Ottertail did better and brought down a big buck. When they went on the next morning, each horse was additionally burdened with meat.

It was past noon when they sighted the village, the tepees pitched in a little valley, sheltered by high hills. At first glance, the camp looked normal. It was only as they came closer that something strange became apparent.

"I do not understand," Ottertail confessed. "When we returned the other time, all was not well, but this seems worse. Look how many are about for the time of day—men who sit idly, instead of being out on the hunt." His glance ranged over the entire valley, and he sucked in his breath. "And where are the horses?"

Johnny had the same premonition of disaster. At least some of the horses should be in sight, with all the men in camp. He could see none. The grass stood tall, with no sign it had been grazed.

Under such conditions, there could be no reason to keep the animals a long way from the camp. Something was wrong.

12

Excitement stirred through the loungers like strong wind as the great ghost animal was sighted; then the riders were recognized. Most of the men rushed out, staring in mingled curiosity and doubt. Some were eager with their welcome, but not all. Running Wolf, Mink Woman and Fawn Who Runs left no doubt as to how they felt, exclaiming at the fine horses, openly pleased. Kathleen greeted Johnny shyly, her eyes as warm and bright as the sun overhead.

There was considerable awe as it became clear that Ottertail really bestrode the Ghost Animal, the legendary Hungry Horse. Here was proof that his medicine was strong.

Eyes brightened even more at sight of the haunches of venison, and no time was lost in dividing up the meat and getting it into the cooking pots. The eagerness to get a meal prepared troubled the boys almost as much as what they failed to see, or the insistent question: Had *they* found any sign of the buffalo?

"No, we have seen no buffalo," Ottertail confessed. "But have you not found them, or other game? Surely the hunters, riding widely, must have had better luck. Why else was the camp moved here?"

Soberly his uncle answered.

"Not one of our hunters has found a buffalo all this season. The big ones have vanished like mud before wind. We moved the camp here in the hope of finding game, but there has been only a little—not enough for our needs even in summer. There was a colony of beavers in the creek. While they lasted, they were good eating."

Such an admission was as stunning as it was revealing. Beaver tail was a delicacy, but it was almost unheard of to kill a beaver in summer. Their fine pelts were too valuable to waste by slaying the animals in hot weather, and Indians did not believe in waste. Only hunger could drive them to such expedients.

The Hungry Horse! If there was hunger even before the moon of harvest, what would the winter moons bring? At this time of year, everyone should be busily drying pemmican, laying up stores against the winter's need. Nothing was being done. The situation was far worse than when they had ridden away.

"But what has happened?" Ottertail was insistent. "And where are the horses? Or the dogs?" It came to Johnny that there had been no clamor of barking hounds, that a strange silence pervaded the camp.

"Are the hunters ranging far from camp?"

Running Wolf no longer tried to hide his discouragement. He lifted his arms, then let them fall.

"Ai-ee, but I must confess that we are the foolish ones." He sighed. "It shames me, but the horses which you ride are the first ones on which we have set eyes for many days. The very first night after we came here, raiders, Crows, stole every horse we owned, stampeding them before we could do anything to prevent it. There was a great bluster of thunder and storm, and they made use of it.

"Once we were afoot, they could laugh at us—as they must still be doing! I led a war party in pursuit, but it was hopeless. They were not so foolish as to fight us, not when they had obtained what they wanted without losing a single man of their party."

Johnny shared the dismay reflected on the faces all around him. It had been bad enough for Ottertail and himself when their horses had been stolen, putting them afoot. But that a raiding party should manage to steal all the horses belonging to the tribe—that spelled disaster.

The Crows had planned well, depending on surprise, aided by the storm. That was a feat which would make the Blackfeet a laughingstock.

In the old days, all the tribes had been forced to travel on foot, and dogs had been the only beasts of burden. The coming of the horse to the plains had changed the red man's way of life. For many years, splendidly mounted, able to roam and hunt with new freedom, they had grown so accustomed to riding that it was a disaster to be set afoot.

The loss of the horses accounted for the untimely killing of the beavers, even the dogs. All game within a walking radius of the camp had been cleaned out. Even the hunters who were bold or strong enough to venture far afield did no better. When they had found game far from the camp, it was impossible to bring back much meat. Without horses, they could not move the camp to a new location.

Trouble had been in the air, like a storm cloud, when Coyote Man and his companions had set out to find the Gros Ventres with an appeal for help. Soon afterward, the horses had been stolen.

"It appears that the Great Spirit looks upon us with disfavor." The chief sighed. "What we may have done to displease the wise ones, I do not know, but our troubles increase with each day. All game has vanished, as you know. All too soon winter will be upon us —a winter in which, unless there is a change, we will surely perish. Our medicine men have prayed and danced, but nothing does any good."

In his words was no reproach, but Johnny sensed that many of the others were more critical. Ottertail had been certain of his medicine, and as though to prove its power, he had returned, riding the ghost animal, the fabled, awesome specter of famine. But the others were still afoot, and there was no sign of the buffalo!

Discouraged and hungry, they were in a questioning mood. It was true that Ottertail had returned with the white king, but with him, as before, was the white man—and bad luck had come with him at the beginning! Even The Hungry Horse—was it a good sign, or was his arrival untimely, bringing famine even before the snows?

It might be true that Ottertail had been befriended by the white man, also that the medicine of the chief's nephew was strong. His dreams had come true. But that was true only for Ottertail. For everyone else, troubles multiplied.

The looks cast toward Johnny were increasingly hostile. Ottertail, indignant, went out of his way to show his belief and friendship. But that would not help Johnny achieve popularity. It would only bring the same dislike upon the son of Seamus O'Casey.

Someone set up a cry. Plodding on foot, Coyote Man and his companions were returning. Like all the others, they were discouraged and hungry. They too had been surprised, their horses stolen. Coyote Man pointed an indignant arm at Ottertail and Johnny.

"They are the cause of all our bad luck," he charged. "The son of the white man has never been a true Blackfoot. Now he brings another white man among us. If you doubt that they are bad luck, then listen. All was well with us until we crossed their trail. After that, our luck was all bad—just as it has been here for all our people.

"We have a dreamer of dreams among us—but dreams can be bad! I say that it is time for the rest of us to awake, to face the truth. It is time to drive out the evil from among us before we all perish!"

There were approving grunts, distrust and active fear in the glances turned his way. Ottertail, who had listened in silence, sprang to his feet.

"What is this squawking of disaster which blows against my ears?" he demanded. "Have the Blackfeet become a nation of squaws? Are there no warriors who can recognize the deeds of a warrior?" He looked about challengingly.

"Have we come to the point where we accept even the Crows as being greater than we? They have proven themselves good stealers of horses, but because they put us afoot, must we howl from our tepees like beaten curs?"

When he finished, some looked shamed, but there was no real change of attitude. Debate continued, confined now to small groups. The hostility centered on Johnny. The disastrous return of Coyote Man had nullified any good feeling.

They were hungry again, and bitter. Night came down, and Johnny prowled restlessly beyond the rim of the camp. The silence was eerie. Before, there had been the dogs, the sounds of rodents large or small. All these had vanished.

"Bee in a bonnet," he grunted aloud, "that's me—stirrin' up trouble whether I like to or not. Guess I can't blame them—much. I'd probably feel the same way if I was in their place. Maybe I'd better just go away and give them a chance to settle down. Without me, it should be all right for Ottertail. I'm the one they don't cotton to."

Still, it was not so simple merely to get on his horse and head for Fort Benton. He'd be leaving behind a passel of trouble. Ottertail would be up to his ears in it—and what chance would he have of bettering the situation?

A stealthy sound warned him, and he swung about. Figures were hurtling at him from both sides, coming with a rush, grabbing before he could dodge or run. Johnny tried to fight back, but they swarmed like ants on a beetle, giving him no chance. Disgusted at being taken by surprise, he found his hands jerked behind his back, tied with a thong of rawhide. Now they jabbered excitedly, triumphantly. There were at least a dozen, made up of younger dissidents, and as he had expected, Coyote Man was in charge.

"Did I not tell you that there was nothing to fear from Ottertail and his medicine?" Coyote Man demanded. "It is bad medicine for true Blackfeet, but only if we fear it! This white man has worked a spell of evil upon him, to encompass all of us. Now that has been broken. Things will be different. No longer will he ride proud and high while we crawl in the dust. Now it will be the other way around."

Johnny said nothing, knowing that he would be wasting his breath. These rebels were virtually flouting the chief and established authority, and if they could do something spectacular, most of the village would probably back them.

Some of the group, eager as a result of the small victory, clamored that the white man should be sacrificed, so that the angry gods of the Blackfeet might be appeased.

"Is he not white, leading Ottertail astray to think white?" Big Bear demanded. "So is their medicine evil, bringing The Hungry Horse upon us in an untimely season! Nothing short of death will wipe out such sacrilege."

Coyote Man had other notions. Perhaps, as leader of the rebels, he was apprehensive of the chief's anger, should they pursue such a course. His refusal was firm.

"We will do nothing like that," he insisted. "There is a better way. Did I not promise you that it will be the other way, that we will ride tall? Come."

Hustled unceremoniously along, Johnny began to understand as they approached the picketed horses.

"Loose their hobbles," Coyote Man instructed. "You and I, Big Bear, will ride. As for you—" he turned directly to Johnny for the first time—"you have brought evil upon this land, upon our people. But we leave you your life. Whether the wise ones will do as much is for them to decide. Go! Set your face away from this camp and turn not back. If you do, you die."

Johnny was not surprised at the ultimatum. He was to be driven forth, to plod until exhausted, then stumble and die. Ottertail, freed of his influence, would be given another chance, but relegated to a very secondary place.

It was the further folly of what they proposed which alarmed him. Because he and Ottertail had ridden the wild horses, Coyote Man assumed that he could do the same without much difficulty.

They would certainly be in for a bad surprise, which might be enjoyable to watch. The Hungry Horse and his own big bay were trained and docile where Ottertail and himself were concerned, but where others were involved, they remained wild. If the hobbles were removed, without Ottertail or himself to handle them, they would run and vanish beyond the horizon, never to be seen again. As for either Coyote or Big Bear supposing that they could ride them—

But to protest would be to waste his breath. The horses snorted, drawing back nervously as strangers crowded around, but because of the hobbles, they did not resist. A couple of the braves stooped to loose those, while the others watched excitedly.

Now when their attention was distracted would be his best chance. He could not afford to make any mistake. Johnny's fingers were loose, even though his bound wrists afforded scant leeway. He moved and closed his hand on a knife hilt stuck in the sash of one of his captors. It came free without attracting attention.

The next move was vital, and could be even more difficult, but no one was paying any attention to him. Johnny dropped onto his back, striving to twist the knife, to bring the blade upright against the thong which held his wrists. Momentarily he had to forget the horses.

Both animals were nervous and frightened, and they sidled away as soon as the hobbles were removed. Triumphant in the realization of a long-held dream, Coyote Man could not resist a shout as he placed his arms on the back of The Hungry Horse and, with a jump, was on his back.

He went up swiftly, but his descent was even faster, as The Hungry Horse twisted and pivoted. Coyote Man sailed even higher, then hit the ground and lay without stirring.

Both horses, finding themselves free, were running. Johnny came to his feet, his arms free. His impulse was to run after them, but it would be a hopeless chase. It was probably just as useless to call after them, using the voice of command which his own pony had learned to understand and obey. But that was his only chance. If it failed, then The Hungry Horse would indeed stalk through the frozen moon of famine.

To his surprise, his call sounded confident as well as loud; he used the inflexion which he and Otter-tail had practised. Johnny repeated it, disregarding the dazed and leaderless group who had been so confident only moments before. They stared uncertainly from where Coyote Man sprawled to the vanishing horses, then back to Johnny, no longer in bonds.

The ghost animal continued to run, but the bay hesitated. As Johnny called again, he broke stride, circled, and looked back. Johnny walked toward him, calling again, repeating the sounds which had been effective in working with the wild ones.

Finding himself alone, easily outrunning all threats, The Hungry Horse slowed, then halted uncertainly. Old instincts were battling new loyalties. Once he had been the king, the unquestioned leader of the wild band, making all the decisions, and the temptation to return to such a life was strong. But opposed to that, an even more ancient heritage had asserted itself, the mastery of a man, a new-old companionship.

Johnny's knees felt shaky, but he moved steadily to where the bay waited. Its feelings were much like those of the white king. He allowed Johnny to come up, repeating the sounds which held reassurance, and Johnny fondled its ears and nose. Then, though he had no bridle thong, Johnny was on its back.

From behind sounded enraged shouts. The entire village was not only awake but stirring, suddenly united in a single emotion—hatred for the pair who rode while they had to walk, and to whom they attributed all the bad luck which had come upon them, centering in Coyote Man who lay outstretched and unstirring. Crying wildly that such evil medicine had murdered him, they were seeking to vent their rage upon Ottertail—who fled desperately in a losing race.

13

The whole outburst was unplanned, but no less furious for that reason. Taken by surprise, Ottertail was in a desperate plight. Sticks and stones, even a few arrows were showering at him, some finding their mark. He went to his knees, dazed, but struggled up again uncertainly. The cry that Coyote Man was dead, struck down by evil medicine, drove the others to frenzy.

Johnny stared, appalled. Then he leaned forward along the shoulders and neck of the bay, fingers clasped in the silky mane, guiding with voice and the pressure of knees and thighs. The bay responded, and Johnny swept alongside Ottertail as he faltered again and stood dazedly.

Here was another test to see if he could stop the big horse in mid-gallop only with his voice, without the pressure of the thong about its nose. It obeyed, and as he reached a hand and yelled for Ottertail to jump, Ottertail managed it and was up behind him.

The mob was close, maddened beyond reason, and a stone struck the horse. There had been no time to wonder whether it would resent a double load or not, but at the blow it ran, and the pursuit was soon left behind. Johnny soothed the frightened animal, gradually slowing, then, seeing the ghost animal waiting uncertainly, swung to come up with it. Ottertail's arms clasped Johnny's waist desperately; he was almost a dead weight against him.

It was ironic but hardly reassuring, as they stopped again, to be able to see and hear enough to know that Coyote Man, momentarily dazed by his tumble, was on his feet once more and far from dead. As far as Johnny could tell, that discovery was doing nothing to abate the fury of the others, to whom Coyote Man was suddenly a hero.

"Are you well enough to ride The Hungry Horse?" Johnny questioned. He was far from certain whether he could drive the ghost animal, or how long he might follow. And if they should lose him, as had so nearly happened, then The Hungry Horse would indeed be a portent of famine and disaster.

Ottertail straightened, drawing a deep breath. He sounded dazed, but no longer confused.

"I think so," he replied. Then his voice broke on a note of despair. "But where can we go? What can we do? My people have turned against me!"

"Not all of them," Johnny said grimly. "The others

were too enraged to reason or understand."

The trouble with so logical an answer was its truthfulness. Ottertail, always volatile in his emotions, was crushed. That they should so misunderstand, blaming Johnny and himself for all their misfortunes, was almost more than he could bear. But his friendship and loyalty remained unswerving.

"It's me they fear and hate," Johnny said soberly. "All they see is that their bad luck has grown worse, everything has become increasingly bad, ever since you brought me back with you. Maybe if I leave, they'll forget the rest and take you back again."

"And do you think I would return on such terms?" Ottertail demanded indignantly. "Sure and I'm not that sort of an Irishman—or Indian! You have been good medicine, not bad. Besides, how would that help anyone? They would still have no horses, no meat and no hope!"

Johnny halted the bay alongside The Hungry Horse. Ottertail was feeling better, and he made the change. Then they rode silently until they halted finally to rest. Johnny could see no ray of hope. Coyote Man and his followers had been jealous of Ottertail, ready to take advantage of circumstances without thinking of possible consequences. They had brought on a crisis, and an already desperate situation had certainly not been improved.

Warm sunshine on his face was hardly reassuring.

They were outcasts now, and to Ottertail, the tragic part was his certainty that his medicine was both strong and good, but rejected by the tribe. Not only he, but everyone, must use the medicine, or disaster would result. But what could anyone do in the face of prejudice and blind antagonism?

"Perhaps they may feel differently by now," Johnny suggested hopefully. "After thinking matters over, they may regret their outburst, even be ashamed of themselves for the way they treated you."

Ottertail was eager to find even one straw to clutch at. He wanted only to help, and rejection by his people was hard to endure.

"At least we can return and see," he agreed. "On horses such as these, we can outrun them, if we have to."

Perhaps that was part of the trouble—the superiority which such horses gave them, and the resentment which the others felt at seeing them so splendidly mounted as they drew up at the edge of the village. Johnny prudently remained silent, and Ottertail tried to reason with them but was shouted down by Coyote Man and his followers. The evil of their course, the curse which he had brought upon everyone, should be apparent even to him. Unless he conceded that and changed his ways, he was an enemy!

The fact that a small handful, including the chief, Kathleen and others, stood apart and refused to join in the condemnation was meager comfort. When, again working themselves to a high pitch of rage, most of the camp ran shouting at them again, there was nothing to do but ride away, more glumly than before.

"It's me they hate," Johnny repeated. "I'd better head for Benton, and stay away. I'm too big an albatross for you to carry."

"Albatross?" Ottertail repeated. "What is that?"

Johnny explained, and Ottertail shook his head. "It is not so," he insisted. "I know it, and you know it. With you, my medicine is strong. Without you, it would be nothing. But how can we help them—how can anyone, when they refuse to be helped?"

He turned to look back at the village, now but a speck against the plain. But though they could ride away, they could not forget.

"A few deserve what is coming—but why should others perish with them? Soon comes the moon of harvest, but there is no crop to gather!"

Johnny's thoughts were along the same lines. What of Kathleen, huddled in the tepee while blizzards raged, cold, starving—

"Maybe we can still do something," he suggested. "We came back here because we planned to have the braves ride with us to round up the wild bunch and drive them to the camp. That would have been the best way, and much easier. But since they can't ride with us, and we have the only horses—why don't we drive the wild bunch back to them? On horses such as these, we can do it! Then, when every man has a horse, many mounts, they can hunt widely before the deep snows come, perhaps even find the buffalo—"

The old gleam was suddenly back in Ottertail's eyes, a fire of wild excitement.

"Sure, and haven't I said all along that you are good medicine, John Hawk! Begorra, and why not? It will not be easy, but have we not many times done the impossible, working together! And when we bring the wild band back to them, then everyone will understand, as I do, that you are no enemy, but the friend of the Blackfeet!"

He had been riding aimlessly, allowing his horse to pick its own pace and direction. Now, laughing exultantly, he again swung it toward the southeast, putting the ghost animal to a stretching gallop. Johnny shared the thrill as he raced alongside.

They rode steadily until mid-afternoon, when they came upon game—a muskrat, poised at the edge of a deep pool in a creek. Ottertail's arrow stopped its leap, and they rested, roasting it and eating, while the horses grazed. Then, still eager, they went on, since an hour of daylight remained.

"We have time enough for what must be done, but none to spare," Ottertail ruminated. "Once we have the wild bunch back there, safely corraled, every man can train his own animal—"

He paused suddenly, his face falling. Johnny sensed his sudden dismay.

"What now?" he asked. "Is there something wrong?"

"Ai, but what a fool I am!" Ottertail wailed. "We have thought only of our part, of rounding up the wild bunch and driving them back—and not at all of how they can be corraled, once we have them there! How shall that be, when there is no corral, no place in which to hold them—and no one to assist us? Such things have been done before, but everyone worked together! Those who remained in camp worked for days or weeks to prepare an enclosure, to be ready to help so that the wild bunch, once headed into a trap, could not break out or escape. Thus they were brought safely into the corral!

"But no one knows that we are going after the horses, no one will be ready—and even if they knew, they fear and distrust me so much that they would not assist!"

14

Excited by the possibilities of rounding up the wild bunch and bringing them back by themselves, both Johnny and Ottertail had been too preoccupied to think of journey's end. But holding horses after they had them there was vital. If they could find them, drive them for several days, the wild ones would be slightly tamed and trained—but at the same time frightened and resentful, desperate, eager to escape.

The climax of such an effort would come when the attempt was made to corral them. There would be one chance, and only one. The animals, with the instinct of the wild, would sense a trap, be frantic to break out. If they were able to break and run, they would flee wildly, scattering widely. They would be wary of men on horseback, so that it would probably be impossible for two horsemen alone, however well-mounted and skillful, ever to round them up or drive them back a second time.

Ottertail was thinking hard, loath to give up so good an idea. Buffalo were sometimes stampeded, guided so that scores or hundreds would plunge over a high cliff to their death, providing meat for a whole tribe with a minimum of effort.

"And sometimes wild horses were driven into a trap in much the same fashion, though that was a long while ago, before my memory. There is such a place, a natural trap, not very far from the camp. Use was made of the hills and the coulees, the natural slope of the land, to turn the wild ones, as they approached, and lead them naturally into the corral! But much work would have to be done to restore it to usefulness now. Poles would have to be laid across openings, or walls built of rock, at spots where the horses might break out before the corral is reached. Men, women, even children, must be ready, hidden but strung out for miles in two lines, so that, once the horses find themselves between those lines, they will run faster and faster, straight to the trap—the corral."

In such an operation, everyone had an assigned role. In position along the sides of the V, it was their task, as the animals swept past, to rise up suddenly, shouting and waving blankets, adding to the band's terror, increasing their speed.

There was always the chance that the leader of the wild bunch, or any one, might suddenly swerve, trying to escape, and lead the others to freedom. Flimsy poles would not hold them in the rush.

At such times, the people deployed along the line had to see that no such break was allowed to occur. For everyone it was an important, potentially dangerous job, until the band was safely inside the corral.

There was a natural corral which had been used in the old days, a sort of blind canyon, walled on three sides. Once animals were inside, the entrance could quickly be closed by poles. But a lot of work and time would be required to have everything in readiness.

"It could be done!" Ottertail clenched a fist impatiently. "But it will be useless to bring the horses unless everyone is ready to do his part! And they are so angry that they will not even listen to what we have to say, even should we return again."

That was the bad part. They were outcasts, feared and resented. Yet everyone would have to work together, if there was to be any hope of success.

Night had closed over the plain as they rode, the horses slowing now to a walk. Even these great wild ones had their limitations.

The bay snorted, a questing sort of sound, but Johnny was alert, his skin prickling at a sense of wrongness. His tense whisper brought Ottertail and his horse to a stop; they were suddenly alert as well.

"Off there," Johnny whispered. "Isn't that a fire—or the remains of one?"

"Ai," Ottertail agreed. "I grow careless, thinking too much of one thing, forgetting others."

They dropped into a coulee and hobbled their horses safely out of sight, then advanced cautiously on foot. Johnny was experienced enough to see that they had almost stumbled upon a camp of considerable size, one which there had been no attempt to conceal. That indicated that the enemy was of considerable strength, sure of themselves, confident that they were in no danger from the Blackfeet.

Ottertail's interest increased as they had a better look. Returning toward their own village a few days before, they had missed this camp by at least a score of miles; today they had taken a slightly different route. Apparently it had been here for some time, at least several days, and was more than an overnight stop.

There were a number of tepees and other appurtenances of a camp such as had lately been absent from the village of the Blackfeet—dogs and horses, the latter in a gathered bunch off at one side. It was a fair-sized village, perhaps half a hundred people in all. And Ottertail had no hesitation in pronouncing them to be Crows.

"They grow over-bold, these Crows," he complained in an angry undertone. "Soon they will think of themselves as the Lords of the Plain, and even now they have scorn for the Blackfeet. If they should guess, or discover, that our village is but a long day's ride from here—"

Johnny understood. An attack, mounted warriors against hungry men on foot, could wipe out the Blackfeet. Those not killed would be made slaves.

The cooking fires had burned out, but at least some in the camp were still awake, moving about, in some cases at work. Voices reached them dimly where they crouched. Faintly, there was the sound of a blow. Ottertail grunted.

"They have slaves," he said, "captives, whose life will be made as miserable as possible. Let us get a better look."

He crawled closer, and Johnny followed, despite his uneasiness. Should they be discovered, the hunt would be on. However, the darkness was increasing, as clouds scudded, blotting away the stars. There was a feel of storm in the air. And such wind as there was was in their favor.

The camp was either asleep or about to settle down to slumber, but a few slaves still toiled at completing some assigned task. Momentarily, the moon broke through a rift in the clouds, and Ottertail caught his breath, having a good view of someone not too far off. Johnny felt him tense. Then the camp before them was silent, and they drew cautiously back until they were far enough distant so that it was safe to talk.

"Did you recognize someone?" Johnny asked. "A Blackfoot?"

"More than that." Ottertail's voice was tense. "There are two of them, their slaves—and Blackfeet, as you say. But they are *more than that!*"

"More? How—"

"One is Lazy Horse. The other is Eagle Wing. Have I never told you their names? They are the ones with whom I rode last spring—the friends who were lost that night when the Dakotas attacked and killed my horse! Apparently they were not killed or captured by the Sioux. But the Crows have made them captive, enslaved them!"

The fact that they were alive was surprising, but being slaves was certainly an unenviable fate. Johnny knew that Ottertail was already figuring how they might free them. They were not merely Blackfeet; they were his friends and comrades, for whose loss many of the tribe held him more or less to blame.

"We cannot ride on and leave them to such a fate," Ottertail explained. "Besides, it is not safe to leave these Crows unmolested so close to the camp of my people. If they are put afoot, there will be no danger from them. I grow a little tired of what the Crows have been doing all this long summer!"

"I know," Johnny agreed. "If we can set them free and get horses for them, that will be the answer to our problem."

"What problem? I—"

"If they return to the village, they can explain how you set them free from the Crows. Also, they can tell your uncle, Running Wolf, that we are going after the wild bunch, and to make preparations for corraling them when we come with them."

Had he been other than an Indian, Ottertail would have given vent to a wild whoop.

"That will do it!" he agreed. "It is the answer, the perfect one. I had thought that they would be of great assistance to us, but this will be much better. Besides, after being slaves so long, they will be nearly starved, weak and sick. It will be better for them to carry the word, then rest and get back their strength."

He looked about calculatingly. The storm was building fast, a vast blot of darkness to the north. The wind was strengthening to sudden gusts.

"There will be rain, lightning, high wind. Under cover of that, we can go into the camp, find them and free them. Each will be held in a different lodge, of course—but it should not be too hard, eh?"

Johnny grinned.

"Reckon we can manage," he agreed.

As ever at such times, Johnny's pulse beat to match the hoofs of a running horse, but the tightness was gone. He was pleasantly excited at the prospect. There was risk, but the challenge was exciting.

The approaching storm had blotted out the moon and stars, and the wind, fitful and uncertain, swirled and twisted. Rain slashed with a savage slap. The darkness was torn by lightning, a blasting white sheet which ripped the night and hung poised for an instant, overly bright, blinding in the next moment as its crash seemed to shake the ground under their feet. Ottertail was gone, and he was alone in a wilderness of storm.

Lightning licked and flickered again, and he picked out a lodge which loomed at the side and stumbled toward it. There was not much risk of being detected while the shower lashed, but it would take luck or chance to find anyone under such conditions. The rain was driving so hard that it was like the creek where he had lain submerged, except that this was hard and blinding.

Another crash of the thunder seemed aimed at him, and it was matched by a frightened howl from some-one even more frightened than he was. He narrowed his eyes against the rain so it was easier to see when the lightning flared. Directly in front of him was wreckage and destruction. The tepee, which had been erect but quivering under the wind and driving rain, now was a tumbled mass of poles and soaked skins.

The storm had collapsed it, and the inmates were crawling out, bewildered and uncertain. Johnny glimpsed what was happening, and saw something else before the brief light was gone—a prone figure lying with folded hands at the edge of the collapsed tepee.

It took an instant to appreciate the meaning of that posture at such a time. This was not someone in an attitude of prayer and resignation, as the others tried wildly to get free of the wreckage. This man lying thus had no choice. His wrists were tied, and very likely another long rope or thong ran from them to a tent pole. Chance had led Johnny to one of the prisoners.

Someone bumped heavily against him, grunting, then veered off without apology. There was less wind now, and the lightning was more infrequent, though the rain drove down relentlessly. Fumbling in the solid night, he found the prone figure and dropped to his knees, locating head and shoulders by feel. The tumult of storm, of collapsing tepees, running people and destruction was matched by the beat of the storm. He spoke swiftly in Blackfoot.

"Are you Eagle Wing or Lazy Horse?"

There was a bewildered moment of hesitation, while the surprised captive sought to understand, surprised at hearing his own language again. Then he answered briefly:

"I am Lazy Horse."

"Good. I am a friend." Still by feel, Johnny had located the bonds. Working quickly, he slashed at them with his knife and felt them fall away. "Take my hand," he added urgently, "so that we do not get separated—"

Something monstrous hurtled past in the blackness, with more wild outcries. This was more than he had bargained for.

15

Johnny led the way, Lazy Horse holding to his hand so tightly that the grip was painful. After being a prisoner for several months, abused, overworked and underfed, he was both hopeful and frightened, bewildered and helpless.

Among other things, Johnny had discovered that he had an excellent sense of direction, even under adverse conditions. Neither darkness nor storm made too much difference. It was an instinct, like a bird's. Some people had it; others did not. He was one of the fortunate ones.

The thunder and lightning were muttering in the distance, the wind had subsided, and the rain was slackening. A lighter patch of sky was followed by more clearing, as the clouds were swept along with the wind. In the half-light, the village, orderly by Indian standards only minutes before, was a shambles. Many if not most of the tepees had been blown down, and an equally destructive force was adding to the carnage. This time Johnny saw what it was, as another terrified horse plunged headlong past them.

He wondered briefly if this might be Ottertail's work, but realized that it could not be. Ottertail would have had neither time nor opportunity to get to the horses and turn them loose, much as he might like to. Like Johnny himself, Ottertail had had another job to do.

But in the storm and confusion some if not all of the horses had gotten loose, perhaps picketed on ropes rather than hobbled, and they were running wild, adding to the havoc. That was fine, for the Crows would be left on foot and helpless, but they had need of a couple of horses for Lazy Horse and Eagle Wing.

Another cayuse tore past, but there was no stopping or catching them now. Past the rim of the village, Johnny quickened his pace. The Crows had been taken by surprise, but they would be working to restore order after discovering that one or both of their prisoners had escaped. It would be better if they assumed that they had gotten loose by themselves, instead of being helped.

They walked in silence until they reached the coulee where he and Ottertail had left their own horses. Johnny was relieved to find both the bay and The Hungry Horse waiting, but he was suddenly uneasy that Ottertail had not returned. The havoc of the storm had aided them, but it had also hindered. Something might have happened to Ottertail—

Here it was safe to talk, and he explained partially to Lazy Horse how he and Ottertail had discovered them to be prisoners, and how Ottertail was looking for Eagle Wing.

In the night, Lazy Horse apparently had no inkling that Johnny was not a Blackfoot, and he was eager for news of Ottertail and of their people. Concerning his own and Eagle Wing's adventures there was not much to tell. They had become separated from Ottertail when the Sioux raided, only to be captured by Crows a few days later. They had survived slavery and ill-treatment, but both were weak, half-starved, all but hopeless.

Others were coming, and Johnny and Lazy Horse fell silent until Johnny made sure that they were Ottertail and Eagle Wing. They had been delayed by the confusion, but in one sense Ottertail had had less trouble than Johnny. He had watched as Eagle Wing was herded to a tepee, carefully noting its location, going to it even in the rain and darkness. Johnny wondered why he himself had not been equally observant.

The reunion of the three friends was joyous. Ottertail had been oppressed by a sense of guilt regarding them, which had been increased by the criticism that he and not they had returned. Now he was jubilant.

"Ai and begorra, John Hawk, again my medicine

is proved strong—working with you. Always, even for the bravest and strongest warriors, there are trials and hazards, but each time we overcome!"

He was particularly pleased that the horses of the Crows had escaped, leaving them virtually helpless. To his way of thinking, that was also a part of his medicine.

"We had better takes our horses and catch some of the others before they stray any farther," he suggested. "Then all will be well."

Leaving Eagle Wing and Lazy Horse to wait, they mounted and set off. The sky was cloudless now, star-studded, the air washed and sweet. A few miles beyond the wrecked camp, they sighted a couple of horses and started them back without much difficulty. There was no sign of the others, who by now were ranging so widely that it was unlikely that the Crows, on foot, would be able to come up with them or recapture any of them.

The pair of ponies, as was natural, were among the poorer animals from the Crow remuda, little inclined to run fast or far. But they would do well enough for the former captives who wanted to return to the camp of the Blackfeet, since they were in poor condition for walking. Apprised of the events of the summer, viewing the magnificent ponies now owned by Ottertail and Johnny, they listened incredulously, forced to believe the evidence of their eyes.

Ottertail gave them careful instructions as to how to find the camp and what had to be done to make ready for the wild bunch. He was in high good humor when he and Johnny again resumed their journey. Not only were his friends alive, but they had freed them. Therefore the message they brought could hardly be disregarded.

The mood of exultation soon gave way to a more sober attitude, occasioned in part by Eagle Wing's anxious question, once he understood what they planned.

"We three were untried when we set out last spring," Eagle Wing said soberly. "Since then, you have found your medicine accomplishing many things. Perhaps I, who have been a slave, should not question one who has made captives and rides The Hungry Horse. Still, I cannot but wonder. Do you think that the two of you can manage to drive such a wild bunch?

"They will not be easy to handle, and there are only the two of you, even though you ride fine horses. I have listened to the horse hunters many times—and such wild bands have sometimes broken away even from a hundred men who pursued them."

"We don't expect it to be easy," Ottertail admitted. "But since it must be done, we will find a way."

"I am sure you will. But there is another matter. Your Hungry Horse has been the king, the leader of this band. Long before you find them again, he will have been replaced by a new king, one who was once under his rule. Each king will resent the other."

"He is still a king, but he knows his master," Ottertail said confidently. "Make ready for our coming."

The day was perfect, following the storm. They skirted the devastated camp of the Crows at a distance, and Johnny unexpectedly felt sorry for the suddenly riderless Crows, whose fortunes had altered so radically in a night. Ottertail had turned sober and thoughtful.

"I know," he agreed. "One must be strong to survive. And in my dream there was a great dark cloud, such as came with the storm last night. Now I understand that in my dream, that dark cloud meant all of the Blackfeet. Their welfare, even their lives, depend now on what we do and how we manage. Without horses, they will go hungry—"

Johnny shared his concern. Until now, the summer had been a long adventure, exciting at times, pleasant for the most part, but involving only themselves. Now far more was at stake. Failure would involve everyone—those who had befriended him and believed in him as much as those who had been motivated by hate and jealousy.

If they failed, they could not return. Indeed, in such a case, there would be nothing to come back to.

Ottertail, having lost his recent high spirits, was sunk in a dark mood, appalled by the responsibility, the many things which might go wrong. Johnny tried to cheer him.

"Your medicine saw all this, and not merely our journey, or even The Hungry Horse," he pointed out. "And has it not proved strong?"

"Ai, that is so," Ottertail admitted. "Sure, John Hawk, and I would be lost without you. But it is the thought of the buffalo that worries me. For a long while I was sure that they would come streaming over the horizon, that someone would find them and bring word. But there is never a sign of them, and the summer is waning. Where could they have gone to? It is as though they had vanished from the earth.

"Having horses for our people to ride will help, but horses alone will not be enough. Our people must have meat, for without it the moon of hunger will be long and bitter. And what other meat is there?" He made a despairing gesture. "Only the buffalo can save them now."

Johnny had been pondering the same question for the past several days, wondering whether or not to mention his theory. Now he decided to do so.

"I've been thinking about them," he admitted. "Do you remember that day when I climbed a high hill to look around? What I saw that day may be the answer."

"Speak freely," Ottertail encouraged him. "Did not your rope catch The Hungry Horse? Was it not your arrow which killed the great bear? And you who decoyed our enemies away, when otherwise they must surely have found the horses? No warrior among the Blackfeet has a better right to be heard."

"You're part Irish, all right." Johnny grinned. "Your Dad must have kissed the Blarney stone. That day, beyond the river, for as far as I could see, the land was black. That means there was a big fire last spring, burning all the grass for a mighty long distance. No telling how deep or wide that burnt strip was —but it may have turned the buffalo, when they were heading toward the Yellowstone and on north. With so wide a waste and no grass, maybe the herds swung off again south or east where there was grass.

"That may be the way of it," Ottertail grunted. "Such a wasteland could stop even the big herds. Who knows but that some of our enemies, who are jealous of the Blackfeet, burnt such a wide strip for that very purpose, not only to keep more game in their country, but to keep it away from us? Only by now the grass has grown again, and there is nothing to keep the big ones from moving as they please."

"So perhaps they will be coming beyond the river now," Johnny agreed. "But don't you think we ought to have a look, to find out what is going on?"

"As usual, you are right." Ottertail grimaced

thoughtfully. "Last night, in the heavy darkness, it was foolish to move when I had no idea where to go or what to do, and this is much the same. Yes, we need to find the buffalo, who are just as important as the horses.

"We can spare a few days to look about, for it would be a mistake to return too soon with the horses, before the people can prepare the corral and do all the necessary work. We will have only one chance to capture them, and that must not fail."

Though still heading east, they swung more to the south, traveling mostly by night, resting during the day. This was enemy country, and the ghost horse could be seen for a long way. So striking an animal would certainly excite intense interest. To most of the tribes, a white animal, whether a buffalo or a horse, was not only rare but almost sacred, and they would go to extreme lengths to capture or kill one. It was well to ride warily.

On two occasions they sighted other riders in the distance, too far off to be identified. But since their own people now had no horses, any others must automatically be counted as enemies. Careful not to be seen, they reached and crossed the Yellowstone.

Even here, at a point well to the east from where Johnny had viewed it, the fire had extended, making a vast sweep, while the old grass was dry. Under the new coat, the ground was bare of humus, the story easy to read. Ottertail nodded grimly.

"So wide-ranging a fire was surely set on purpose," he agreed. "Otherwise it would never cover so much country. Even a big fire will usually die of its own accord before it spreads so far."

The country was green again, though the new growth, juicy and succulent, showed little signs of grazing. Clearly there had been no buffalo along here this year.

"But they must turn this way soon," Ottertail muttered anxiously. "Such great herds cannot vanish overnight, and because they are so big, they have to keep ever on the move to find enough to eat. With so much range burnt last spring, crowding many into a smaller territory, by now they should be hungry and on the move."

Johnny's eyes were half-closed, his head cocked in a listening attitude. Ottertail eyed him sharply, then broke off and listened as well. Presently a smile eased his tight-set lips.

"You are true kin to the old one," he breathed. "Perhaps they *are* coming!"

It was only a faint whisper at first, like the distant murmur of wind high in the tree-tops. Here there were no trees, and this was not wind, but something stronger, muted by distance. It held a suggestion of thunder, a steady, unending roll, a growl, a mutter.

"It is a big herd, a herd on the move, the great

ones," Ottertail asserted confidently. "Always a thousand throats give forth a bellowing, the cows calling to their calves, the calves bleating for their mothers, with others joining in for whatever reason seems good to them, or just to be heard. And when they break into a run, the pounding of thousands of hoofs shakes the earth."

Excitedly they swung their horses. Now dust began to puff to the south and west, a growing cloud. There could be no doubt but that a vast herd was on the move. Presently they could make out the dim outlines of the herd, a vast brown blot which seemed to spill and run like ink. Johnny caught his breath, swallowing. He had heard many tales of the great herds, some of which required hours to pass a given point. But the actual sight of such a mass was beyond description.

For as far as he could see, the herd was on the move, thousands, tens of thousands of great, shaggy beasts. They were not running, but they maintained a steady pace, as though the leaders had some objective in mind and were determined to move along.

Now they were close enough to make out individuals, to catch the sheen of glossy black horns, the sea of humped backs. They rolled like the waves of the ocean, and if this course was maintained, the herd would reach the Blackfoot country within a few days.

The danger was that at the river they might turn again, since there was now ample grass on every hand. Ottertail breathed an audible prayer that they should not be swerved, but even as he did so, there was some sort of commotion along the vanguard of the herd.

At least a score of horsemen were braving the onward sweep of the big herd, making a sudden appearance, though half-hidden by the heavy dust stirred by so many hoofs and swept along by a pushing breeze. Clearly, others also had ideas and desires regarding the buffalo and were trying to influence their course.

They were waving blankets and yelling, hoping to frighten the leaders and stampede the herd, to swing them back southward once more, away from the river.

Here was a further explanation why there had been no game in the Blackfoot country that summer. Fire and now terror were being used as weapons. Ottertail exclaimed angrily and put The Hungry Horse to a gallop.

"So that is what they are up to!" he grunted. "It is not enough that they steal our horses and leave us afoot! Now they would drive away even the buffalo! We must stop them."

16

Johnny rode with a similar sense of outrage. It had been bad enough for a Crow to steal their horses and put them afoot, and insult had been added to injury when all the horses belonging to Running Wolf's band had been taken. What made it worse was that the Blackfeet looked upon the Crows as not quite as good as themselves at anything—and the Crows had turned the tables at every opportunity.

"Bee in a bonnet, reckon that gives them something to crow *about*," Johnny muttered, admiration struggling with dismay. "But there's sure enough got to be a limit."

These riders apparently were Crows. Whether or not they belonged to one of the groups with which he and Ottertail had already tangled was of no importance. What they were up to was what mattered.

He had no notion what Ottertail might have in mind, or how the two of them could battle or thwart ten times their number. The Crows would react savagely to any interference. Yet what happened with this big herd might spell survival or starvation for Running Wolf's band.

From what he knew of buffalo, they were stubborn, and not easy to turn once they had an objective in mind. The riders were having trouble, which might give them a chance to make a counter-move. They reached the river, shallow at that point, readily ford-able, and plunged in. Pestered by the Crows, the vanguard of the herd had more or less divided, but were still coming.

Ottertail brought his horse alongside, shouting. It was hard to hear above the noise of the approaching herd, but Johnny understood. They would try to turn one prong of the advance, swinging it against the other prong which the Crows were trying to turn in the opposite direction.

This could be highly dangerous, with the result in doubt. But the shouting and blanket-waving were beginning to have an effect. Some of the big animals were hesitating, starting to mill. They might break and plunge back upon the mass of the herd at any moment.

They came out on the far shore, both horses running again, then hit one prong, shouting and shoving to create a counter-pressure. By now, a big bunch of the main herd was between them and the opposing riders, so there was no immediate danger to themselves from the Crows. The contest was centered on who would direct the herd.

Being shoved and shouted at from two directions bothered the buffalo. They were confused and angry. Should they panic and stampede, anything might happen.

Johnny's big bay seemed to sense what was involved, to enter into the spirit of the occasion. He was suddenly a demon cayuse, ears laid back and jaws gaping, screaming, biting, whirling at times to lash out with both hind hoofs when a plunging bull refused to heed or turn. Johnny lay low along the neck, one hand wrapped in the heavy mane, barely able to keep his place as the pony twisted and jumped. Such tactics terrified the lumbering monsters as nothing else could have done. They swerved to escape the savage attack, breaking into a run. Others followed their lead.

Though he had no idea how it had been managed, Johnny saw that the whole herd was smashing straight across the river as though it were no barrier, on to the far shore and ahead, relentlessly pushed by the mass behind. This was what they wanted, what the Crows had tried to prevent. They were headed toward their old, neglected range, into the Blackfoot country.

Johnny's sense of triumph was tempered by awe and a sense of unreality. The press of bodies on every side was too great even for horses such as they rode to fight against. They were caught up in the mass, carried back across the river, on and on, almost lost in the rumbling sea of horns and hoofs. Anything which faltered, slipped or fell would be pounded to oblivion.

But the land was wide, the herd spreading as they ran, and they gradually worked toward the rim. Finally, still together, they got free and pulled up, watching the cavalcade, which seemed as endless as ever. With the bulk of the herd between them and their rivals and fog-like dust everywhere, they had little to fear from the Crows.

Ottertail was jubilant, his Irish heritage battling the stoicism of the Indian.

"Talk about medicine!" he exulted. "Sure and begorra, but I wish those at the camp could see this! Now they will keep on, spreading out, grazing as they tire, and nothing will turn them back."

There would be buffalo for the hunters, once the warriors were mounted again. With that now certain, it was imperative to get the wild bunch corraled.

Turning back, they followed the river. Ottertail was confident that the angry Crows would expect them to keep on with the herd and would look for them there. In an encounter, the superior speed and stamina of The Hungry Horse and his bay might save them, but even at best, that could waste time, might even ruin their plans.

They recrossed again, camping south of the river.

The herd was out of sight, and the dust had settled. Here was meat for the taking—stragglers who had dropped out when the pace of the stampede became too fast, victims who had fallen and died. The coyotes were feasting well, for the first time in months.

They crossed once more in the dark just short of the first sign of dawn, then headed toward the mountains looming to the east. The horses were eager to run, sensing that they were approaching their old range, back to where the wild bunch roamed.

Their eagerness was something to ponder over. A horse was an intelligent animal, friendly and eager, anxious to please when they understood what was wanted of them. That held true for those raised in the wild as well as for a rancher's bunch. But The Hungry Horse had been king of the wild band. How would he act when confronted by them?

It was the middle of the second morning when they neared the isolated valley where the wild bunch had summered. From a hilltop, they had a look and glimpsed them, miles away, but still in the same general vicinity.

Finding the band still there was almost as great a relief as sighting the buffalo. In the interval spent returning to camp, then coming back, the horses might easily have been frightened, a new leader deciding to find new feeding grounds far removed from former associations.

"That would surely have been the way of it, had this Hungry Horse still led them," Ottertail observed. "He would lose no time taking them well away from where danger had lurked. But the new king has not had much experience.

"We must be doubly careful," he added, "to keep out of sight. We want to be right among them before they discover us."

The precaution proved wise in a way they had not expected. Johnny's big bay, moving almost with the daintiness of a rabbit despite his size, threw up his head, ears cocked at some alien scent or sound. Moments later, they saw what had attracted his attention.

Less than a mile away, near the far rim of the valley, a trio of horsemen moved at an easy pace, following a course which led toward the wild band. From there, the natural terrain, as well as their leisurely pace and lack of excitement, indicated that they had not yet sighted the wild horses. No one could make such a find and remain unmoved.

If they kept going as they were, they would soon discover them, and that would mean more trouble. It seemed to Johnny that there was something familiar about the three. Then Ottertail spoke excitedly.

"Those three are Crows also, and look—they ride our horses, the two which were stolen from us long ago!"

He was right. One man rode Johnny's old hammerhead; another was proudly astride the medicine pony which Running Wolf had given Ottertail, though that pony, Johnny knew, had originally been stolen from the Crows.

Here was both a problem and an opportunity. If they could get their horses back, that would be a real coup, wiping out the humiliation they had suffered, erasing at least part of the disgrace which the Crows had inflicted upon the Blackfeet. If at the same time they could put their enemies on foot, then the trio would be helpless to interfere with the wild bunch.

But they were three to two, and night, which might work in their favor, was a long way off. Long before that, the Crows would see the wild ones, and everything could be changed.

"Bee on your nose!" Johnny's startled exclamation made Ottertail turn quickly. He followed Johnny's pointing arm.

Some distance farther to the side, seven other horsemen moved at the rim of a coulee.

17

It seemed to Johnny that the big valley was suddenly like a prairie-dog village, looking empty and deserted one moment, then with heads popping up everywhere. Odds of three to two were not too bad, but ten to two were nasty. How could they possibly drive the wild band, or do anything with them, with the country suddenly aswarm with enemies?

"Seems to be a whole flock of Crows," he muttered with a feeble attempt at lightness, then was startled at Ottertail's retort. After a careful look, he seemed excited rather than dismayed.

"Our medicine is still good," he breathed. "Those are not Crows, but Dakotas."

Johnny could discern no particular difference, either in appearance or dress, at that distance, but the actions of the larger party quickly confirmed Ottertail's appraisal. Obviously, the seven Sioux had also sighted the Crows and were working to approach as close to them as possible before being discovered.

It had been sheer luck that this valley of the wild ones, remote though it was, had gone so long with no visitors other than themselves. This was a summer of little game, and as fall approached, more and more hunters would be widely on the prowl. And this was a sort of no man's land, territory claimed by many tribes, loosely held, fought over by all.

There was a sudden wild gabbling as the Dakotas made themselves known, the sound reminding Johnny of the time when the *Oregon* had been attacked. Then they swept out at the startled Crows.

Caught by surprise, the three gave dismayed glances at their dreaded enemies, then lost no time in putting their horses to a run. Distrustful of the valley ahead and what traps it might hold, they headed uphill, to top the crest and find more running room in the country beyond. The Sioux, yipping excitedly, followed. Within moments, all ten were over the rim and out of sight, on a course away from the wild horses.

Excitedly, Ottertail pushed to the crest; Johnny was equally eager to see what might happen. All had vanished in a big dip, but presently they reappeared, first the Crows, then their pursuers, still the same distance behind.

"Your old pony and my medicine horse are good runners." Ottertail grinned. "Not that I wish the Crows good luck, but the farther all of them go in that direction, the better for us."

"None of them seem to have guessed that the wild horses are anywhere near," Johnny observed. "If they did, those would have come first."

The chase might continue for hours, with the outcome uncertain. Since it tended away from them, they had nothing to fear, at least for the present.

They turned again, riding more warily, picking their course with care. The mounting excitement in their horses showed that they had sensed the presence of their former comrades. How would they behave when asked to drive them?

Ottertail had no worries on that score. Each new manifestation of what he confidently believed was the strength of his medicine reassured him. Johnny was not disposed to argue. Medicine was as good a word as any, but as Jonathan Wilde had once remarked, a man had a lot to do with making his own luck.

These hills had changed since they had last ridden through them. Here and there on the hillsides, particularly in the sheltered spots, clumps of brush flamed redly, and the aspens were burning gold. Frost came early to the high country.

Such reminders of fall were almost a shock. The spring and much of the summer had passed since he had found Ottertail, pinned under his dead horse. The *Oregon*, if its luck and the captain's drive had held, would long since have reached Fort Benton, then backtracked down the river. He had probably been reported missing, lost.

That was no particular worry, since no word would reach anyone likely to be much concerned. Once this summer's business was out of the way, he could complete his journey. On the whole, it had been quite a summer.

For the Blackfeet, it had been a long moon of anxiety, with conditions showing no improvement as the seasons changed. Since the threat of hunger and death was imminent, it was easy to understand why some of them looked on him with suspicion. In their minds, white men were enemies, bringers of bad luck.

Still, not everyone felt that way. Running Wolf, Mink Woman—Fawn Who Runs. Kathleen! Either name was mighty pretty. He had a strong hunch that he'd be making more visits to the tribe after all the misunderstandings had been settled.

It was still vital to drive the wild bunch to the village, to get them safely corraled. It would make no real difference to Running Wolf's people that the buffalo were back, unless they had horses with which to hunt and pack in the meat.

They sighted the horses again and spread out, grazing a wide section. They had as peaceful and contented a look as ever. The main difference was that a big red stallion, alert against peril, now watched from a hilltop instead of the ghost horse.

At sight of the new king, the Hungry Horse snorted, but when Ottertail spoke soothingly and stroked his glossy neck, he quieted, tossing his head but neither rearing nor neighing a challenge across the intervening space. Obviously the Hungry Horse didn't like it, but he seemed to recognize that the old days, the old ways, were gone. Conditions would never be the same again.

"Actually, he likes it this way," Ottertail observed. "Ai, but it is fine to be free, to be a king, as he was. But a horse's real heritage is to serve man, and he is happy and proud of his new place."

They made a wide circle down the valley, keeping out of sight, to get beyond the grazing animals.

"We must start them moving in the right direction," Ottertail explained. "If they set off running the wrong way, we would have a lot of trouble and long delays. Our big test will come when they recognize their former leader, or if the new king tries to challenge him. The red one will want to lead them where we do not want them to go—if he can decide which way that is. But maybe we can fool him."

Ottertail understood horses. Johnny had never seen anyone to match him in handling them.

"It is not far to the river," Ottertail added. "If the red one is smart, he will try to reach and get across it. We must prevent that."

The grass to the south of the Yellowstone was now

rich, ripening in the hot suns, blotting away the burnt strip, mostly ungrazed. South of the river, the mountains fanned out, range upon range, valley following valley. If the herd could reach and scatter through such a maze, rounding them up would be almost impossible.

As they moved into the open, the nearer animals raised their heads, sensing change. Discovery ran through the entire band like a strong wind. They stopped grazing or playing, turning, staring with an air of expectancy. They recognized their former leader, along with Johnny's big bay; the boys too were familiar, both in appearance and scent.

But things were not as they had been. In the interval, all of these had become alien, and now they were trespassers if not interlopers. If they were not actually to be feared, neither were they to be trusted.

The band's reaction was different from their first sight of two-legged creatures, when The Hungry Horse had challenged, then charged them. They waited, while the new leader came galloping, then halted at a distance, no more certain what to do than his followers. This time they were riding other horses, and Johnny knew that they found these aspects both unsettling and perplexing.

Then the red one made up his mind. This was not a time for challenge, but for caution. He lifted his head and neighed, then set off, running, clearly intending to go elsewhere. After a momentary hesitation, the band started to fall in behind him.

This was what they had feared, and he was taking a course which would end up wrong. The Hungry Horse was plunging to cut them off, and Johnny's big bay galloped alongside, catching the excitement, eager to run.

The valley was widening, with a long, gradual rise toward the rim, an easy route over which to travel. It could be a long run, for these ponies were as wild as the buffalo and able to travel as tirelessly. A gradual veering one way or the other could completely alter the course within a few hours. And the decisive difference in such an endurance contest might lie with the added burden of riders carried by the bay and the white.

Ottertail pointed and shouted. They had to sweep along one flank of the band, gradually shoving, turning them from south to north. Once the push became serious, the new king might turn on them in challenge, initiating a clash between The Hungry Horse and the red.

They broke over the crest into more open flat country. The valley was finally left behind, and the silver gleam of the Yellowstone was far off toward the south.

Shouting, crowding and pushing at the flowing line, Johnny saw that they were working toward the lead.

But the red one was running easily, making a wide sweep but managing to turn toward the south. Such a course would bring them to the river where it ran wide and shallow, an easy ford. Once they started across, there would be no stopping them.

Johnny swung alongside and spoke to Ottertail. This was a desperate plan, and his own part in it was risky. But he could see no other chance.

Ottertail looked uncertain, but only for a moment. There was no time to lose. This called for speed— a decisive test.

18

"This is it, old horse." Lying stretched along his horse's neck, Indian fashion, Johnny spoke to the laid-back ears. He no longer used the Indian talk which had proved effective, but his own. After all, horse and man understood each other pretty well now.

"Burr in your ear, but you've got to show them," he added urgently. "This is one race we've got to win!"

The bay seemed to understand. Never before had Johnny covered either ground or water so fast. On the lower river, not far above St. Louis, the *Oregon* had encountered another river packet, and both captains had promptly raced, crowding steam and speed to the limit.

This was faster, more breath-taking. The Hungry Horse and Johnny's bay matched step for step, passing the others, making them look like stragglers. They reached the head of the line, and the red one swung furiously, jaws wide in raging defiance. His former leader, now his rival, was daring to challenge him. Eager to meet the test, The Hungry Horse started to swing, and in that instant, Johnny urged an extra burst of speed from his bay and swept between.

With human royalty, such interference between kings would have been an insult, and the wild horses had their own royal pride. But leadership belonged to those able to take it, and the bay had his own pride. At Johnny's voice and the pressure of knees and rein, he made a sudden lunge sidewise straight toward the red one, and the surprise worked. Before the king could swerve or steady to meet the onset from an unexpected quarter, the shoulder of the bay hit him broadside.

Johnny twisted his fingers in the heavy mane, clinging desperately. The shock almost sent him flying, but it worked. The red one was knocked to the side, almost off his feet. But now, though still running, he was no longer leading. The bay was staying beside him, pressing him relentlessly farther and farther, forcing him to swerve. Yelling wildly, Johnny used both hands, flicking a rope's end in vicious darts, and the sorrel was shoved down a sudden steep slope.

The maneuver was not a clear-cut victory. For now both horses were sliding, barely able to keep on their feet as they plunged down the hill. Stones and showers of dirt spurted away from gouging hooves.

Johnny eased a deeper breath into straining lungs, grinning. He had not only forced the new king to give ground, but had cut him out from the band, so that the slope of the hill hid him from the others. They were still thundering ahead, but following almost automatically a new leader who was also their old one, long habit reasserting itself. The Hungry Horse was showing the way.

Thus far, the shift had been almost mechanical, the change so gradual as hardly to be noticed. The test for Ottertail with The Hungry Horse lay ahead. He must make a wide turn, to lead the band away from the river back toward the north. Would they continue to follow?

So much hinged on the next few minutes, on old habits and the natural leadership of The Hungry Horse, that Johnny scarcely dared to think. But he still had a job to do.

The hillside, steep at first, was easier now. Guiding his bay, Johnny kept crowding as they neared the foot of the slope. The sounds of the main herd were receding, growing faint. Bewildered, the red one hesitated and tried to turn, only to be balked by the bay, the swinging rope buzzing before his nose. He swung away, but his course was no longer toward where the band were being led, but to where he had intended to guide them. Having lost sight of them, he was not sure where to find them.

It took several minutes of circling and climbing for Johnny to reach a point where he could see. The horses were strung out behind the ghost animal, running steadily, without question.

Ottertail had flattened himself low on the neck and side of The Hungry Horse, clinging with hands in mane, almost invisible to most of the band. Johnny cut across, swinging behind the stragglers, shouting, driving now to keep them bunched. The herd was being driven as well as led, and they moved as a matter of course.

It was nearly an hour before the red one caught up. Johnny saw him coming at a tireless lope, flinging up his head at intervals to neigh a challenge and a command. The challenge was ignored by The Hungry Horse, controlled as he was by Ottertail, and the lesser ones paid no attention to the command, being too tired or too well satisfied to be following their long-time leader.

Johnny swung to meet the red one, and again it was man and bay against a deposed and uncertain leader. The flicking, lashing rope, a man on a horse, was too much. Finally, ignored by his ex-subjects, the sorrel was content to straggle along at the rear, one of the bunch.

Ottertail was apprehensive lest he make a later try at regaining authority, for he and the Hungry Horse could not run ahead indefinitely. He fell back gradually, allowing several to take the collective lead, making sure that they kept in the right direction.

The strategy, with guidance from the sides and behind, was working. The problem now was to keep them moving, not allow them to rest or spread out for grazing. If they could be kept moving until they were very tired, they would be easier to control.

"Ai and begorra, sure but we've done it," he called gleefully. "Such medicine, John Hawk—what could be stronger?"

"Shake well before using," Johnny returned, and saw his friend's puzzled look at the incomprehensible phrase. Neither was deceived. Getting the band headed properly was a big step, but the long drive back would be a test of endurance for them. They would have little chance to stop and cook, probably even less to rest and sleep, until the horses were safely in the corral.

This was all new to the wild ones, who were accustomed to being led, but had never before been driven. They were growing restive, showing that they had run far enough. They wanted to stop, to rest and graze, but the white and the bay, the shouts and flicking ropes, forced them ahead.

Johnny sympathized with them as the sun set; then darkness spread across the prairie. It was a clear, warm night; the high stars were luminous, casting enough light to travel by. He, too, would have liked nothing better than to halt until a new day. It was hard to keep awake, doubly difficult to be alert, to make sure in the gloom that the big herd remained bunched.

They had long since slowed to a walk, refusing to trot, more and more indifferent to these two-legged creatures, obeying only when forced.

"It is hard on everyone, but we must keep moving," Ottertail said. "There comes the moon, so there is light enough. We must not let them rest, for they are still wild and would be hard to start moving again, to go where we want them. Also, if they are fresh when we near the corral, they are more likely to take alarm and break away."

It became an endless ordeal, not merely to keep awake and on their own horses, but to keep the bunch moving. At this point there was no sign of wildness. They could push close alongside, shout, flick the ends of their ropes, and the horses would pay no more attention than had they been a domesticated herd. They snatched bites of grass at every opportunity, but could not stop for steady grazing.

When a stream was crossed, they allowed them time to drink. As was common, there was almost no sign of other life, certainly not of buffalo. But that meant nothing in particular. This was a vast land, even for such a herd as they had seen heading into the north.

The Hungry Horse and Johnny's bay did their part,

obedient, seeming to take a new pride in their roles. They crowded loiterers into place, squealed and bit at rebels.

Passing a clump of tall bushes, Johnny snatched a handful of service-berries, stripping off the purple fruit with quick grabs. Some crushed in his palm, but they were sweet and tasty. The few bites hardly eased his hunger, but the effect helped keep him awake.

The horses plodded with lowered heads as dawn grayed the horizon, giving way to the sudden blaze of sun. Rousing, Johnny blinked. The terrain was vaguely familiar. Cloudy with distance, a rougher line notched the horizon. Somewhere in there was the village.

Ottertail grinned, but his face was tired and drawn, like a mask. Johnny tried to shout at a straggler, and his voice sounded like the croaking of a frog.

19

It was mid-forenoon when they spied a welcome sight—a single horseman, riding to meet them. It was too far for recognition, but neither had any doubt that this was a friendly messenger from the camp. No lone rider would approach under ordinary circumstances, but this proved that they had been on the alert, had recognized the wild bunch as they approached.

It was Lazy Horse who joined them, a person transformed from the exhausted, half-starved and hopeless slave they had rescued some time before. He was a man again, wildly excited as he viewed the horses, trying not to show it.

"You have managed," he said. "But I knew you would."

The return of the two, long given up for lost, with their report on how Ottertail and John Hawk had freed them from a large Crow encampment, then had scattered the horses of the Crows, putting them on foot, had created a profound impression among the almost hopeless people. Johnny suspected that the story had not suffered in the telling.

At any rate, the response had been prompt and unanimous. If the wild bunch could be driven here, the least that they could do was make preparations and help in every way possible. Coyote Man and Big Bear, suddenly in disfavor, had obeyed Running Wolf's orders, and much had been accomplished.

"The old corral is ready, with poles to bar the gate, once they are inside," Lazy Horse reported. "The course will be guarded by the people, strung out, hidden along the sides. It is not too well prepared, for there was less time than we had expected, but everyone will do his best."

They had had good luck the day before. Lazy Horse and Eagle Wing, taking the horses and hunting, had come upon a small herd of deer, and had gotten two of them. Everyone had feasted.

It had clearly been a time of work and excitement, of orderly but frenzied preparation, with everyone working well into each night. No one scoffed now. The nephew of the chief had dreamed, and his dreams, like his medicine, were proving strong.

Lazy Horse described the corral in detail, so that Ottertail had everything well in mind from past experience in the country. The horses would be held in it until they could be tamed and broken to ride. It was a natural, rock-walled gulch which ended in a blind pocket. There was a meadow of good grass, ample feed for several days. A spring of water near the far end formed a series of ponds.

Ottertail elaborated for Johnny's benefit. At one point, the natural cliff walls narrowed, to make an opening of less than sixty feet. It was big enough to crowd the horses through, small enough to be closed after they were in.

Stout logs were piled at either side, ready to be raised, to close the gate. Shorter poles could be set up swiftly, resting against one another in the manner of tepee poles, to hold the ends of the bars. Properly placed, these would be strong, and could be further braced with additional poles from the outside.

So well had the work been done that there was nothing new or unusual to see which might cause alarm. The spreading slope of long natural ridges, or hogbacks, acted as natural guides toward the corral. Wherever possible, gaps had been closed, the barriers concealed by covers of sagebrush or evergreen boughs. The wild bunch must not suspect the trap or take alarm until it was too late to break away.

Both the warriors and young men had worked late the night before, taking advantage of the moon and of a good meal to give them strength. It had been as they started wearily to return to the village and rest that a scout had spotted the dust, distant but hanging like a beacon against the horizon, stirred from a thousand plodding hoofs.

All thought of sleep was instantly forgotten. Such a cloud could mean only one of two things. Either the horses were coming, or else buffalo.

Those who had been asleep were soon aroused, including the squaws and children. Everyone wanted to have a part in what was to be done, and there was work for all. They hurried to take their places, squaws and boys along the guides and ridges, the braves venturing farther out on the prairie, concealing themselves at strategic places. Once the horses came along, they could leap up, shouting, waving blankets, gradually closing a ring and harrying the band toward the corral.

Now, in the full light of day, there was no room for doubt. These were horses, the wild ones, plodding and weary but pushed along by the two who had been outcasts. All at once that had become a shameful memory.

Ottertail and the white man had done their part, accomplishing what many had thought would be impossible. Now it was up to them, and everyone had to remain hidden. Any premature sound or movement, which might alarm or stampede the band, could still spoil the venture.

Johnny blinked, sitting straighter on the back of the big bay. He felt like stretching along its neck and back and going to sleep, but at least the hot sun and Lazy Horse had stirred him fully awake. He blinked, stared, and pointed as Ottertail came alongside.

"Off there!"

Ottertail looked and grew more alert. At the rim of the prairie, distant but unmistakable, was a crawling, spreading mass—buffalo!

"We can't have anything go wrong now," Ottertail said hoarsely. "For other hunters will be coming, along with the buffalo!"

Johnny nodded his understanding. It had been a long spring and a longer summer, with game almost at the vanishing point, not alone for the Blackfeet, but for others. The others would be after the big ones, mounted braves, and Running Wolf's people must be able not only to get in on the hunt, before the buffalo were frightened to new pastures, but to meet invaders on an equal footing, to be able to defend themselves if necessary.

Once more the straggling line of horses were turning stubborn, wanted to stop. The brief energy stirred by a new day was more than offset by their determination to graze. The plain was rich with grass, and if they were half as hungry as he was, Johnny could understand. Having grown accustomed not only to The Hungry Horse, who no longer ran in the lead, but to the men, they had lost their fear.

Johnny's voice came out between a squeak and a

roar when he tried to yell. But someone took his shout for a signal. Men sprang from the grass, cavorting and yelling, closing behind and on either side of the band.

At least it was well-timed. The sudden materialization of so many two-legged creatures was startling, and the horses plunged ahead, taking the one direction still open. Squaws and children added their shouts to the pandemonium.

It looked like success, but the red king had other notions. For part of the day and through the night he had moved with the rest, not trying to lead, but biding his time. If the others had already forgotten that he had been their king, he had not, nor had he forgotten a leader's responsibility.

The suddenly jumping, shrieking figures enraged but did not terrify him. He sensed, even if the others did not, that this was a trap, seeing the danger in the closing lines.

Casting aside weariness, he flared into sudden action. Rearing on his hind legs, his front hoofs pawing the air, he opened his mouth in a screaming challenge which was equally a command. Coming down, he struck the ground so hard that the earth seemed to shake, though that might be the impact of the whole herd in a sudden run. Then he dashed for a break at the side in the rocky wall.

The corral was still quite a distance ahead. If he

could get out, the others would swing and follow, and the red one would be king again.

More braves were jumping up, waving and screeching, trying to turn the rebel. They were forced to jump for their lives as the sorrel drove at them with gaping jaws, then tore through the gap, crashing among the poles placed in the way, sending them flying like matchsticks.

Ottertail saw the danger, and The Hungry Horse responded to his shout. The red one was out, but there was room and a chance to overtake him, and the ghost animal seemed, like his rival, to shed his weariness, sweeping alongside in a desperate surge. Johnny, coming also, saw that the two kings were ready to battle for supremacy, just as they would have done under normal conditions. There was enmity, sharpened by rivalry, a sense on the part of the sorrel that his former leader had betrayed them.

Ottertail had other notions, and The Hungry Horse obeyed him. As they hurtled alongside, he risked the one chance which held much promise of success, reaching out and flinging the loop of his lariat. This time it was the neck of the red one which felt the sudden constriction as the noose found its mark.

Ottertail was counting on the surprise as well as the painful effect. He needed every possible advantage, for today there was no convenient tree about which to snub the end of the rope, not even a saddle and horn with which to get purchase and control. There was only himself, grasping the rope with bare hands, pitting such strength and skill as he might against the maddened frenzy of the big red.

The shock of the closing noose worked as he expected, the painful surprise checking the sorrel's rush, but not quite sending him back on his haunches as Ottertail held on desperately. The red's attempt to trumpet fresh defiance was a gasping wheeze.

The tug of the rope and its surprise slowed him, but only for an instant. He spun about furiously, surging for his tormentor, jaws wide and savage.

Ottertail had made his try, and it had been a good one, but he was in a desperate spot, helpless now to help himself. Calculating the odds, Johnny drove in with his bay, turning suddenly to hit the maddened red broadside, much as they had done at the start of the drive.

The smash of the impact almost jarred Johnny loose, for this time the ex-king was down in a welter of flailing hoofs. The blankets and the shouting had checked the rush of other animals as they tried to follow. Milling briefly, they were caught, absorbed by the rush of the main herd, carried on toward the corral.

Johnny and Ottertail pulled back, Ottertail dropping the lariat, leaving the red one to his own devices. He came unsteadily to his feet, badly shaken, hampered by the rope, the noose still dragging from his throat. For once he was unsure. Most of the herd were vanishing down the run. Johnny signaled and jumped the bay, and The Hungry Horse surged as well. Almost meekly, the sorrel galloped after the others.

The wild shouting was giving way to a new note, exultant with triumph. Men rushed to close the gate, erecting poles as a barrier, bracing them against a backward rush once the milling band discovered that they had reached a point of no return.

What happened was an anticlimax, disappointing. The red one, with the spirit of a king, was ready to lead them back in a rush, but another horse stepped on the dragging end of the rope, almost throwing him. The others, tired and discouraged, had little inclination left to run. Ahead was grass and water, a chance to stop, to rest and feed.

Johnny slid wearily to the ground, staggering with stiffness. Ottertail was being acclaimed from all sides. Then Fawn Who Runs was beside Johnny, the warmth of her welcome not to be misunderstood. Johnny sighed contentedly. There would be no hurry about heading for Benton, or anywhere in particular. He scarcely heard the words of Running Wolf as he addressed the throng.

"The buffalo are returning, one of the greatest herds ever to move across the plain. Now we have horses, and soon we will hunt! This winter, there will be meat in every lodge!"

THE RANCH AT POWDER RIVER

1

The sun cast slanting long rays across a rough and broken land, but the sharp chill of dawn clung to the air. Off to the south, breaks in the hills afforded Montana Abbott occasional glimpses of the Yellowstone, running as turgid as its name. The water and the cottonwoods which lined its course were partly obscured by rising mists from the river, looking curiously like puffs of gunsmoke. As if to add to the reality of the illusion, a gun growled throatily from considerably closer at hand.

The big bay cayuse on which Montana was mounted snorted its dislike, jerking its ugly hammerhead. The horse seemed to have as deep an aversion to guns as he did, and Montana had long since learned that their booming was usually a portent of trouble.

The gun rasped again, followed by a sharper, even more chilling sound—a keening, high-pitched wailing, once heard never to be forgotten. It reminded him of a werewolf's cry, the war whoops of

Indians on the attack.

The long leanness of his big body went tense, as much from surprise as the ever-recurring emotion which came with the threat of danger. This thumb-screwing of the nerves was not exactly fear, and no man had ever questioned his courage. But after a dozen battles and a score of lesser skirmishes, it was always the same: a dryness of the mouth, tightness which squeezed like a bulldog's jaws, the prickling of apprehension. Like the river mists in the sun, such tensions evaporated when threat became action, but he had long since realized that he'd never outgrow the initial chilling impact.

The big hammerhead paused at the sound, while a shiver worked up from its hoofs as though it, too, had heard such sounds before. Nightmare noises went ill with the morning sun.

Also, technically at least, there was a truce if not peace between red men and white. This absence of active animosity was of recent origin, but like a worn rope, quick to fray. Young bucks had to prove their manhood, riding adventurously, satisfying ancient cravings. Such rovers found temptation hard to resist when they came upon a few straggling white men who offered the promise of easy scalps.

"Reckon we'd better have a look," Montana told the horse, and the hammerhead, obedient to a pressure of knees and reins, swung as he directed. Which was probably a foolish thing to do, and might well prove foolhardy, since he could as easily have kept going, closing his ears to sounds of strife and despair. But in so lonesome a country, and with fellow-men in such a fix, a man did what he could.

Once more, in the next few minutes, the gun growled its defiance, but the long spaces between shots bespoke desperation and perhaps a shortage of ammunition. Here the hills peaked a couple of miles back from the river, long and half-naked ridges like loaves of bread baking in the sun, their timber cover of evergreens scanty and remote. If any of these trees had echoed to birdsong at the approach of the sun, such lilting had hushed in dread before the harsher assaults.

The big cayuse climbed a final slope, hoof-falls muted by the grassy carpet, then halted at a touch. Twin bowls were spread out below. The nearer was directly ahead, a rock-walled enclosure of no great size, less than a hundred feet across. As though nature had envisioned what was now taking place and prepared an amphitheatre, the first bowl provided an excellent fortress, overlooking the larger bowl, considerably farther down the hill.

Leaving his horse on the sheltered side of the crest, Montana made use of the lookout, assessing the situation.

The view was reasonably good, and what it disclosed was not too different from what he had expected. The larger bowl, below, was nearly a quarter of a mile in width, sufficiently broken and boulder-studded to afford some shelter both for fugitives and attackers. He made out a couple of the besieged near the middle of the enclosure, crouched amid a tangle of stones. The ripple of the early sun along a gun barrel served as a focus.

A couple of horses stood nervously in a partly sheltered screen of brush, not far to the side. He had the picture. The two had been surprised. Forted up, they were besieged.

It took another couple of minutes, studying the bowl above as well as the one below them, to decide that at least half a dozen warriors were spread around it, occasionally loosing an arrow, endeavoring to slip from one covering boulder to another, closing the ring. Not much was actually to be seen, but enough to give him the picture.

Both groups had fallen silent, growing more deadly as the climax neared. The stones which afforded cover also made it easy for the attackers to creep in. If any help was to be given, it would have to be soon.

There was the rub. Even should he take a hand, the odds would remain heavy, almost overwhelming. The end result could well be not the saving of the threatened scalps of the besieged pair, but the addition of his own to the collection.

The warriors blended well with the terrain and were difficult to locate. Perhaps deceived by the hush, a magpie came winging, to veer abruptly and increase the beat of its wings. Guided by what it had seen, Montana made out part of a bared brown back, a half-shaven head adorned with a single feather. It was good enough as a target, but too far off for him to be sure whether the brave was Blackfoot or Sioux, Crow or a wanderer from some more distant tribe. Not that it made a great deal of difference. A tame house cat never lost its lust for mice or birds, and the comparison extended to this case.

He sensed a restlessness, a stirring, as though the attackers were about ready to chance a rush, a finish marked by overwhelming power. He might delay if not avert that with a few well-placed bullets, but as a former captain of cavalry, he preferred a battle plan which afforded at least a chance for victory.

Surprise would favor him. If he could build upon that—

Montana worked swiftly. The six-shooter in his holster he set in position beside an upthrusting finger of stone, tying it with a short length of fish line. Always, as a matter of prudence, he carried a coil of such cord, along with hooks. Together they had provided many a meal of trout, and it had been in his mind to cut a willow for a rod and whip some small stream for his breakfast, when the fight sounds had interrupted.

A slip knot at the end of the line curved around

the trigger. Drawing back the hammer of the Colt's to full cock, he moved across to the far side of the small bowl, playing out the fish line as he moved. At the halfway point of the natural wall, a round boulder, as thick as his body, suggested a plan. It was already upon the rocky shelf, and required only a little adjustment to be poised so lightly that a nudge would set it rolling and bounding down-slope.

Here was the mix for a devil's broth. Having at times been forced to sup such a brew, Montana found it more palatable when he was the cook. From the far rim of his own bowl, he selected a target, thrusting the snout of his rifle into position. He curled a finger around the trigger, and the instantly responding yell, mingling pain and consternation, accompanied by a wild scrambling, attested to the fact that the shot had not been wasted.

Promptly, from another point, the revolver boomed as he jerked the trip line. He fired the rifle again, as surprise startled another warrior to make an incautious move, then snatched a stone the size of his fist. His aim was good, and the impact of the missile against the delicately balanced boulder worked precisely as he had hoped. It went tumbling, crashing and bounding in a noisy frenzy all out of proportion to what damage it might wreak.

A third shot from the rifle was followed moments later by another from the Colt's, as he reached and snatched it up. A couple of extra bullets served as good measure but were otherwise wasted, since by then the demoralized besiegers were in full retreat, already out of sight and range. They fled with the certainty that not only the tables were turned, but that a sizable rescue party was above.

Recoiling his fish line and reloading his weapons, Montana descended to the larger bowl, leading his horse. That the two men had been in dire straits was immediately apparent. One lay outstretched in a pool of his own blood, an arrow protruding from both chest and back. He was unconscious, if not already dead.

His companion was in better shape, but not much, from the standpoint of effective resistance. Another arrow had gashed his right arm below the elbow, a bloody if not otherwise ugly wound, but bad enough pretty well to spoil his marksmanship. A reddish stubble of whiskers, the grime and dishevelment of battle, disguised but could not conceal the marks of an old soldier. He eyed Montana with surprise, incredulity and gratification.

"I'm pleased to see you, stranger," he observed. "Which same goes for Bill Jameson here, even if he can't speak for himself. But you didn't create all that unholy ruckus by your own self, did you now?"

"Such as it was," Montana acknowledged. "A diversion seemed to be called for."

"It sure was. Them red devils jumped us without

no warnin'—risin' just like the sun. They was just nervin' themselves to come on in and finish us off— which they could have done, easy enough. Is he— dead?"

Montana was examining Jameson. Of medium build, he was wiry, muscled like a cougar, with thinning hair of a cougar's pale tawniness. Montana's head shake was grim at thought of the chore yet to be done.

"Not yet, at least. But this arrow has got to come out. Which operation he may or may not survive."

In preparation, he stripped off his own shirt, tearing it into long strips. Mercifully, the wounded man remained unconscious. But a groan was twisted from white lips as Montana took the protruding barb of the arrow in both hands and broke it with a swift motion, then, seizing the haft on the opposite side, pulled swiftly and strongly to extricate the crimson rod. Its removal was followed by twin gusts of blood.

Moss grew on the side of one of the boulders where the fugitives had sheltered. He used chunks of it to cover the arrow punctures, bandaging the wounds as well as possible with the strips of cloth. Presently, when the bleeding was reasonably well checked, he made sure, with some surprise, that the injured man was still breathing.

Inquiry widened the eyes of his companion.

"Has he got a chance?"

Montana was tempted to make an admission of the

stark truth. Under the best of conditions and care, the wound was ugly, and survival would be uncertain, the odds against it high. Lacking such care and the skill of a doctor, there was even less possibility.

"Sure'd hate to see the cap'n go under now, in such fashion," the other man went on, his words confirming the impression which Montana had already received. These two had been soldiers, the one probably a sergeant. The stamp of the army was as indelible on a man's character as the loyalty which non-coms sometimes felt for the commanders with whom they had served across years of strife. "Folks used to call him Old Indestructible. And for a measly arrow to do him in—"

"You never can tell," Montana said. "We'd better get going, see if we can find help."

The old sergeant's gaze was bleak with comprehension.

"And the chances of that, hereabouts, ain't half as good as stagin' a snowball fight in Hades." He nodded. "But still, *you* turned up in the nick of time—"

On his own horse again, cradling Captain Jameson in front of the saddle, Montana swung toward the river. If any hope existed, it would be along the watercourse. Not that his expectations were any higher than those which the sergeant had voiced.

Then, from near the crest of the line of bluffs, with the river a gleam of silver in the sun, he stared, shook his head and marveled. Old Indestructible! Perhaps there was something in the name, after all.

So far away as to give the appearance of a bird on a pond, a river packet was breasting the current of the Yellowstone. River boats were increasingly common on the Missouri, but they rarely ventured onto the dangerously taboo waters of the forbidden Yellowstone. By tacit, sometimes even formal agreement between the angry red men and the Great White Father, the territory abutting the flowing yellow waters was reserved for the red men and forbidden to the white.

Not that all white men obeyed governmental injunctions or were impressed by threats.

A river packet here, under such circumstances, seemed in the nature of a miracle. Montana was of no mind to question or argue. There might even be a doctor aboard the boat. If they could signal her and get the wounded man on board, then he would have discharged his responsibility.

2

The gentleman who promenaded the available deck spaces of the river packet Star of the West preferred to be known as the Right Honorable Henry Tiller-Parsons. Clad elegantly if inappropriately in spats, he gazed about with the air of a monarch surveying his domain. Perhaps rightly, for what he had done during recent weeks certainly could have been rated as an accomplishment, the crowded condition of the packet furnishing additional proof of what had been or was still to be.

Practically the entire capacity of the stern-wheeler, whose captain boasted that she could run, if necessary, on a heavy dew, was given over to a variety of freight. Its ultimate destination was tagged or lettered as the Powder River Ranch. Stacks of lumber, boxes of tools, cartons of hardware were piled under and around a sleek-looking buggy. A pair of heavy wagons had their double boxes already loaded with staple groceries. Household furniture vied with other items of a surprising nature. All of this was being brought as far as the mouth of the Powder River at Tiller-Parsons' direction.

Removing a glove, he gave a complacent twist to a small, neatly waxed mustache, watching the slow alteration of the landscape as they churned against the current. To attain his present position had taken some little while, together with a mixture of servility to his betters on the one hand, and effrontery to all others whom he could afford to bully; there had been as much luck as ability, almost as many downs as ups, but he was finally reaching the goals which he had set for himself. The Star and what it carried was proof.

Most of the merchandise had been loaded at St. Louis. For one man to charter a river boat for the long passage up the Missouri was unheard of and had excited comment. He had made the commitments and paid necessary bills in the name of the Powder River Ranch Company, as its manager. Sums, little short of staggering even to himself, had passed through his hands. But such expenditures had been necessary. Money spoke with a convincing voice, especially where Captain Ira Shaumut was concerned.

"You must have good backing for this ranch," Shaumut had observed. "A syndicate, I take it?"

"A syndicate of English gentlemen," Tiller-Parsons confirmed. "Sir John Crispin is one of the directors." He added with easy complacence, "By another spring, the Powder River Ranch should be the largest operation of its type in the territory of Montana. Our ranch headquarters are back in the hills, half a hundred miles from the Yellowstone. A house is already in the process of erection, but some of these supplies will be used to finish and furnish it."

"A house, did you say?" Shaumut gibed. "Wouldn't a mansion be closer to the fact?"

Tiller-Parsons preened his mustache, his somewhat prominent eyes goggling.

"There will be some resemblances, certainly," he confirmed. "While I will occupy it as manager, the real purpose is to provide adequate accommodations for the owners, when they may see fit to visit the ranch. For that, something along the lines of an English country estate is called for. I would not want to disappoint them."

"Naturally not," Shaumut agreed, regarding Tiller-Parsons with a grudging respect. Something about the man was not quite right; there was some quality which grated, for all the superficial smoothness which he exuded. But if he possessed the trust of his employers and had the ability to manage a ranch of such proportions, there must be more to him than met the eye.

Fort Benton had been the original destination of the Star of the West, but the charter and full consignment of cargo had persuaded Shaumut to turn into the little known waters of the Yellowstone and proceed as far as the mouth of the Powder, a stream which in appearance he found far less impressive than its name. Having made fast near the shore, they proceeded with the business of unloading, under the watchful and somewhat nervous eye of Tiller-Parsons.

Setting foot on solid ground again, this apprehension he carefully concealed, along with the immediate reason for the apprehension. In fact, he took pains to hide it under a stream of light and airy conversation with the lady herself. Miss Alicia Fredricks had proved a charming companion during the long miles up from St. Louis.

Her original destination, booked prior to the chartering, like that of most of the other passengers, had been Fort Benton rather than Powder River. But when the matter of the freight had been explained, along with the need for haste in delivering it, Tiller-Parsons had proved convincing. Captain Shaumut had offered to return any fares paid in advance, or to secure the passengers accommodations aboard another river packet. But Tiller-Parsons, with an eye to the considerable sums involved, had suggested that the Star first proceed up the Yellowstone, then return to the Missouri and so on to Benton, affording everyone several extra days of voyaging and scenery at no extra cost. To that there had been general agreement, the others following where Alicia led.

That they should do so was not surprising. Not only was she an extremely good-looking woman, of an adventuresome disposition, as taking such a trip, attended only by a maid, attested; in her native New Orleans she was an arbiter of fashion and society. That sprang partly from her own good looks and accomplishments, in part from the wealth belonging to the Fredericks.

Hearing the proportions of that wealth, Tiller-Parsons had been as dazzled by the possibilities as by the lady. At the outset he had hesitated, though briefly, uncertain what course he should take, weighing the rewards against the risks. An easy compromise had been to accommodate the original list of passengers.

By the third day out from St. Louis, he had made his decision, encouraged by the graciousness with which Alicia Fredericks accepted him as an equal, or perhaps as a suitor. Complacently, he had given an added twist to his mustache, surveying himself in the mirror of his room. Men might, in fact often did dislike him, but with the ladies it was a different story. He was where he was today by reason of his ability to charm the fair sex.

One example had been Sir John Crispin's lady. She had swung a close balance in his favor, approving him to manage the big ranch for the syndicate, persuading her husband to influence the other

stockholders. And she was but one of several be-
dazzled ladies.

That the effect had a way of wearing off, on
longer acquaintance, Tiller-Parsons had discovered
to be an asset rather than a liability. The process
enabled him, on general principles, to love them
and leave them, which was also profitable.

Now, though giving no outward sign, he found
himself on the long horns of a dilemma. The considerable load of supplies had to be transported to
the ranch headquarters, and the work pushed with
all possible speed. The house had to be enclosed
before the advent of bad weather, and enough
accomplished along other lines to confirm Sir John's
judgment and reassure the others that he was the
proper man to manage the enterprise. Failure could
bring an unwelcome probing into the lavish manner
in which he had been spending the assets of the
syndicate.

He should go along with the loads of freight,
supervising the work. Just as imperatively, he must
go back down-river on the Star, continuing to dance
attendance on Alicia Fredericks. Such an easy gesture on his part, signifying affluence along with a
careless ability to manage everything, would, he was
certain, accomplish the desired result: to wit, to
stand before a parson, perhaps at Fort Benton, with
Alicia by his side.

The immediate difficulty was that by taking such

a course he might lose his position as manager of the syndicate, which at this particular juncture would be highly undesirable. But to get his hands on the Fredericks wealth was at least equally tempting.

There should be a way to do both. But his mind, usually agile, was slow in coming up with a solution.

Hopefully he noted a pair of new arrivals and, excusing himself, hurried to meet them. One he recognized as a cowboy already in his employ at the ranch. The other he took for a second hand. He had left instructions that his ranch foreman should be at the Powder on or before this date, to await the arrival of the chartered craft. Anxiously he confirmed that there was no sign of the foreman.

Timothy O'Donnell, ex-sergeant of cavalry, C. S. A., was bluff and hearty, not to say capable. He gave Tiller-Parsons the bad news in one stiff swallow.

"Jones wa'n't able to come. He's dead."

"Dead?" Tiller-Parsons echoed, and swallowed painfully. He had almost persuaded himself that it might be safe to entrust everything to Jones, in addition to the work with the cattle. Jones was only a cowboy, but he was a man who knew cattle—and so essential, since Tiller-Parsons did not. But when that had been said, all the facts were encompassed. Jones was—or had been—a cowboy. That was all.

O'Donnell nodded, his face carefully blank. "He got the herd you wanted up from Texas. But there was a smidgin of trouble, a gun battle. We had to bury him."

Tiller-Parsons digested this news, carefully asking no questions. It was a relief that the herd had been delivered, even if Jones had lost his life in the operation. Tiller-Parsons' long-range plans, like those of his employers, were centered in a big beef herd, and he had made promises which might have fallen short.

So that part of the report was a relief. But it was highly inconvenient that the foreman had gotten himself killed at this particular time.

From being a lonely spot in a wide land, this mouth of the Powder was suddenly becoming populous. Another contingent of riders was coming up, and Tiller-Parsons, always observant and sharp of wit as necessity demanded, noted that one man held another, who appeared to be either sick or wounded, on the front of his saddle.

During the next several minutes, as Montana Abbott made the welcome discovery that there was a doctor on board the packet, then carried Bill Jameson and delivered him into the doctor's care, Tiller-Parsons learned in his turn that this man was Montana Abbott. Though his wispy mustache was his closest physical resemblance to a fox, Tiller-Parsons' ears figuratively perked up at the news.

Presently he found an opportunity to introduce

himself, extending his hand.

"I've heard of you, Abbott," he said. "It's a pleasure to know you, sir."

Montana accepted the handshake without particular enthusiasm. Ladies might find Tiller-Parsons attractive. He did not.

Tiller-Parsons went on to explain himself, also the considerable amount of freight which was still being unloaded. He had already come to a decision.

"The Indian attack of which you speak, and its consequences, was certainly regrettable, but the end result of it, which was to bring you here at this particular time, I find most opportune," he said smoothly. "Except for the business of the Powder River Ranch and this cargo, the Star of the West would not have arrived at this particular place in Mr. Jameson's hour of need. Nor would you in *my* time of need."

Montana's eyebrows lifted in faint inquiry.

"I've just received bad news," Tiller-Parsons explained. "My ranch foreman was killed in a gunfight with cattle rustlers. His loss, especially at this particular time, puts me in a bad fix. Not every man—in fact, very few—is capable of doing what has to be done."

That, judging by the scope of operations suggested by the mountain of freight, was perhaps true. Montana waited politely.

"I've heard of you—favorably," Tiller-Parsons went

on, with only faint condescension. "You are an experienced cattleman, and as a former army officer, also experienced in leadership; in short, the sort of man I require. I hope I find you at loose ends, sir. I'd like to hire you as foreman of the Powder River Ranch."

Montana was incredulous. He had not expected anything of the sort.

Such a position might be quite a job—and he could use a job. On the other hand, he could feel no enthusiasm at the prospect of working for Tiller-Parsons. His prejudice might be irrational, but it had been formed. He didn't like the man.

"I have to return down-river with the boat, then up to Fort Benton, after which I will journey to the ranch," Tiller-Parsons went on. "As foreman, you will be in charge of all operations during my absence, not only as regards the cattle and the running of the ranch, but also when it comes to seeing that the buildings are properly erected with the least possible delay."

"But you don't know a thing about me, or whether I could handle such a job," Montana protested.

"On the contrary, I've heard quite a lot about you, Mr. Abbott—and I flatter myself that I am a judge of character. The job is yours if you will take it." He played his trump card.

"Your salary will be two thousand dollars a year, plus board and quarters, starting as of now."

Montana drew a deep breath. He'd intended to say no—but this sounded challenging as well as interesting. And the pay was far above what he would be able to command as a cowhand.

"You've hired yourself a man," he said.

3

Tiller-Parsons was elated. There was no doubt in
his mind that Abbott was a good man, who would
be able to handle affairs at the ranch during his
absence, and that was fine for the immediate present.
But it was the long view which chiefly concerned
him, the carrying out of plans which had been set in
motion a long while before. The killing of Jones
had posed a threat, but by this gesture he had pretty
well retrieved the situation.

Montana Abbott was well known beyond the
Territory as an honest man of unimpeachable in-
tegrity. Such a reputation was precisely what Tiller-
Parsons required at the moment.

A measure of his pleasure showed through as he
introduced Montana to Alicia Fredericks. He dis-
played a ponderous playfulness akin to that of a
dancing elephant.

"My dear, this is Montana Abbott, of whom you
may have heard. He has quite a reputation for
getting things done, and I'm particularly fortunate
in having him take charge at the ranch so that I
can devote myself to other matters of equal or even

greater importance—affairs such as roses and moonlight."

His meaning could hardly be misunderstood, as
Alicia showed by blushing in emulation of the rose.
Clearly she was not displeased. Montana shrugged
and put it from his mind. It was none of his business, though he found it somewhat incomprehensible.
He had wondered more than once why the most
lovely women seemed to be attracted by worthless
men—though in view of his position, perhaps that
was unjust as applied to Tiller-Parsons.

The physician on board the Star of the West was
taking such care as was possible of Captain Bill
Jameson, and perhaps his reputation as Old Indestructible, along with the doctor's skill, would
carry him through. In any case, there was nothing
more that Montana could do for him, and the series
of events had led to his acquiring an unlooked-for
job at a very good salary.

Tiller-Parsons filled him in on the general situation, giving some last-minute instructions, along
with funds for expenses. Then the Star of the West
backed to midstream and began the return trip to
the Missouri. Timothy O'Donnell was displaying
the qualities of a sergeant, getting the freight loaded
onto the wagons, with the excess stored for a later
date, as they made ready to head for the ranch.

"It's an amazin' set-up," he confided to Montana.
"Them crazy Englishmen must be made of money,

judgin' by the way Tiller-Parsons has been throwin' it around. Likely they've heard of lots of land and big herds in this country, and figure that it adds up to a deal where they can't help but make fortunes. Cows have calves, they eat grass and grow up, your herd gets bigger and bigger!" He grinned sardonically. "Of course it could work out that way, but I'd want somebody else managin' the job, if it was me."

Montana volunteered no comment, although the opinion jibed with his own. Undeterred, O'Donnell went on:

"Tiller-Parsons! What sort of a name is that? Sounds like a horse's snort. Sure he's the boss, and I'm takin' some of the money he's throwin' around, and I'll do my best to earn it. But all I've got to say is, I figure those Englishmen have got a lot to learn."

While that might be true, it should be interesting to work for a syndicate whose notion of a cattle ranch was perhaps entangled with ideas of English country estates and hunting expeditions along the frontier.

By nightfall, the laden wagons had left the river well behind. The next day's journey was uneventful, the slow miles unrolling along a wide and empty land. Besides himself and O'Donnell, there were eight other men to handle the teams and wagons. They halted short of sunset, and the cook soon had a tempting collection of aromas rising, much as the mists had risen above the water. His grin was a little awed.

"I've been kind of pokin' into the supplies we unloaded yesterday, and samplin' some things that I've heard of but never come across before," he explained. "I ain't never seen the like of it, not for grub. We'll eat like a hog in a 'tater patch."

Hunkered back from the fire glow, with a tin plate and a coffee cup, Montana agreed. For one thing, this was real coffee, ordinarily difficult to obtain. A well-cured ham was easily the best that he'd tasted since before the war.

Something stirred among the brush at the rear. Montana turned swiftly, gun in hand, then lowered it uncertainly at a startled gasp. His own reaction was one of equal surprise. Whatever he had expected, it had not been a woman, her eyes rounding at sight of the gun.

Not only was she a woman, but by no stretch of the imagination could she be classed as ordinary, or belonging to the country thereabouts. She was a shade above normal height, dark hair accenting the fairness of her skin, and a wistful quality of eyes and mouth adding an elusive charm. She might be twenty, possibly a year or so older.

Her face had paled. "I'm sorry," Montana said quickly. "You surprised me—but I didn't mean to startle you."

Tim O'Donnell, on the opposite side of the fire,

was staring as though beholding an angel.

"It's all right," the girl said reassuringly as Montana holstered the revolver, and her poise was complemented by graciousness. "You have reason to be alert, to be suspicious, with outlaws close at hand—dangerous ones."

Such words might be a warning, or they could serve as a distraction. Long-standing familiarity with risk had taught him to regard everything with the same suspicion as a fox circling a trap. A partial answer came with unwelcome promptness. From the closing darkness, off in the sunset's last glow, there was a commotion, shouts and snorts and the pounding of hoofs. Their horses were there, mostly the work animals, unharnessed and left to roll and graze before being herded closer for the night.

Even as the girl spoke, raiders were attempting to stampede the horses, to strand them on foot. Not having expected anything of the sort, he had been caught napping. With a remuda of riding ponies such as accompanied a trail herd, such an attempt might be logical. But that anyone might attempt to steal heavy work animals had not entered his mind.

Whatever the object, the raid could be crippling if successful. Already, judging by the sounds, the horses were being put to flight. Overtaking them, much less recovering them, might be difficult.

His own horse, still saddled, was grazing close at hand, dragging the bridle reins. Montana had come late to supper, intending to bunch the others before it grew too dark. Now the girl was speaking again, this time to O'Donnell.

"Here, take my horse," she offered. It had been hidden by the brush and dusk as she dismounted, but she still clung to the reins. Tim O'Donnell nodded, but wasted no time in words. He was up as quickly as Montana; then they spurred in pursuit.

"What a woman!" O'Donnell breathed. "Here, take my horse—just as I'm needin' one, and never a waste of time questionin' and answerin'. It's like she was an angel, droppin' in on us from nowhere!"

Montana was willing to accept his opinion, but his mind was on the business at hand. He urged his cayuse to a burst of speed, glimpsing a flowing huddle of movement ahead, the running animals like spilled ink in the lighter gloom. The shouts of the raiders, as they sought to push the plunging horses to greater speed, suggested perhaps half a dozen men. Initially, favored by surprise, they had succeeded, but the heavy draft animals ran lumberingly, and the swiftness of the pursuit was disconcerting. They had probably hoped to get away with every horse, leaving the men on foot. After that, all the advantage would be with them.

Odds of three to one could be touchy, though in the gloom they did not matter so much. The gap was swiftly closing. Sensing that, the raiders closed ranks, swinging to face their pursuers; then flames stabbed the night like spiteful fireflies. The crack of guns was succeeded by the whistle of a bullet.

The closeness was probably more the result of chance than of a sure aim, and Montana paid no attention, returning the fire. The raiders were shooting in panic, and that was a mistake. Their gun flashes provided targets at which to shoot back.

Like himself, Timothy O'Donnell was demonstrating that he was an old hand at forays of this nature. He knew how to pick a target and make his shots count. Or it might be that, inspired by the sight of an angel, he was outdoing himself.

Their fire was proving uncomfortably accurate, almost devastating. The others continued to blaze away frantically; then panic had its way. One man screamed wildly that he was killed. The loudness of his protestation left some doubt regarding the assertion, but it had its effect on his companions. The sudden neigh of a horse was high with terror. With a common impulse, those who were able to flee did so, swinging, riding with no thought beyond escape.

Their numbers apparently included the man who had thought himself killed, for only one darker huddle remained as they were swallowed by the night. The blotch against the earth was a downed cayuse, an error which Montana disliked. But in the heat of battle, with poor visibility, mistakes had a way of occurring.

The stampeded work animals, already tired from a long day in the harness, finding themselves no longer driven, were coming to a halt. Montana dismounted beside the downed horse, O'Donnell coming to stand beside him.

A dragging sigh of pain and weariness testified that the rider was still alive, but perhaps not much more than that. A closer look showed the correctness of such a guess. He lay, caught and pinned by the dead horse he had been riding, and the grayness already spreading over his face confirmed Montana's initial opinion that freeing him from the weight would be largely a wasted gesture.

But O'Donnell, not waiting for instructions, was removing a coiled lariat from the saddle which he had borrowed, attaching one end to the nearest hoof of the sprawled cayuse and the other to the saddle-horn. Mounting, he applied leverage, tipping the dead animal over so that the trapped man was freed. Montana knelt beside him.

The injured man's eyes opened as the crushing weight was removed. Pain-washed, they gazed vacantly. The light grew better as the moon, nearly at the full, rolled into sight over the horizon, in the manner of a gopher pushing a mound of dirt from its hole.

The vacancy of the stare gave way to a sort of recognition; the weary eyes focused. To Montana's amazement, there was both resignation and a sharp scorn on his face.

"You made a good shot," he observed. His mind seemed clear, though the tone was hardly above a whisper.

"The luck of the game," Montana agreed. "It might have been the other way."

"Not my luck, mister. It don't run that way—never did. Guess I've got it coming, though we had figured to fool you."

"You almost did."

"Almost's not good enough." The bitter scorn seemed as much for himself as for Montana. It welled up in searing laughter, and with that he choked, and a foam of blood appeared on his lips. But presently he controlled himself.

"Likely you're wondering why. But why not? Why not steal from you blasted thieves? It makes us plain rustlers—but you syndicate skunks ain't lily white."

He seemed impelled to talk, to explain if not to excuse his actions. Montana opened his mouth to caution him, then left the words unsaid. This fellow had very little time to talk left, and further words would not make any particular difference.

"Yeah, we're cattle thieves, all right—tryin' to steal that big herd, and we sure enough botched that, too." Montana supposed that he was referring to the attempt on the trail herd from Texas, the one in which Jones had been killed. Then the dying man's words drew his startled attention.

"Why is it any worse for us to steal the herd from you fellows than for you to rustle those critters from their owners in the first place? Or did you figure nobody'd find out about that massacre down in the Wind River Country?"

His mocking voice stopped. The eyes were still staring up, wide, but no longer angry or sardonic. Montana got slowly to his feet, looking questioningly at O'Donnell, who had overheard. The ex-sergeant slowly shook his head.

"I wouldn't know, Cap'n Abbott," he said, and his voice as he articulated the title held respect. "A crew delivered the trail herd that we'd been expectin' to the ranch. And as far as I know, the papers on them were in order. But I suppose they could have been rustled somewhere along the trail up from Texas."

Montana considered the matter with a bleak distaste. He'd taken the job as foreman, and that entailed a certain loyalty to the outfit as well as responsibility, but he did not like any of these implications, although the dead man's last words helped explain certain recent events, including the try at stealing the horses.

His assumption that the theft and massacre had been at the orders, or at least with the connivance, of the syndicate might or might not be true. Jones, who had been the man in charge, was dead. Tiller-

Parsons was the agent for the syndicate, made up of supposedly honorable men, who were certainly too far away, too strange to this land and its customs, to have much inkling of what was going on.

Nor had Tiller-Parsons been on the ranch or in its vicinity at the time. And that, too, might or might not be pertinent.

O'Donnell helped load the dead man onto Montana's horse. It snorted and sidled, not liking the burden, the smell of blood making it nervous. But the fellow deserved a decent burial before they went on, at least for his cynical honesty if not for his revelations. Montana led the horse back to camp, and O'Donnell brought in the horse herd.

The night was soft with the hush of summer, the moon lending a mellow quality sharply in contrast to the strife it had witnessed. Montana's thoughts reverted to the woman, who had appeared so strangely, immediately voicing a warning, then lending her horse to O'Donnell. Except for that extra animal in addition to his own, they would probably have been stranded, vulnerable to ambushment and bushwhack.

Who was she, and where had she come from? For any woman, especially any white woman, to materialize in such fashion and at such a time was a reason for surprise. And for a woman apparently of the quality of Alicia Fredericks to come riding into their camp was doubly bewildering.

But probably she could explain herself; he was certainly curious. Brighter crimson flared like a beacon where the dying cook fire had been restored. The rest of the crew were alert and uneasy, awaiting their return. The girl stood near the fire, finishing the supper with which she had been provided.

Tim O'Donnell reached the camp ahead of Montana. He came leading her horse, sweeping off his hat.

"Here's your horse back," he said. "And many thanks for the loan, ma'am. I don't know whether Montana could have managed that rustlin' crew entirely by himself, good as he is at such chores."

The woman gave O'Donnell a quick smile, but her regard was for Montana as he came up and halted, waiting at the rim of the fire glow. Her eyes were appraising, judging.

"You are more than welcome," she informed O'Donnell, then swung toward Montana. Her voice held a pleasant muted quality. "You are wondering, of course, who I am, where I came from, and why I am here."

Montana did not dissemble. "I guess we are all of us a bit curious, ma'am," he conceded.

"And naturally so. I had heard that your group would be on the way to the ranch with supplies. So it seemed reasonable and proper, under the circumstances, for me to try and join you. I am Rose Tiller-Parsons—Mrs. Tiller-Parsons."

4

O'Donnell, listening eagerly, overheard. He stared blankly, a comical look of dismay spreading slowly over his face. Montana was equally startled. The woman's assertion that she was Mrs. Tiller-Parsons was at least as surprising as her sudden appearance.

Rose seemed fitting as a name, but Tiller-Parsons did not. Seeing their bewilderment, she explained in more detail.

"My husband has been busy, what with buying supplies and looking after a great many details. I did not accompany him on that trip down-river. Isn't he here now?"

Montana shook his head. "He stayed with the boat as far as Fort Benton. Said he had other business to attend to."

He had an increasingly uneasy feeling that there was more to this than misunderstanding. What Tiller-Parsons chose to do was of course his own affair, but each new report on the man was less favorable.

Rose intended to accompany them to the ranch, but she offered no further explanation. She made no effort to take advantage of her position by remaining aloof or demanding special privileges. Instead, she helped prepare breakfast, then rode on one of the wagons. By daylight, she was even prettier than in the fire-lit dusk, and Tim O'Donnell fetched a long sigh as he and Abbott rode out ahead.

"That sun beatin' down feels just as hot as it did yesterday, so the chances are that it's just as bright," he observed. "Only somehow I don't appreciate it quite the same." He shook his head, then squared his shoulders.

"I guess dreams—especially the pleasant sort—are generally brief and are just that—dreams. And a man can wake up when he has to go ahead with what has to be done. Still, there's times when dreamin' comes as natural as breathin'."

He was silent for a long moment before ending his thought.

"But I just about stopped doin' even that when she proclaimed herself a lawfully wedded wife."

Montana sympathized with him. He liked this big ex-sergeant, and it was clear that the sudden materialization of so much beauty had affected him. Unlike Tiller-Parsons, O'Donnell was no ladies' man. For him to look twice at the same woman would be something of a record. Abbott changed the subject.

"You noticed what that outlaw had to say last evening about the trail herd?"

O'Donnell removed his hat to scratch his head. He resettled the hat at a rakish angle, a perplexed look on his face.

"Yeah, I heard. Seemed like he felt he had to explain himself. Could be he knew something, I suppose. There was some trouble with the herd, Jones being killed and so on. But what might have happened along the trail wasn't our business at the ranch or known to us. The only thing I can say for sure about that herd is that there's three thousand head of them, and they're better than average stock."

The dying man's suggestion that the herd had been rustled rather than rounded up or purchased, taken over through a deliberate massacre so as to leave no witnesses, was serious. Such a statement, made as a dying declaration, could not lightly be disregarded. On the other hand, he had been an outlaw himself, and he might have believed a report which was more malicious than accurate.

To Montana, the double-barreled name of Tiller-Parsons sounded affected if not pretentious. He wondered if, with its suggestion of prestige and family, it might have helped influence the members of the syndicate in their choice of him as manager of their American properties. Their standards for judging would hardly match those of Tim O'Donnell.

The increasingly big question, with each fresh disclosure, was why? The chartered river boat, the big beef herd, the freight which they were transporting, all proved that the financial backing for the enterprise was ample. As manager for the syndicate, there would be no point in Tiller-Parsons resorting to dishonesty, but every reason he should not. Also, it was unlikely that men of position would place the handling of their resources in his hands without first checking carefully.

The scope of the operation had appealed to Montana, and its overseas backing had seemed to assure a solid background. In any case, he decided, having taken the job, along with an advance in pay, he would be foolish to shy at shadows. If later on he didn't like the job, he could always quit.

Rose was no chatterbox. Seated beside him that afternoon while Montana drove one of the wagons, she seemed composed, slightly pensive. But she volunteered nothing more than what had already been said, and he did not ask.

They followed a wheel trace which might soon develop into a road. Ranch headquarters came in sight on the afternoon of the third day. Montana studied the setting in surprise and approval. If Tiller-

Parsons had picked the site, he had shown good taste.

A house such as might grace a country estate two thousand miles to the east was in the process of being erected, with workmen busily hammering and sawing. A big barn thrust arrogantly above lesser outbuildings. Montana noted that, quite properly, the first priority had been given to structures required for the efficient operation of the ranch.

These nestled in a little valley, fringed on two sides by massive cottonwoods which were watered by a slow-running creek. Twin corrals had been built to hold the horses, their poles making a checkerboard pattern of sun and shade.

The big house was set apart, long and wide rather than high. Peeled logs gleamed, with the imported lumber being used for roofing, floors, windows and a wide porch.

Cattle grazed in the distance, as though this had been home for more than a few uneasy days.

At their approach, a tight-jawed man left the house and advanced to meet them. O'Donnell explained:

"That's Jim Anderson, in charge of the carpenters. He's a good man—though it don't look like they've gotten much done since I left here the other day."

"You're right, Mr. O'Donnell; we've accomplished next to nothing," Anderson declared heatedly. "I'm at my wits' end, and near the end of my patience as well, with a crew made stupid by booze."

"Booze?" O'Donnell repeated. "I didn't know there was any of the stuff closer than Benton. Jim, this is Montana Abbott—the new foreman, in charge during Tiller-Parsons' absence."

Anderson surveyed Montana with sharply grudging appraisal. Clearly the name meant nothing.

"It's about time that we had somebody in charge," he growled. "My only authority is to see that the carpentry work is done right, and with no one to back me or throw the fear of the devil into some of that crew, that has been no cinch. There was no liquor, but some turned up almost as soon as you fellows were out of sight. There were jugs and bottles, filled with rotgut enough to stock a saloon. The crew found them before I did, as was no doubt intended, and by the time I realized what was going on, they were drunk. They've been guzzling the stuff ever since, paying no attention to me. And the work's at a standstill."

The former sergeant shook his head, but eyed them with an understanding gaze.

"That's not so good. But they've worked hard and well for a long stint, Jim. It's in the nature of such men to go on a spree every so often."

"Sure, but not to have the stuff dropped right in their hands by someone who wants to hinder the work," Anderson pointed out. "That whisky didn't get where they couldn't help finding it by accident."

"Well, if they've been drinking the way you say, the supply should soon be running low," O'Donnell suggested philosophically.

"That's what I've been counting on. They are next to worthless until they sober up."

He paused as someone gave a delighted, if somewhat maudlin whoop. It was echoed by the others as they turned, then crowded around him. Montana pushed forward for a look, the others at his heels.

If the original supply of liquor had been running low, now it had been almost magically replenished, or so it seemed to them. Going after a board, the man had lifted it from where it lay on the ground a little to one side. Under it was a freshly dug trench filled end to end with more jugs and bottles.

To the men, this was a gift to use and enjoy, with no questions asked. The possibility that the cache might not be intended for them was not troubling their minds. Here again was largesse, to be accepted and made the most of. Bottles were being opened and upended. Anderson's shrill wail of anger and dismay was ignored. As he persisted, one man placed a big hand on his chest and shoved. Taken off balance, Anderson went down.

"Jus' cause you don't like the stuff 's no reason to spoil our fun," the other man chided. "We do like—"

The smash of a bottle, coupled with the roar of the revolver in Montana's hand, startled them to bewildered attention. The slivered flask, disintegrating as it was upended, showered half the group.

"What's going on?" the dazed carpenter protested. Then anger flared in already reddened eyes as his bemused mind grasped cause and effect. "What the devil do you think you're up to?" he demanded.

"You fellows are here to work, not to drink," Montana informed him shortly. "Smash those bottles right where they are. Every one!"

This was trouble of an unlooked-for nature. Someone clearly was out to delay the work on the house, to obstruct the operations of the syndicate. Difficulties of this sort were an old story.

The sodden workmen eyed him resentfully, but before the gun and the sharpness of his tone, they offered no further protest, as Anderson and O'Donnell caught up hammers and smashed the jugs and bottles. Their sorrowing glances confirmed their opinion that this was a waste if not a desecration, but since the liquor had been an unexpected boon in the first place, the loss was not too personal.

"Montana Abbott's foreman here, and what he say goes," O'Donnell explained. "It's a point to keep in mind."

"You men are hired to work," Montana reminded them. "You might as well knock off for the day. Get some sleep, and be ready to get at it again tomorrow. One other thing. If any more of this stuff turns up, show it to me first! I'll deal personally with any man who takes another drink until this job is finished!"

What that deal might amount to, he did not elaborate, but from the nervously repectful glances bent upon him as the men shuffled off, it was clear that he had impressed them.

5

Montana was impressed in his turn. This ranch had a great potential, and undoubtedly much of the credit belonged to Tiller-Parsons. What had been done required imagination as well as ability.

He had a look at the herd the next day, and here was more proof of selectivity. They were long-horns, almost as strange to that range as its owners would be, but there was a wide difference between cattle from so vast a state as Texas. Some had run wild for generations, reverting almost to the savage, creatures of bone and horn, lean and rangy and tough and stringy as to meat. Others had retained a natural sleekness, despite necessary fighting qualities.

These were above the average for a beef herd, about evenly divided between cows and steers, but dry cows had been selected for the long trail, without calves to tag along. In consequence, they were as sleek as the steers. Now they were putting on fat on the rich grasses which were being cured in the sun.

Intrigued, Montana had a look at the books in the office. Since these were piled on a desk, instead of under lock and key, he felt that as foreman he should be familiar with them. He found what he sought, and everything seemed to be in order. But certain details made him wonder.

It was still possible, as it had been during the war years, for a crew to go into the bush country, along some of the back-country reaches of the Lone Star State, and to round up a bunch of mavericks, establishing ownership by applying their own brand. The syndicate ranch had been more businesslike as well as selective. Papers testified that this herd had been purchased from a local owner for eighteen thousand dollars, paid in cash.

That seemed a fair price for such stock, since prices were beginning to rise as twin lines of steel opened up the heartland of America. Yet in it was a smell of extravagance. A good crew could have had such stock almost for the cost of wages.

Apparently the syndicate was owned by wealthy men, and Henry Tiller-Parsons had no hesitation when it came to spending their money.

Whatever else he might be, Tiller-Parsons was a student of character, at least reasonably familiar with the class of men who employed him. Also, it seemed a fair guess that he had added either the

Tiller or the Parsons to his own name, believing that a double-barreled moniker would impress them.

Which is likely his notion of giving them value received for their money, Montana decided sardonically. He had yet to find the vitally important answer to the riddle. A man might be extravagant yet basically honest, and do an excellent job. Or this might be larceny with a high polish.

Even these papers might be faked. Though properly signed and witnessed, they had not been notarized. The average buyer or seller would accept them at face value, especially since Montana was a long way from Texas.

On the whole, it appeared that a good beginning was being made at establishing the ranch and its basic commodity of meat. Yet it was a start which, even with the best of intentions, might end in catastrophe, due to a lack of foresight and experience.

The difference lay in the difference between Texas and Montana.

In their native state, running half-wild, the cattle could not only survive against odds, but flourish. Northers did sweep portions of the country, with heavy snow and blizzard cold, but they were infrequent, and normally of brief duration. Even a heavy fall of snow would usually melt soon enough so that hungry animals could feed again.

The plains and hills of southeastern Montana were

a different story. The grass was shorter, less lush, but such deficiencies were compensated for by its quality of rich nourishment. Here the heat of summer could be almost as intense, but the cold of winter was longer, more enduring. Without additional care, Texas cattle could hardly hope to survive.

That was the immediate problem. Tiller-Parsons was perhaps assuming that the cattle could look after themselves as they would in Texas. So no grass had been cut for hay, and no hay would be obtainable, at any price, unless they put it up themselves.

It was already too late to do much about that. Summer was well advanced, and the chill which betokened the approach of autumn knifed the air with each dawn. However benign the summer, winter could pounce fast and hard.

An examination of the supplies on hand was partially reassuring. Montana found two scythes, the questioning of the crew elicited the information that a couple of the men had had at least a limited experience with swinging a scythe. While not too happy at the change in occupation, they set to work as he directed, where the grass stood tall and untouched in the meadows. It was browning, sun-cured as it stood.

Two men with scythes would be able to cut enough hay to carry the horses through the winter.

The irony was that horses could and would forage for themselves, where cattle would not.

The carpenters, sober now, were making use of the lumber brought in on the Star of the West. Outwardly, the ranch was a beehive of activity. Yet aside from the house, there was little productivity.

"You've sure got them working," O'Donnell observed. "Everybody busy as bees."

But there was a difference in bees, Montana reflected. Honey bees stored provisions against the coming winter. Bumblebees bumbled—and accomplished nothing.

He could not rid himself of the feeling that the pattern had been deliberately set up that way, that the Powder River Ranch, for all its outward appearance, was a place of contradictions.

"I may be borrowing trouble, imagining things," he admitted. "But if it turns out that way, I could turn out to be the man in the middle—the one that gets stepped on."

Feeling a strong aversion to such a role, he set out again to ride more widely, to take a comprehensive look and familiarize himself with the ranch and with conditions. In any case, that was a necessary part of his job.

Circling beyond the cattle, which were scattered over a wide area, he came to territory that seemed as remote and lonely as might be found anywhere.

But it was there, extremely surprising in such a place, that he came upon a trail, as remarkable for its freshness as that it should be there at all.

At first glance it was seemingly only a set of wheel tracks, a wagon drawn by a team of horses. In settled country, or along a road, that would excite no suspicion. Here it seemed alien; moreover, the depth to which the wheels had sunk where the soil was light and the grass scanty suggested a rather heavy load.

Even more odd, the equipage had moved to make a V—heading toward the ranch buildings, then halting and swinging off at another angle, almost directly away from the headquarters, but not retracing its former course.

Moreover, the wagon had been there very recently, probably that same day. Montana followed.

His speed would be several times that of a plodding team dragging a laden wagon. He had ridden less than an hour when he sighted the wagon ahead, and another quarter-hour was enough to catch up.

Though it had a canvas top, weathered and stained, it was in no sense a prairie schooner or covered wagon. This was an equipage not often seen so far west of the river, a light spring wagon, pulled by a tired team of ponies, who in size and build seemed more suited to the saddle than to such a chore.

A lone man perched on the seat, eying Montana

with wary suspicion as he approached. A stubble of salt and pepper whiskers splotched his face, his jaws moving mechanically above a chew of tobacco, whose juices seeped like the overflow of a creek from the edges of his mouth. A Sharp's buffalo gun was on the seat beside him.

He was clearly of two minds as to what course he should pursue, but his horses solved the matter by halting of their own accord, glad of an excuse. Pale eyes surveyed Abbott, and his nod was as jerky as the jump of a frightened rabbit.

"Howdy!"

"Howdy," Montana returned, and matched the other's stare unblinkingly.

The wagoner endured its challenge for a space of heartbeats. Then he squirmed uncomfortably, loosing a stream of tobacco juice over the right front wheel.

"You want something?"

"Kind of like to satisfy my curiosity," Montana admitted. "I'm wondering what you're doing out here and what you're hauling."

There was another speculative period, while the eyes ranged the holstered gun at Montana's side, the calmly waiting face above. The man sighed resignedly.

"I ain't got nothing to hide. Besides, it's a free country—or so I've heard."

Montana's nod was noncommittal. Riding closer,

he lifted the loose rear flap of the canvas and peered into the murky interior. He was not much surprised at the array of jugs and bottles, carefully packed against the jolting of the wagon. They were similar to the cache which the delighted carpenters had discovered.

Montana allowed the flap to fall. "You changed your mind?" he suggested.

"A man's got a right to, ain't he?"

"No law against it. What I'm curious about is why you were giving away good liquor in the first place without even asking credit."

"No law against that either, is there?"

"That could depend. You wanted to get those boys drunk, and you did. Went to a lot of trouble to do it. Why?"

"I was hired to."

"Makes rather a reverse twist," Abbott conceded. "Usually whisky is a big-profit deal. Furnishing it for free don't often happen."

"I guess I might as well tell you," the other man said resignedly. "One of the fellers that was murdered down Wind River way was my pard. I couldn't fight back, not the way your crew does. But he cashed in with a wad of money in his pocket. I don't know whether he had any folks anywhere or not. He never said. Anyhow, I couldn't send it to them, but I thought of this way to use it. Maybe I'd botch things up with that house, with a bunch of drunks on the job. Sure, I guess it was a crazy notion."

"You figure the Powder River crew had a hand in what happened at Wind River?"

The mottled face darkened.

"What happened there was murder. And where does the herd end up? What the devil should a man figure?"

Reduced to so simple a philosophy, it was damaging—but there were middlemen among outlaws as among honest men. An opinion, however disturbing, was not proof.

"So you decided to heap coals of fire, eh?" The blankness in the pale eyes told him that the man did not understand. "You've enough rotgut left to go into business for yourself."

A cunning gleam replaced the blankness as the driver chirped the horses into motion.

"Yeah, that's a notion. I might just do that."

6

The long days of summer were giving way to the
shorter ones of autumn. The leaves on trees and
shrubs seemed to have absorbed the color if not the
warmth of the sun. Birds, having sung themselves
out, swept by in increasing flocks. The moon of
harvest flamed nightly against wide horizons.

Tiller-Parsons, heading ranchward across-country,
traveling with a retinue of horses, vehicles and men
in almost princely fashion, was elated. His plans
were working out excellently, as was attested to by
the fact Alicia Fredericks now journeyed with him,
rather than he with her. By such phrasing, he felt,
was marked the change in his life, a demarcation
from a period which he would as soon forget. He
had been an overseer, a hired hand. Technically it
was still that way, but actually he was taking an
ever firmer grip on the reins.

From Fort Benton, as the Star of the West turned
back down-river, he had forwarded glowing reports
to the members of the syndicate, outlining ac-

complishments achieved or in the process of building, achievements which should leave them well
satisfied. By the following summer, should some of
them take the notion to risk a sea voyage and see
the ranch for themselves, fantasy might almost have
become fact. By then everything would be ready for
them.

The early dusk had closed down, with the sun
setting in what, on another night, Alicia had described as a blaze of glory. He had agreed, reflecting
with some wonder that all women seemed to have
romantic notions and a disposition to indulge in
flights of fancy. Certainly it was pretty enough; still,
a sunset was merely a going down of the sun. It
was like lumping two names together to form Tiller-
Parsons, a lot of foolishness, to be indulged in only
because a hyphenated name seemed to impress some
people.

The sudden sunset had caught him some distance
from the evening camp, strolling by himself as he
awaited the call to supper. Alicia usually walked
with him, but tonight she had been busy with a
womanly chore, that of washing and putting up her
hair.

"Since we're due to reach the ranch tomorrow, I
want to look my best," she had explained, and he
had agreed helplessly, refraining from remarking
that none of the cowboys or other hands would
know the difference in any case.

Shadowy figures were suddenly all around him, emerging from the gloom like phantoms. Two men seized his arms from either side. His sharp exclamation was cut off as a hand clapped heavily over his mouth.

Struggling, as he quickly discovered, was useless. His lively fears were only slightly eased as he realized that his captors were Indians. He had been convinced that he and his party were totally alone on the prairie, that there was no risk. Even if enemies should lurk nearby, they were a large enough group to put up a good fight.

Whatever his shortcomings, Hank Tiller had never been lacking in courage. He took a grip on himself and, allowed to speak, ventured a remonstrance which he hardly hoped would prevail.

"You fellows are making a mistake. I'm your friend—Chief Spotted Pony is my friend. I want to talk to him."

One of his captors laughed, a loose, foolish gurgle. The other nodded ponderously.

"Spotted Pony—waiting."

The quality of the laugh and speech, as well as the alcoholic breaths, staggered him. These men were drunk. Not totally so, however, since an Indian, unused to hard liquor, was apt to pass out completely when such a stage was reached. But they were drunk enough to be maudlin, a good-natured phase. The trouble was that such moods could change to ugliness in a hurry.

They did not have far to go. Firelight glowed as they reached the rim of a coulee, and from its depths several figures wavered, ghost-like. The fire was reflected from flasks scattered about.

One of the men was the chief. Recognizing him, Tiller-Parsons made up his mind. He'd take a hard line, as became his position.

That might or might not be the proper way to handle Indians. Actually, he didn't know much about them, or how one was supposed to deal with them. But he did know that Spotted Pony was a chief, though with only a handful of followers. If he recollected correctly, he was supposedly friendly to white men. They had met some months before, even indulging in a game of poker.

Poker was Tiller-Parsons' greatest delight or affliction. Where some men would get drunk whenever the opportunity presented itself, he would play the game, for increasingly high stakes. Often he won. More frequently he lost. In fact, this potbellied savage had beaten him, to the tune of a thousand dollars.

Since Spotted Pony had attended a white man's school, some of his skill in the white man's vices was understandable.

"Hi, Spotted Pony," Tiller-Parsons greeted him. His tone sharpened. "What's the idea of treating me as though I were a prisoner?"

For a long moment the chief regarded him woodenly. It was more than the reflected light of the fire. His eyes were bloodshot; his manner, like his hair, rough. He was clearly as drunk as his followers, enough to be unpredictable or ugly. Evidently this drinking bout had been going on for days.

"You are a prisoner," Spotted Pony returned insolently, but he spoke English. When sober, he was likely to insist on Indian ways, proceeding formally through an interpreter. Now he disdained such methods.

"Why do you think I've had you brought here?" he added. The unwashed smells of camp and tepee made a rank emanation.

Tiller-Parsons' nerves stretched like drying buckskin. This had all the elements of trouble, and he had blundered straight into it. It could mean disaster, not only for himself, but for Alicia as well. But to back down would only make matters worse.

"I suppose you want another poker game," he suggested, and shrugged. "What's got into you, Chief? you're drunk."

Spotted Pony regarded him owlishly. But it was the right approach. An Indian respected courage.

"Sure I'm drunk," he acknowledged, attempting to speak carefully, though the words were slurred. Remote contempt veiled his eyes. "Why not, when white men are such fools?"

Tiller-Parsons sensed that more was back of this

than he had suspected. He took a familiar tone.

"Are they? Some whites are, and so are some red men. Not you or I, though. Tell me about it. Let's sit down and get this straightened out. You know that I'm your friend, Spotted Pony."

The chief hesitated, his mood was wavering as a feather in the wind. Then he grunted and sat down, cross-legged. Relieved, Tiller-Parsons did the same.

"I've been away," he confided. "A long journey, far down the rivers. I'm just getting back. But what's this about whisky?"

The recollection had amused the chief. He was enjoying not only the fruits of his recent action but also the triumph, in retrospect.

"White men are fools," he repeated. "Did you not send this one to trade with us, to get us drunk so that we could be played with as a child plays with a toy bow? He had a wagon loaded with whisky. But instead of paying a big price for only a few drinks of it, we had it all, and at no cost. Now one of my braves has a new trophy in his scalp-lock."

That final reference was as mocking as it was challenging, but Tiller-Parsons disregarded it. Someone had gotten the notion of trading liqour to the Indians, and for his pains he had been killed and robbed. Dead, he was past helping, nor could he offer any contradiction to whatever story they chose to tell. Here again the mood of the chief was lightly balanced, ready to veer either way.

A poker player by instinct as well as liking, Tiller-Parsons knew when to gamble.

"You guessed right, Chief." He shrugged. "He was my man. Only you made a mistake. I was sending him to you with many bottles, as a gift, a token of friendship and respect. Not to trade, but to show my regard.

"You and I met a long way from here, and we had a friendly game of poker. Now, I run a ranch in this country for men who live far across the big water. So when I was told that you were now in my part of the country, I remembered how pleasant is a meeting between friends and sent him. A mistake was made, but it was not mine. Still, what is done is done. At least you received the gift."

To excuse an error which had caused a man to die sounded magnanimous. Sober, Spotted Pony would be too shrewd for such sophistry, but drunk as he was, it might work. Tiller-Parsons held his breath.

The chief pondered owlishly. Then he nodded. The mistake, being past and beyond changing, was of no consequence. But the story had a reasonable quality; it was logical to send a gift to assure his friendship. Moreover, it had an imaginative quality, such as few white men would dare. Whites usually used whisky only for trading, for cheating and debauchery.

He flung an arm across his companion's shoulders. Tiller-Parsons managed not to flinch.

"I am sorry for the mistake," Spotted Pony proclaimed. "It was a fine gift. We have enjoyed it."

Whether or not the last of the liquor had been imbibed, Tiller-Parsons noted that the Indian did not invite him to have a drink to seal the pact. Considering the circumstances, he was as well pleased. A clear mind was vital.

"What is past is past," he repeated. "Since you received and enjoyed the gift, that is all that matters. There will be other tokens of my friendship in days to come; days which may prove profitable for both of us, my friend."

7

Work on the big house was coming along nicely. Sober again, and somewhat ashamed of their prolonged drunk, the carpenters exerted themselves to make up for the lapse. Under the supervision of Jim Anderson, they did an excellent job. Montana was more than a little amazed at the structure taking shape so far from any town, in the heart of a wilderness. Henry Tiller-Parsons might be lavish in the spending of his employers' money, but at least he would have something to show for the expenditures.

The harvesting was also doing as well as he had hoped. Several small stacks of hay had been put up, carefully fenced against forays by the herd or from deer or elk. It would not be enough to tide such a bunch of cattle over the winter, but it would be an excellent hedge against the cold for the horses.

On the whole, Montana was finding the job to his liking. Big already, there was the promise of steady enlargement. Ranching on the scale of the syndicate could be fun. With proper management and a bit of luck, it might even prove profitable for the stockholders.

Some disquieting doubts had been raised, but there might be good answers to them. Until those were provided, he could hardly do less than give his employers the benefit of the doubt.

There had been no further word from Tiller-Parsons, no contacts with the outside world. Montana had an idea that the manager would probably be turning up one of these days. When he arrived, he should be pleased with what had been accomplished.

The nearest thing to a reminder of the outside world had been a few distant smudges of smoke glimpsed on the far horizon. In reality they were not much more than wisps, not signals, but suggesting a possible Indian encampment. That was both reasonable and likely, and as long as there was no hostility from whatever wandering band might be off there, there was no cause for worry.

Tim O'Donnell concurred with his opinion.

"Indians, more than likely. There are other outfits of white men no more'n a day's ride from here, and that could be from some of them, but more likely it'd be Spotted Pony's band. He's a Pigean, kind of a lone wolf. Not exactly a trouble-maker, maybe—but he'll bear watching."

The extent of the supplies which had been planned, purchased, then transported some two thousand miles and were now going into the house was astonishing. Not only were there several glass windows, but some of the glass was colored. Other touches, such as square white pillars for the porch, were equally luxurious. Powder River Ranch was intended to vie with English estates. Tiller-Parsons intended not only to impress his employers when they should eventually pay a visit to their holdings, but to make them feel at home.

There was much which was right here, and only one thing which seriously troubled him. That was Rose Tiller-Parsons, as she had proclaimed herself to be, and how Tiller-Parsons might feel about her presence when he arrived. During the interim, there had been no real problem. Mrs. Sally Miller was the housekeeper, a competent, bustling lady, settled in a small adjoining house prior to Montana's arrival. Such a place as was being built would require the service of someone like her, and Tiller-Parsons had not overlooked that angle.

Upon Mrs. Miller's invitation, Rose had moved in with her, pending the completion of the big house and the arrival of Tiller-Parsons. The two women had become fast friends.

If Montana was apprehensive on general principles, Tim O'Donnell was even more troubled, and more personally. He expressed his feelings with some heat.

"The little lady's an angel, Montana—as fine as

they come, and on that I'll stake a stack of blues! She's as quiet and tidy as a brown grouse, but what she is just sort of shines! Which leaves us up against the rest of it—and that beats me; I just can't figure matters."

Montana elevated a quizzical eyebrow.

"You're suggesting that Tiller-Parsons may not be equally angelic?"

The reply was explosive.

"Him! All I know for sure—beyond my remarks concernin' her—is that I'm a fool. Was I any less a one, I'd be pullin' stakes and betakin' myself to a far country, beyond the bewitchin' glance of such a pair of eyes! But I'm intrigued to discover certain answers which'll sooner or later be forthcomin'. And who knows? When that time comes, she might even need a friend."

"In which case you'll be around."

"In which case I'll sure enough be around," O'Donnell agreed emphatically.

They were riding together, somewhat farther afield than usual. Lacking a survey, which would probably be far in the future, no one, Montana included, had any firm idea regarding the boundaries of Powder River Ranch. Such descriptions as he had found among the papers were grandiose but vague. And the lines did not matter too much, as long as the country remained uncrowded.

But sooner or later others would come, and when

that day arrived, familiarity with the range would be vital. Whether or not he would be there then Montana had no way of knowing, but as long as he was foreman, he wanted a working knowledge of the territory.

It was off in this section that he had encountered the man with his wagon and stock of liquor some time before. Whether or not he'd realized it, whisky could be a dangerous cargo.

O'Donnell was staring into the distance, shading his eyes with a hand against the sun.

"Something sort of odd off there," he suggested. "Something that don't quite fit."

Montana had noticed it also. As they drew nearer, the strangeness became understandable. The thing had once been a wagon, the light spring type, next to a saddle pony the fastest means of transportation available. Now there remained only a charred and twisted wreckage, a lonely hulk which seemed to crouch close to the ground as though to hide its shame, perhaps cowering in terror.

The wooden parts, including the box and running gear, along with the spokes of the wheels, had been pretty well consumed. Tire irons and metal parts remained. The grass had been consumed close to and around the wagon, but in still green grass the fire had not edged far beyond. Since the fire, rain had caused a thin new growth to tint the blackened are with its freshness.

Still, this fire and destruction were of recent origin. Montana was not positive, but he felt reasonably certain that this was the wagon he had seen before.

One broken bottle lay among the ashes. There was no sign of the team or the driver.

"Everything looks mighty peaceful as of now," O'Donnell observed, his gaze ranging the horizon. "But appearances can be as deceivin' as judgin' from a frog's looks which way he'll jump."

Abbott explained his encounter, the reason for the load of liquor and the new purpose for which it had been intended. He drew no conclusions, but with the ex-sergeant a blueprint was unnecessary.

"One time in a book, I got to readin' about termites," O'Donnell murmured. "Seems they're sort of a little bug that likes to eat wood. An old house can be full of such critters without nobody even suspectin' it, till one day the place comes clatterin' down about your ears; what you'd call a case of being et out of house and home. Ain't a thing to see here, neither—but such varmints as you don't see can be as obnoxious as the kind that barge in and outstay their welcome."

"What do you know about these neighbors of ours?" Montana asked.

"They're part of the larger tribe of Blackfeet, a sort of independent bunch under Spotted Pony. I gather that he carries a grudge against just about everybody, whites in particular. Somebody got hold of him as a boy and sent him off to a mission school. Trained him like a white man—only it didn't take. Or maybe it did. Learned all our bad tricks on top of his own. This could be his work."

The Blackfeet had always been independent, generally distrustful of the white man. That they had been given reason enough for such an attitude over the years, Montana was not inclined to dispute. Probably Spotted Pony was no worse a neighbor than most, but the wreckage of the wagon was a warning to keep in mind.

"Makes me shiver," O'Donnell observed, breaking a long silence. They were halfway back to the ranch buildings. "I cain't get out of my mind about Rose —Mis' Tiller-Parsons—turnin' up all by herself, out of nowhere, like she did. I reckon where she came from and what she does in *her* business—it sure ain't mine. But sashayin' around alone in such country ain't what I'd recommend as healthy. A wife ought to be with her husband," he concluded violently, "special if she's going to travel in country such as this! What's a man thinkin' of to let her go without him?"

As they topped a slope, the headquarters came into sight. The house was taking on an air of livability. Inside and out, finshing touches were being applied, and the over-all effect was impressive. The owners would be hard to please if they did not approve, while as for a woman—

For the twentieth time, Montana found himself wandering what Alicia Fredericks would think, since her position in Eastern society had obviously entitled her to move in exalted circles. And as for Rose—

Montana had asked no questions, nor had she volunteered any additional information concerning herself or her claim. Living with the housekeeper, she had quietly assumed the place of mistress, as wife of the ranch manager. But she made no demands, advanced no claims. Yet answers would have to be forthcoming presently.

Anderson reported the job finished. Together they inspected the work of a spring, summer and early fall. The carpenters' foreman was justifiably proud.

"It's the biggest job I've ever worked on," he admitted, "and one of the fanciest. This house is the sort that you'd expect to find in upstate New York or New England, or down South before the war. Out here—well, I'll confess that it is beyond my understanding, but that's not my affair. I hope somebody gets some good out of it."

Like his crew, he was anxious to get away, to make the trek back to civilization before the coming of winter. Montana paid them off, as Tiller-Parsons had arranged if they left before his return. In addition to the barn, bunkhouse and cook house, three small guest houses had been erected. Without the clatter of hammers and saws, the cluster of buildings seemed suddenly silent, a lonely oasis in the wilderness.

The term was hardly an exaggeration. The gold camps of Helena, Diamond City, Virginia City or Bannack were flourishing centers, and a few other settlements, including Fort Benton, had their reasons for being. Also, some ranches were being established. But for the most part Montana remained a wide and lonely territory, no section more so than this one along the Powder River.

With a comfortably substantial headquarters established, the English syndicate was, at least theoretically, in a position to exploit the situation, to build big. And if this house was a fair indication of what Tiller-Parsons could do, it might come to pass.

Montana felt a loyalty to the outfit, to his absent employers. He wanted to see the venture succeed. But the future of the ranch was in the hands of the manager and, to say the least, Tiller-Parsons seemed to be taking his responsibilities lightly.

One of the cowboys rode in to report he had sighted a small caravan of horses and wagons trekking steadily toward the headquarters; also a single-seated, high-topped buggy, drawn by a team of matched ponies.

"Reckon you'll want to sort of have a welcomin' committee," he added, grinning broadly. "I hustled to let you know."

Rose appeared at the corner of the house, listening. As usual, she was neat, as unobtrusive as a beautiful woman could hope to be, asking no questions, volunteering nothing. But the usual color had fled her cheeks, leaving them as stark as frost at dawn.

She don't know what to expect, Montana thought, considering that buggy with its fancy team. And neither do I.

They would not be long now in finding out. The wagons were in sight, a considerable amount of freight and supplies, obviously being brought against the needs of the coming winter. Tiller-Parsons had not overlooked the welfare of the ranch.

The buggy was in the lead, the team coming on at a swinging trot. Red wheels flashed in the sun. Then the horses were pulled up with a flourish along the curving driveway, the wheels cramped open with easy skill. Wrapping the reins about the whipstock, Tiller-Parsons jumped down and hurried around to assist his companion, extending both arms. Montana and O'Donnell recognized her without surprise. Eyes sparkling, with vivid color whipped into her cheeks, Alicia Fredericks was gazing about eagerly.

Tiller-Parsons held her a moment longer than was necessary, then set her on her feet, turning with a broad smile.

"Welcome home, my dear," he said. "Folks, allow me to introduce my wife, Mrs. Tiller-Parsons!"

8

The words fell like a cold breeze, though Montana was hardly surprised. Tiller-Parsons' conduct was like a well-woven piece of tapestry. But again and again the precise pattern was disturbed by irregularities.

Nearly all of the ranch hands had gathered, eager to welcome their boss, as much because of the break which his arrival afforded in the monotony as anything else. Most of them enjoyed working for the syndicate. Powder River Ranch was remote, but the accommodations were comfortable and the food better than average. For so big a crew, the work was light, with few of the usual chores to be found on a big spread. There had been no fall roundup, no branding. Such work as was necessary could be done by a third as many men. Montana suspected that the extra hands were for protection against possible Indian attacks.

At Tiller-Parsons' announcement, they stared, slack-jawed, wondering if they had heard aright.

The radiant look on the face of Alicia convinced them.

Rose was standing frozen, her face drained of color.

The booming welcome which the crew had intended to provide failed to erupt. It was Timothy O'Donnell, a hard undercurrent of anger in his voice, who broke the silence.

"Mrs. Tiller-Parsons, you say? Now how in the devil can that be, with Mrs. Tiller-Parsons already here?"

The chopping gesture of one big hand took in Rose, leaving no doubt as to his meaning.

The rich autumnal color faded from Alicia's cheeks, as color faded from a flower at the touch of frost. She gazed around, hurt and bewildered, then looked at Tiller-Parsons for an explanation and reassurance. Neither was in his face. Surprise, consternation, disbelief and horror made a mixture which left him temporarily wordless. He had been taken completely off guard.

He stared at Rose, at least as surprised as Montana had been when she had first appeared. Anger and contempt blazed in her eyes, but she did not seem to share the universal surprise.

Tiller-Parsons swallowed, but Montana gave him credit for courage. Faced with a crisis which not only spoiled his triumphant homecoming but threatened his career, his recovery was swift.

"Mrs. Tiller-Parsons?" he repeated, and the blankness on his face was gradually replaced by an excellent approximation of amazement. "I'm afraid I don't understand. There's some mistake here—there has to be." He bowed to Rose with stiff formality. "I have never seen this lady before."

Alicia had been about to question him, but she stood silent, still holding onto his arm, looking from one to another, as much doubt as bewilderment in her eyes. A touch of color returned to Rose's cheeks, and she took a step toward them.

"So you disown me now—after robbing, then deserting me? After that, I'm not too surprised. But I am no less your wife."

A pained look pinched the brow over the pale eyes of Tiller-Parsons.

"I'm sorry," he said, and spread both hands in a wide, disarming gesture. "Obviously there is some mistake, some misunderstanding." Then his face darkened at the gaping interest of the crew.

"Whatever it is, let us discuss it in private and reasonably," he added. "I'm happy to be back—or at least I was. But I'm sure you men have work to do. These supplies need to be unloaded."

He looked at Alicia with mingled anger and contriteness.

"I'm more distressed than I can say, my dear. But this is clearly a misunderstanding, or perhaps a case of mistaken identity. Yes, that must be it—it has to be," he went on confidently. "So let us go inside and try to straighten it out. You, of course." Again he bowed to Rose. "And you, Mr. Abbott, if you will be so good."

"I'm coming, too," Tim O'Donnell growled, and placed a big hand under Rose's elbow. But she required no assistance, walking proud and straight. Tiller-Parsons favored the ex-sergeant with a sharp glance, but shrugged.

The big house was obviously ready for his arrival. The front door stood open, the housekeeper beside it. Though she had waited welcomingly, she now remained discreetly in the background. Tiller-Parsons cast a swiftly appraising glance about, but whether he was pleased or otherwise, it did not show in his face or voice. Not until all except O'Donnell were seated did he speak. O'Donnell remained grimly standing.

"You, madam—" Tiller-Parsons bowed a third time to Rose—"claim to be my wife, which is a manifest impossibility. But I'm certain that this is a case of misunderstanding or mistaken identity. If you will be so good as to give us your story—"

Rose's eyes were hot with anger, her voice brittle with scorn. Hers was the terrible quality of the aroused meek.

"There's no mistake, Henry Tiller," she said. "You married me a year and a half ago, back East, professing to love me. Fool that I was, I believed you and allowed you to get your hands on my money. As soon as you had that, you walked out on me."

"Aha, money," O'Donnell cut in. "Was it a great deal now, Rose ma'am?"

"A great deal to me," Rose admitted. "Twenty thousand dollars."

"And you robbed, then deserted her—"

Tiller-Parsons' hand raised imperatively.

"I can understand your feelings," he said. "In fact, I share them. But I believe I have the explanation. Though I'm certainly not proud of it, nor have I been inclined to mention it to anyone, I have a twin brother. For most of his years he has been a ne'er-do-well type, but in appearance he is astonishingly like myself. Apparently he is not above playing so despicable a trick, even upon a woman. The only additional explanation that I can see is that he took advantage of you, madam, also of me, using my name and reputation, deceiving you, then deserting you. Certainly I do not doubt your veracity. The whole affair is extremely unfortunate."

The English had a habit of understatement, and in this he aped them. It seemed to Montana the understatement of the year.

Rose eyed Tiller-Parsons sharply, but he had implanted at least a shade of doubt.

"That's too incredible to be true," she protested.

Tiller-Parsons fetched a convincing sigh. He had found himself in tight fixes on a number of occasions, most recently when Spotted Pony had been of two minds as to whether to treat him as a friend and ally, or instead rob the supply train, acquiring a collection of hair trophies as a bonus. But with each crisis he acquired increasing adroitness.

"It does seem so," he acknowledged. "But it appears that both of us have been victimized by my scapegrace brother. Unfortunately, he is not at hand to be compelled to face up to his responsibilities. Under the circumstances, dear lady, I can only sympathize with your perfectly natural mistake. Beyond that, it seems that I have gained a sister-in-law. That being so, Alicia and I extend you our sympathy and affection, and of course our hospitality. I shall certainly attempt to locate my graceless brother and see to it that he makes restitution."

Once again, his luck had held. If the others did not entirely believe him, at least they could not disprove his version. Tiller-Parsons was sweating, but breathing more easily.

It might become necessary to change some of his long-range plans, since he must be prepared for any possible eventualities. Whatever happened, he had to keep control of the situation. His eyes seemed to grow more colorless and remote, staring speculatively into the future.

There were possibilities, means to an end, which might be used, should it be necessary; methods which would insure a permanent solution. But for the present he preferred not to think about such things.

With an abrupt change of manner, he turned to some immediate tasks. An inspection of the house brought his enthusiastic approval. Alicia, sobered by what happened, managed only a tremulous smile when he reminded her that she was now its mistress, but he knew that she was reassured as well as pleased.

"I never dreamed to find such a place, way off here," she admitted. "It's almost like a transplanted fairyland."

"I was hoping that you would like it." He smiled. "Again, I'm sorry about this other matter—sorry for everyone, for you that you had to be involved, and especially for her. The thing is monstrous."

"What I can't understand is why your brother would use your name or want to involve you," Alicia protested.

"I can understand that part only too well." Tiller-Parsons shrugged. "As I told you, he's a graceless scamp. Clearly, he married Rose only to get his hands on her money, intending to desert her once that was accomplished. By using my name and reputation, it was easier for him to manage. And once he walked away, he was in the clear."

Which, he reflected, was almost the truth. It had worked out that way, except for Rose turning up again, thousands of miles away. That was the last possibility he had ever dreamed of.

Rose was at least silenced, and he felt that he had removed Alicia's doubts. As for what the ranch crew might think, he simply did not care. In any case, it was none of their business.

Tim O'Donnell thought otherwise. He was explosively frank with Montana.

"The man's a liar and a scoundrel," he declared, "takin' advantage of trustin' women in such fashion! He's the same as saying that Rose is a liar, and that she would not do. She's not that kind of a woman."

"It's not quite that way," Montana pointed out. "If he should have a twin brother—"

"There never was a brother, and you don't believe that wild story any more than I do!"

"For the present, I'll give him the benefit of the doubt," Montana decided, "though there's a heap of doubt involved."

He rode with Tiller-Parsons the next day to look over the cattle, along with improvements of the past several weeks. He noted his quick interest in the stacks of hay, his approval of what had been done. One fact was apparent. Tiller-Parsons was well fitted for the position he held. He had ability. To what uses he turned such talent was the question that loomed increasingly large.

The haystacks served as a starting point for the problem which worried Montana most.

"Winter up here's not at all the same as down

Texas way. The herd is in fine shape now—but I'm worried as to whether they can survive a Montana winter."

"You're right, of course, and I've had that on my mind. Almost as soon as I had made arrangements for the herd, I saw that it was a mistake, that we couldn't be ready to care for them properly." A sly smile lightened his face. "So I made other arrangements. There are the gold camps—where meat will be in short supply."

What he was suggesting was at least feasible. "You intend to sell them to the camps?"

"That's the general idea; only we will drive them part way to market, then turn them over to a buyer and his crew. He has agreed to pay cash for the herd, and that way, it will be his responsibility to get the cattle the rest of the way, then to turn them into beefsteaks. I always prefer to do such jobs with a minimum of risk and a maximum of profit."

It appeared that all the arrangements had been concluded. Montana would set out, with six men, to move the herd about a hundred miles, to the vicinity of Pomp's Pillar, up the valley of the Yellowstone. There, the buyer would take over.

"He will pay you cash," Tiller-Parsons emphasized. "Thirty thousand dollars. That amount will give us a substantial profit on the deal and make a nice report for the owners, eh?"

"They should be pleased," Montana agreed. It

was almost too neat, with the risks of winter swept aside, and a handsome profit insured. Certainly it was bold and imaginative.

A rider had come in while they were making the inspection, bringing mail from the latest up-river boat. There were three letters from England, and these carried news which the manager found startling but not particularly unsettling. He relayed it to Montana.

"I've been meaning to tell you, Montana, how well pleased I am with what you've accomplished since taking over as foreman. With the buildings done and everything in order, we're in shape to entertain company—and that is most fortunate.

"I had been counting on some of our stockholders paying us a visit by next summer, but my reports must have been more optimistic than I intended. Or perhaps they have a feeling for adventure, and think that they'd enjoy a bit of roughing it. At any event, several of them are already on the way, to enjoy a vacation, look over their property and, as they put it, to enjoy some good hunting.

"Sir John Crispin, Mr. and Mrs. Silvanius Drew, also the Right Honorable Thomas Noonin and his lady, along with Mr. Byron Fancher, who is the London manager of the syndicate, will be here by the first possible boat up the river, which may of course well be the last of the season. We'll have to try and show them a good time."

9

"Somehow, sir, this is all too pat—too blasted handy, the way things work out." Tim O'Donnell spoke with a restrained formality, sure proof that he was deeply troubled. A deepening friendship had developed between the two former soldiers, and the ex-sergeant was far more frank than he would ever have dreamed of being with his captain. The news concerning the herd, the buyer who would be waiting along the Yellowstone, and the coming of the owners from England served to perplex rather than reassure him.

"Tiller-Parsons prides himself on careful planning and foresight," Montana returned mildly. "And he seems to get results."

"Yeah, he does so," O'Donnell agreed gloomily. "Such planning is almost too good. I don't like the man or trust him. I'd feel better if I was going along with you to deliver that herd. I hope you'll watch your step."

Montana was genuinely amused.

"If you weren't the man you are, Tim, I'd have to accuse you of being an old maid, of seeing a ha'nt behind every bush. Seven of us are enough to move the herd for a few days, after which we'll be coming back. There's little enough risk. Besides, you and I will both feel easier in our minds, having you here to keep an eye on thngs."

"Well, there's that," Tim conceded. "Him treating Rose so fine, like a sister-in-law—which ain't fine at all, when the man's a bigamist, and what more there's no telling. There's just one thing I'm sure of. He's no ordinary villain."

Montana was inclined to agree. He liked the ranch and the job, but he was increasingly distrustful of the manager. Once the cattle were delivered, he would give serious consideration to moving on.

A day was spent gathering the herd. Then they set out, and the animals looked fat and sleek. No longer rangy, they plodded sedately, giving no trouble. That seemed to confirm Tiller-Parsons' judgment that seven men were a big enough crew to handle them. On the other hand, an attack such as had been made upon this herd once before could succeed more readily under such circumstances. And the bulk of the crew had been left to loiter idly at the ranch.

But nothing untoward occurred. A week brought them to the vicinity of Pomp's Pillar, that upthrust of stone which had so impressed the captains Clark and Lewis as they worked their way up the broad valley of the Yellowstone.

Horatio Gates arrived, also on schedule, with a crew of ten to take over the herd. Everything was as Tiller-Parsons had outlined, including the money. Having tallied the stock and verified the papers, Gates handed over the cash.

"Well, I guess that takes care of the legal end," he observed. "We'll go on with them in the morning. Hope you have a good trip back, Abbott. May be kind of a lonely journey, all by yourself."

Here, like the far-off moan of a blizzard, was the first suggestion of trouble. Montana eyed him sharply.

"By myself? There are seven of us."

"Seven of you this far," Gates agreed blandly. "But I'm hiring your men to go on with me and help with the herd. Tiller-Parsons arranged the deal. Didn't he tell you?"

"This is the first I'd heard of it."

"That's funny. He told me it'd be a favor to him if I could give them a job. With the herd gone, he'll only need a few men on the ranch, and he wants to hold costs down, to show a profit."

On the surface, that sounded reasonable as well as logical. But why had everyone so carefully refrained from any mention of such a plan in his presence? The crew members might have supposed that he knew, but Tiller-Parsons should have explained.

It was a hundred miles back to the ranch, and that could prove to be a lonely trail, with thirty thousand dollars to deliver at its end. Having counted on the six as a bodyguard, Montana had not been worried. But this was a horse of a different and very dark color.

The sale and delivery of the cattle had been planned well in advance, ostensibly with an eye to the oncoming winter. With every detail worked out, the heretofore casual aspects were suddenly glaringly weak. Thirty thousand was a huge sum of money to entrust to a single man across five score miles of country.

Tiller-Parsons had married Rose, gotten hold of her money, then had walked out on her. Never suspecting that she could turn up at the remote ranch, he had risked another marriage to Alicia Fredericks. And she too, it seemed, was a wealthy woman.

There was the herd, and the testimony which had been given was well above the rumor stage: that it had been obtained not by purchase, but by treachery and murder.

Now there was thirty thousand dollars in cash—which he alone was to be responsible for.

Montana had experienced too many shadows to start at one more, but the chilling part was that everything was in order, according to careful planning. If something happened, and the money was lost—

Dead, he could hardly be held responsible—but there was scant comfort in that reflection. His reputation, along with the fact he had been killed, would demonstrate that it had been a bona-fide robbery. No real blame could attach to Tiller-Parsons.

The important difference would be that the dividend would not be paid to the ranch and its owners. Instead, most of that thirty thousand would probably find its way into the private pocket of Henry Tiller-Parsons.

Montana's face betrayed none of his suspicions. But he was thinking back to the route just traversed, reviewing the miles which would lie ahead, regardless of which direction he might choose to ride. In every direction the country stretched wide and lonely. There would be plenty of time and chance for bushwhacking.

They would of course credit him with seeing the trap and trying to avoid it. So they would have planned accordingly.

It struck him that the combined crew were more than usually jovial as they ate supper and cracked jokes. He joined with the rest, betraying no outward concern, then rolled in his blankets near the remnants of the cook fire. He slept, but presently came awake as he had intended. A faint high wind rustled the leafless branches of the cottonwoods, and not far to the side the river murmured.

Snores and heavy breathing were all about him. Moving carefully, he slipped away for a hundred feet before pausing to tug on his boots. As he came erect, a prowling coyote was briefly outlined against the sheen of the river.

The herd was bedded down a mile away, one man riding night watch. Should he think, when the watch was changed, to inspect Montana's blankets, he would find them empty. But that was a small and unlikely risk which had to be taken.

The buyers had brought along a big horse remuda. Those animals, along with the mounts belonging to his own former crew, were also bedded down for the night according to individual preferences. Some stood heads down; others sprawled on the ground. As he neared them, he saw that two were awake, having grazed to the edge of the bunch. All of the animals were hobbled.

Montana chose the pair, removing their hobbles. Knowing him, they did not shy. Riding one and driving the other, he swung away, causing no disturbance.

Circling on the back trail, he was tempted to alter course and keep going. With a change of mounts and a few hours' start, he'd stand a fifty-fifty chance over the long haul. But the certainty of pursuit, of murder once they came within rifle range, held no appeal. He was playing for better odds.

A few miles out from the camp, he hid the extra horse, picketing it among a clump of cottonwoods. Then he returned.

More than half of the night had been used up, but the men still slept, though most of the horse herd were awake and grazing. Leaving the horse he had ridden, Montana crawled into his blanket. This second nap was as brief as the first, before the stirring of others around him brought him yawningly awake.

Breakfast, like supper, was a friendly meal, the cordiality of his fellows a shade too warm, their casualness somewhat overdone. He doubted that all of them would be in on the planned operation of which he was the center, so for their benefit, things must be made to look right.

The cook smothered the remnants of his fire as packs were rolled and tied, the horses brought in and saddled. They saluted one another gravely; then the herd got under way, while he jogged in the opposite direction.

The fact that he had taken no alarm, making no effort to slip away, had made them overconfident. Apparently no one had bothered to count the remuda, to discover that one horse was missing.

Nothing was likely to happen for a while, in the full light of day, with a long trail stretched ahead. Montana took his time, the probable sequence of events reasonably certain in his mind. The terrain had pretty well fashioned that in advance, and he had a hunch that this had been taken into account when the Pillar had been chosen as the meeting place for the two crews.

At what would be a convenient distance, there was only a single good route through and among rocky, broken country; this ran for half a dozen miles. They had brought the herd along that trail, and he must use it as he returned, or swing miles out of his way, to struggle over a course at least as difficult and inhospitable.

Either way, they could follow his sign, in a perfect country for an ambush.

The likely places for a bushwhack were about the right distance from last night's camp, so that he would pass amid the lengthening shadows of late afternoon. In this again was grim evidence of careful planning.

An occasional look behind disclosed no evidence of pursuit, nothing to excite suspicion, but he expected none. In so well-conceived a scheme for such high stakes, the bushwhackers would be a separate group, posted in advance to await his coming. That way, they could watch his movements and pick their time.

His nerves were like drying rawhide as the afternoon waned and the rough country lay ahead. He had a pretty good notion about where they might post themselves; there were two or three excellent spots. The real risk was that, weary of waiting, they might become impatient and advance the schedule.

Against that possibility he could pit only his skill and the instinct of the hunted. Fall lay across the land. Tree leaves were brown or stained to sharper tints by the frost, but were only partially swept from limbs and brush by the hungry snooping of the wind. The sun slanted with a deceptive warmth, as though denying that snow might replace it in a night. A faint haze hung in the air, lending a luminous quality.

Nothing suggested trouble as he rode. Birds and small rodents, making the most of this remnant of summer, sailed or scurried, intent upon their own affairs. A stream widened into a long marshy pond. A muskrat was busy among the reeds.

A long meadow stretched ahead, the last real open space before the rough country. A scrub of evergreens made a sharp demarcation with the cottonwoods which had claimed the wider valley. At the far side of the meadow, birds took uneasy flight—magpies, apparently disturbed by something or someone sheltered among the trees.

That was what he had been looking for. A man might yawn and stretch, but such movement would call him to the attention of the birds. His hunch seemed confirmed.

He swung aside, finding the other horse where

THE RANCH AT POWDER RIVER

he had left it during the night. It had grazed all available grass within the reach of the rope, and now stood with weary patience, its tail switching at flies. It welcomed him with a whicker of relief.

Having made his own plan to counter the other, Montana worked swiftly. He had already cut a convenient sapling. Now he bent it double, tying the ends to the stirrup skirts on either side of the saddle. Braced at each end from the saddle, it stuck up to the height of a seated man, and across this frame he affixed his hat and coat. At a distance it would look real enough.

The part he disliked was sending his own horse ahead along the trail. With bridle reins tied to the saddle-horn, he put it to a brisk run with a whiplash across its withers. But there was no help for this. The bushwhackers would recognize the pony and be looking for it, be posted above the trail as it came.

It might have been the dress rehearsal for a play, farce or comedy rather than tragedy, except that as the first shots rang out and the frightened pony failed to stop, the next bullets were closer, with grimmer intent. The cayuse faltered, made a wild effort, then spilled down a short, steep incline and lay still, even as the echoes of the long guns whispered to silence.

10

Such a methodical working out of the ambush was chilling, confirming as it did Montana's own deductions and suspicions. In such a deal, no leeway was allowed for human or animal life or the quality of mercy. As far as they could plan, the bushwhackers were taking no chances.

He reflected on this almost with a sense of regret. Such ability might carry a man a long way, to great attainments. It seemed a pity that such talents were not being turned to better purpose; if not for the man himself, at least for the sake of the women who loved and trusted him.

Even the incomplete record was impressive. Hank Tiller, whose name as well as his present efforts suggested a dubious youth, had planned to better himself, socially and financially. Hank Tiller had become Henry Tiller-Parsons. He had married Rose, gotten hold of her money, then deserted her, since she had nothing more to give to further his career.

Apparently he had taken ship for England, and

with ample money to bolster his new role, along with an exercise of charm, he had gained his next objective. Accepted in the proper circles, he had been hired to manage the ranch for the syndicate.

With such backing, and given the spending of large sums of money, he had done a commendable job. Most men would have been satisfied to build solidly from that point, but he was not. At each turn, someone had to pay his personal account. And those payments were exacted in treachery and murder.

It was only too clear now, and loyalty to the man who had hired him was no longer involved; Tiller-Parsons had forfeited any claim to that. But loyalty to the ranch was a different matter.

One question had been puzzling: why Tiller-Parsons, playing for high stakes, should have hired him. Now he understood. Confident that his deserted wife would never find him, Tiller-Parsons had decided to risk another marriage if he could win the lady, again with the same purpose in mind—to get his hands on her money.

In order to have time for his courtship, to remain with the river boat, he had needed a replacement for the slain ranch foreman, and Montana had turned up most conveniently. He was more than handy, in that he had a reputation for honesty.

That aspect was vital to Tiller-Parsons in this particular deal, which he had already arranged. Let the cattle be sold, the cash be paid over to a man of unquestioned integrity. Whatever happened then, no lack of good intentions could very well be laid to Tiller-Parsons.

Circling, Montana came upon the bushwhackers as they were making the unpleasant discovery that the figure planned beneath the dead horse was not himself, but only his coat and hat. There were three of them, and they had ridden up, soberly enough at first, not liking their job. Picking a target at long range was more or less impersonal; they would have preferred to keep it that way, but the money had to be recovered.

One man was getting down from the saddle, moving like an old man. A second remained seated, his eyes fixed between his horse's ears. The third, untroubled by compunctions, walked across to stare down, jibing roughly at his more squeamish companions.

"What's wrong with you two? Ain't you never seen blood before? A hunk of meat's a hunk—"

Jaw slackening, he gaped as realization hit him. His companions were still uncertain as the voice of their supposed victim rapped at them from behind.

"All right, boys, hold steady! No sudden moves—that would be a mistake. After the way you've been setting an example, I might get trigger-happy!"

Carefully, on command, they lifted their guns and dropped them, then stood or sat, painfully reaching.

The shock of finding their victim alive, with a full understanding of the situation, was sobering.

They were oddly assorted, but alike in one respect. Life had dealt harshly with them, as with many during the war years. The gold camps, with their remoteness from established law and the chance for easy wealth, had been a magnet for men of their type.

The camps had proved lucrative, until the Vigilantes had sent them scattering. Now they hired their guns to men who felt themselves above killing chores but did not hesitate to employ others.

Montana's anger was tempered by understanding. Such employment was akin to the hiring of mercenaries to fight a war. By whatever name, killing was a dirty business.

All three were tall. Sharp fox-eyes peered from folds of flesh in the face of the man who had been the first to dismount. A loose grin hung lopsidedly on his mouth.

"You sure enough fooled us," he observed. "But I guess it's all in the game."

"Meaning that I should shoot you and be done with it?" Montana suggested.

They blinked uncertainly. If this was a joke, they had it coming, but he might well mean it.

"Wa'n't nothin' personal in what was going on," the middle gunman protested. "We was hired to do a job. A man's got to live."

"By killing others? It's not a convincing argument, my friend, particularly with me."

One upraised hand sagged, to brush across a stubble of beard in a nervous gesture. "No, I reckon not," he conceded unhappily.

"I *might* be interested in who hired you," Montana offered.

The third man shrugged.

"We got some principles left," he grunted. "Get on with it."

"'*Tenshun!*'" The command, barked in a drill sergeant's accents, startled two of them. The third man snapped to attention, confirming Montana's guess that he had been a soldier. He held the pose a moment, then relaxed defiantly.

"All right," Montana said sharply. "I want to know."

"Hell with you, Yank. I don't have to answer no questions for you. I was a Reb—and proud of being one!"

"Makes two of us," Montana returned quietly. "I led a blue-rescue column to save some settlers at the close of the war. It was over and lost, but they still had their lives. While the war lasted, until I was taken prisoner, I was a captain of cavalry, C. S. A."

The ex-soldier stared uncertainly, wetting his lips. "You was for the South?"

"Just as much as you." He allowed that to sink in

for a moment. "We worked for the same cause then. Now we work for the same man."

"Well, maybe so, only—"

He caught himself sharply, coloring. "I ain't sayin' nothing," he ended doggedly.

Montana shrugged the disclaimer aside. The man had already said enough. There had been no doubt about them, but Montana had felt honor-bound to give Tiller-Parsons the benefit of every doubt. It was almost a new low, to hire a man so that he might be killed, branded a felon and tumbled into a dishonored grave.

Almost, but perhaps not quite. Tiller-Parsons' treatment of women was worse.

He gathered up the dropped guns, loading them into a pair of saddlebags, then mounted one of the horses.

"I'll toss out your guns after I've gone about a mile. You may need them. Sorry that you'll have to ride shanks' mares, but I need these."

The former soldier wet his lips with dawning incredulity, in slow understanding.

"You ain't aimin' to kill us?"

"That wouldn't profit anybody," Montana returned. "In any case, there's already been too much killing."

11

To a gambler, the benefits of a poker face are many, and Tiller-Parsons not only understood but made use of them, though he thought sardonically that the debits more often than not outweighed the benefits.

There were such disadvantages as losing a fortune, virtually on the turn of a card, and betraying no emotion, not even by the quiver of an eyelash. To take such luck impassively was the mark both of an experienced card player and a sportsman. The bad part was that it had a way, when coupled with a losing tendency, to get a man in over his head, often to the point of desperation.

Since adding Parsons to his name and adopting the character which went with the new appellation, this ability had proved profitable, bringing him to his present position through contacts with men of money and prestige. That had been equally true of the ladies.

But the losses had a way of not merely offsetting,

but of outrunning the gains. And in such a stratum of society, if a man was to maintain his standing, he must pay his losses, most especially those at cards.

In other words, he reflected grimly, the higher you climbed, the farther you fell. It tempted a man to go back to the more direct, simpler ways of straight banditry.

At this stage of his career he should be rich, instead of teetering constantly on the brink of disaster. Three separate times when he was threatened with ruin, women had come, however unwittingly, to his rescue. Yet even with such windfalls, and other deals such as the cut he would receive from the sale of the beef herd, he was far from being in the winner's circle.

Now he pondered, considering a few remarks that he had chanced to overhear. The chance had been brought about by carefully putting himself in a position to eavesdrop, which occasioned him embarrassment only in what it disclosed. Timothy O'Donnell had been speaking to Rose, his voice restrained but insistent.

"The Indians call this the harvest moon, and it used to be my favorite time of the year," he observed. "But these mornings, there's a smell in the air. The stench of polecat comes and goes, but this is worse, and it lingers. Tell me true now, girl. Do you believe a word of that tale regarding a twin brother who masquerades under his name?"

As Tiller-Parsons had suspected, they were discussing him. There had been no uncertainty in Rose's reply, though it was touched by hopelessness and despair.

"Not a word," she admitted. "I know him now for the liar he is—but what can I do? He got away with all my inheritance. It was as much from necessity as anything that I hunted him down when I happened to learn about this ranch and that he was the manager. And of course there's Alicia now. At first I was inclined to resent her, but she is just as much a victim as I am. And she's sweet. I don't want to hurt her."

"She's been hurt already; both of you have been," O'Donnell reminded her bluntly. "The man's a scoundrel. And something has to be done about it. I suppose some would say that it's none of my business, but after the way he's treated you, I'm making it mine!"

Walking, heads close together, they passed out of earshot, but Tiller-Parsons had heard enough. As he had suspected, the big cowboy was in love with his ex-wife—or whatever the relationship might be—and he had a forthright way which took no note of and gave no respect to a man's position. While as for Rose—

He'd prided himself on the adroitness with which he'd managed an almost impossible situation, but apparently he had fooled no one—perhaps not even

Alicia. His two wives, thrown increasingly in each other's company, had become good friends. Perhaps they were already confiding in each other. With Rose in her present mood, they would not stop short of discussing him—

Ordinarily, he wouldn't have cared. He could find ways to keep the situation under control. But with the owners of the ranch due to arrive almost any day—

He hadn't counted on such a complication, but there was no question about it: he would have to act. Failure to do so could bring ruin. But how?

There was the rub. There were few, if any, among the ranch crew whom he could trust, particularly in so delicate a matter. The ironic part was that those on whom he could depend had been despatched with Abbott and the herd.

It would not do to be involved personally—

A tight smile did nothing to relieve the sudden cruelty at the corners of his mouth. The solution, after all, was so very simple. Moreover, he had promised Chief Spotted Pony something in return for a favor granted, and this could be made mutually profitable.

Dusk was closing over the valley like a drift of fog, blurring the outlines of the big house, masking the lesser structures. Only the savory smells of a roast of beef and of what he judged to be biscuits hot from the oven penetrated without hindrance, and O'Donnell lifted his head, swinging his eager horse toward the corrals. In that instant he heard a scream.

It came sharp yet muffled, as though choked before the sound could gasp above the throat. Simultaneously there was a quick beat of hooves, as swiftly receding.

O'Donnell was already swinging his horse, spurring. Brief and muffled though it had been, there was a quality to the voice that left no doubt in his mind. It was Rose who had cried out.

He made out the moving blur ahead as his cayuse lined out for a run, as though shadowy ghosts fled before him. The big ex-sergeant crooned in his horse's ear, stretched along its neck, and as though understanding the urgency, lengthened its stride. So they were gaining, since one of the two horses ahead was doubly burdened, and was thus in poor condition for racing.

Now the buildings had been left behind, as they crested the slope and then lined across the easy roll of flatlands beyond. O'Donnell rode in grim silence, his mind busy with a problem. Somebody was abducting Rose, which he did not find too surprising, but who? Well, he'd get an answer.

He gave no thought to the holstered revolver at his hip. In his present mood he felt no need for more than his hands, and in any case, he couldn't chance a shot.

The space between had been halved, then cut again. One rider turned to look back, his face only a dull blankness in the gloom. O'Donnell sensed that panic rode with the abductors. They were bunglers, not having anticipated instant pursuit; also, from the muffled grunts and exclamations, it seemed clear that Rose was far from a docile captive. Apparently she was threshing wildly, kicking, very likely using teeth and fingernails, giving her captor more than he had bargained for.

The unhindered rider suddenly swung his horse at O'Donnell's, lashing out with a tomahawk. That confirmed his guess, which had been growing into a conviction. These were Indians. But a red man could grow just as panicky as a white when things went wrong, and the frantic swing of arm and axe was easy to avoid. For a man who had more than once put his life on the line in hand-to-hand combat, it left a wide and easy opening.

Swinging close, O'Donnell closed his fingers behind the gripping hand. A violent jerk dislodged the rider and sent him flying through the night. A dismayed howl ended as suddenly as had the earlier scream, causing the sergeant to suspect that the wailer had probably gotten a mouthful of dirt.

Then he was alongside the burdened cayuse. The captive had been brought temporarily under control, held face down on the running shoulders in front of the warrior. With frantic desperation he brought up a short-barreled derringer which he had wrestled from his captive, firing at point-blank range. The flame made a crimson blossom, and O'Donnell responded, chopping with the long barrel of his own gun, raking down the skull and across the nose.

As the brave collapsed, spilling, O'Donnell snatched and caught Rose, who in turn was making a desperate if ungraceful jump toward him. Then they were together, and despite the remembered fragrance of food, O'Donnell had lost all desire to hurry.

12

Clouds were piling to the west, a vague dark tumble suggestive of a pillow fight, while an increasing sharpness in the air betokened that the long spell of fine weather might be drawing to an end. Montana, jogging easily, driving the extra horses as he came, eyed the cluster of buildings, then another moving mass just beginning to show from the east. Swinging from almost under the gather of clouds, following the wheel trace which usage was rapidly making into a road, came a caravan of horsemen; behind them were wagons, along with a couple of two-seated carriages, then more wagons with canvas covers.

The owners of the syndicate must be arriving, Montana decided, and found the circumstances to his liking. At the same time, it was apt to bother his employer. Briefly he pondered the complications which might ensue, and his part in them. Tiller-Parsons had hired him, so technically at least he was

working for him. But the Englishmen owned the
outfit, paying his salary as well as that of the manager. Actually, he was working for them.

There had been plenty of time for thinking, as
he followed the long trail back from the Yellowstone.
He was looking forward to what might develop with
considerable anticipation.

He was not supposed to return from this journey,
having been marked for sacrifice. Which was but one
of several matters in which the manager had interested himself, with his penchant for planning.

It was something like a rope artist displaying his
skill with several lariats at one time. That always
made an impressive act, as long as the performer
did not become tangled in a maze of his own
contriving. For a while, Montana was willing to
watch the performance.

The approach of the caravan had already been
noticed. Now there was a bustle of last-minute
preparations at the buildings, a scurry as of hens
at the shadow of a hawk. But it was an ordered
haste. With a manager who planned so carefully and
so far in advance, everything would be under control; everything with the exception of his own return.
Tiller-Parsons would have made no plans for such
an eventuality.

Tiller-Parsons came out from the big house, Alicia
by his side. They had dressed for the occasion more
elegantly than usual, certainly more elaborately than

the natives thereabouts had ever seen. Tiller-Parsons' attitude would be correct, a nice blend of the welcoming host and the obsequious servant.

Tiller-Parsons glanced about, viewing the elegance of the fine house with conscious self-approval, certain of the good impression it must make upon his employers. From that survey he turned to see Montana swinging down from his horse.

A gambler by nature, even if somewhat lacking in the skills necessary to such a profession, Tiller-Parsons was seldom caught off guard. This time he was. Blankness, mixed with consternation, flowed across his face, and the almost colorless eyes became even lighter. He stared unbelievingly. Montana could appreciate what he felt.

Only an instant. Then Tiller-Parsons had control of himself. The mask dropped back in place, although he swallowed uncomfortably. To give him credit, he *was* a gambler, ready to put whatever fortune might be his to an instant test. Smiling, he advanced with outstretched hand.

"Montana! I was just thinking about you! You made the trip without trouble, I see?"

"No trouble at all," Montana assured him blandly, and went on to the next step, which would be at least as painful for Tiller-Parsons as his return. The housekeeper had appeared, also Rose and Tim O'Donnell, as witnesses to the transaction.

"I have the money that was paid for the cattle,"

Montana explained. "So I'll turn it over to you now."

He proceeded to untie a wrapped package from behind his saddle, and for a second time, much like a fish newly pulled from the water, Tiller-Parsons swallowed. His mind worked like the frantic digging of a gopher, as a crisis closed in inexorably.

He had recognized the hazard in involving a man like Montana Abbott, who had a reputation for being able to take care of himself. But that sort of a reputation was vital in lending credibility to the loss of the money, and Tiller-Parsons hadn't seen how it could fail.

Yet fail it had, and now he was faced with a threat far more dangerous. And here was O'Donnell with Rose, smiling and polite like Abbott. What had happened to those darned Indians?

He desperately needed time to think, to deal with one thing at a time, and there was no time. His employers were arriving and must be greeted. They of course would be delighted with so early and sizable a cash dividend from the ranch operations. The painful part was having the money in his hands, but with no chance to hang onto it. He managed a desperate sort of calmness.

"Excellent, Abbott," he agreed. "I'm delighted, of course—both at how you've managed and at your safe return. Right now our employers are arriving."

It was a temporary relief to be able to turn as

the buggies came up and began to disgorge their passengers. A driver was in each, leaving six seats for the guests of honor. His glance ranged quickly. Sir John and Lady Crispin, the former as red-faced and hearty as his lady was thin and ascetic in appearance—one did not apply the adjective vinegary to a woman of such distinction—

Mr. Silvanus Drew, sagging the buggy step and spring, backing out and down as ponderously as a hog for the weighing—Tiller-Parsons' mind recoiled with a start from the comparison, however apt—

The Right Honorable Thomas Noonan, M. P., and Mrs. Noonan, both looking precisely and exactly right, even at the end of so long and wearing a journey—

Tiller-Parsons lost color, gulping a third time. Mr. Byron Fancher, manager of the company as well as the syndicate—and Tiller-Parsons understood that much more than this Montana ranch was involved— Fancher should have been the sixth notable. Instead, he was dismounting, a shade stiffly but with a suggestion of sprightliness, from a horse, while the other passenger—

The pale eyes seemed to recede, blinking rapidly. This was a nightmare, dynamite and disaster. It was as startling and impossible as finding Rose here at the ranch, when he had arrived with Alicia as his bride. Somehow he had weathered that, even though his solution now seemed in danger of falling apart.

But this—

However overweight and ponderous of manner, Mr. Silvanus Drew was reported to be a friend of the Prince. He was one of the manner born, doubly fortunate in being the possessor of a more than ample fortune. He was dressed as he deemed the occasion merited, in boots and rough tweeds topped by a real cowboy hat. Despite his bulk, he looked and felt at home, turning from assisting the final passenger down from the double-seater. His smile was warm as it rested upon Tiller-Parsons— deceptively so, the latter suspected, and could think only of the satisfied, wide-toothed grin of a well-fed wolf.

The lady on Drew's arm was slender, smartly dressed, and as strikingly beautiful in her way as Rose or Alicia, a pale-gold blondeness suggestive of silver and gold. She was painfully familiar to Tiller-Parsons, and Mr. Drew was presenting her, with the air of a man who delighted in happy surprises.

"Look whom I ran across in London, just the week before we sailed, and brought along to make the party complete," he said. "A happy surprise, eh, old boy? Mrs. Jennifer Tiller-Parsons herself!"

It seemed to Tiller-Parsons, gasping again after the manner of a fish, that these low blows were coming unduly thick and fast. For an instant, panic gripped him. But having been through this before, experience steadied him. He drew back a pace, and by then his mind commenced to work again.

"I'm delighted to see you again, sir—all of you. But is this some sort of a spoof? Yet I'm only too afraid that I understand," he added grimly.

"Spoof? Understand?" The solidity of Drew was thoroughly British. "What do you mean? You should be overjoyed to see your wife again."

Everyone was staring, all else held in abeyance, with varying interest and anticipation. Tiller-Parsons' shake of the head was resigned, almost forgiving.

"As it happens, Mr. Drew, I have a wife—but only one," he added. "To my regret, I also have a twin brother, who for reasons of his own, unknown to me, appears to have assumed my name and identity—in a deception of which this lady seems to have been the most recent victim."

Jennifer was eying him with incredulity and anger. She was slightly smaller than the other ladies of his choice, but vibrant now as a too tight fiddle string. Eyes normally violet but now almost black swept him furiously.

"So to top all the rest, you lie about it now?" she demanded. "With you, I'm past being surprised."

"There you differ from me, madam." Tiller-Parsons contrived a sweeping bow. "These surprises still startle me. I only wish that they did not discommode such charming and lovely ladies!"

Montana had to admire his adroitness. The man was a scoundrel; of that he had received more than enough proof. On the broad pattern, he was also a skillful planner, but he was like an overly busy spider in a high wind, weaving so many webs that he was getting entangled in them.

But his alibi had worked once, and it was equally convincing now. If his twin brother had deserted Rose as soon as he had gotten his hands on her money, why should he not use the same formula a second time? It seemed clear that he had taken ship for England, to be well away from Rose. With an ocean between, and his charm for the ladies undiminished, he had considered it safe to marry Jennifer.

As the supposed facts were gradually brought to light, Jennifer regarded the other ladies appraisingly. Then she made a confession which a lady to the manner born might have found humiliating.

"So he rooked you, did he?" she demanded of Rose. "The same with me, I'm afraid. Fifteen thousand pounds, the stinkin' blighter! Told me he had a chance to myke a fortune, off here in America—and myde me believe it! Then he walked out on me—not realizing that I had as much more left!"

She swung suddenly to Alicia, who during the interchange had been a silent onlooker.

"And how much has he rooked you for? For with him, it's just a gyme to steal .That's all he ever wants from any of us is our money!"

Alicia caught Tiller-Parsons' appealing glance, but her own was as considering as it was troubled.

"There was a matter of some forty thousand dollars," she admitted. "These twins seem to have certain traits in common."

"Oh, now, my dear!" Tiller-Parsons' protest was pained.

Alicia's rejoinder was even more devastating.

"Perhaps we might form a club," she suggested brightly. "There are enough of us. We could call ourselves The Cast-offs."

13

There was spitefulness in the remark, but Montana sensed the deep underlying hurt. Along with that, there was the hurt which had not quite been laid to rest with his initial explanation, and now was sharpened almost to conviction. It was the deadly parallel, the wheedling of huge sums of money from each bride, which did it. Had that been an attribute only of the supposed twin, not touching Tiller-Parsons, his alibi would have been acceptable.

Still, it was an alibi, and Tiller-Parsons clung to it with the stubbornness of desperation. The home-coming of the owners of the ranch was marred but not quite spoiled, and one factor on which Tiller-Parsons had failed to count in all his careful planning went a long way to balance the scales in his favor. That was the cash profit, the sizable dividend realized on the sale of the herd, which he was able to present to them.

Nor did he weaken his case by any reference to what his graceless brother might have done with such a sum of money.

Montana might have tipped the scales by telling what he knew or suspected, but that was between the two of them; he owed a certain loyalty to the outfit if not to Tiller-Parsons, and there already was uproar enough. For the present, he would wait.

On the surface it appeared an uneasy draw, with none of those involved quite believing Tiller-Parsons, yet not entirely doubting him. With a half-guilty sense for the fitness of things, each one attempted to restore pleasant relations, with at least outward success.

Tiller-Parsons did not delude himself into any such belief. This had been an incredible chain of events, resulting in all three of his wives turning up on this ranch, and he was still bewildered by the sequence. When he had left Rose, taking ship for England, he had counted the episode as over and done with, to his own profit. Certainly she was a lovely lady, who had believed his protestations, but a man on the make could not afford to let senti- ment stand in his way.

That she might one day read in a newspaper feature about an English syndicate which had ac- quired a Montana ranch and employed him to manage it—or that she would or could make her way to that ranch, he would have dismissed as un- thinkable.

Similarly, it had seemed a perfect opportunity to

repeat the already successful formula by marrying an English girl who was charmed as much by his supposed social position as by himself. Since she would be not merely disappointed but furious at his inability to make good, it had been best conveniently to lose her, by again boarding a ship for the States.

Even should she discover that much, she would look for him along the Eastern seaboard, rather than across a continent. The odd chance that she might somewhere have made the acquaintance of one of the owners of the ranch had certainly never occurred to him.

It had been a long day, and tiring. Tiller-Parsons winced as pain racked his shoulder, a short quick stab, as swiftly gone. A knife had cut there years before, twisting and gouging, and though the wound had long since healed, he suffered an occasional reminder. Now his mouth twisted. That fracas had been over a woman.

Soberly, he took stock of the day's events. They had been unpleasant, but he was sure that he had put on a convincing show. And in a way, it made sense.

"I'd almost have liked to know you," he paid tribute to his mythical twin. "There's no doubt that you're a scoundrel of the first water; still in all, you're a man after my own heart!"

With all three of his wives thrown together at the ranch, the next few days would be risky. He

would have to tread warily. Even his encounter
with the drink-sodden chief had hardly been more
precarious. It would take only a single miscue to
render his position untenable.

A very present danger was Montana Abbott. He
too, had a fund of knowledge which he'd be pondering, and sooner or later, he would demand an
accounting. It was not a reckoning to look forward
to.

Then, like a ripple of heat lightning along a distant horizon, the solution came to him. Tiller-Parsons
stared at the darkness and shook his head, appalled
at the fertility of his imagination. It could be a complete and final way of solving his problems, all of
them, and with little or no risk.

But he wasn't a savage—at least not yet. Angrily
he rejected the thought, which had come unbidden,
frighteningly.

He had managed to slip away, to stroll by himself, to settle his shaken nerves and ponder. This
early in the evening, although it was late in the
fall, the air was almost balmy. Somewhere, from the
hilltop back of the buildings, a coyote's cry quavered,
rising, hanging on a note of mockery.

Still, taking the idea on a reduced scale, it might
present a solution. Actually, something of the sort
would be no worse than what he had already intended to set for Abbott, a trap which he had somehow eluded.

It was time to be getting back to Alicia, to make sure that, despite her comment in which hurt had wailed, she was not too disturbed by the accusations. Somehow, to gain time, he must contrive to keep the three women from getting together and comparing notes. He must be especially nice to all three, each in the right fashion. Also, there would have to be some entertainment provided for his visitors, something to keep everyone occupied. That was it. Appeal to Alicia, as his wife—to her sense of duty as the hostess, let her know how much he needed and depended on her. The planning for the entertainment of their guests would give her something to do—

He was startled to find their room empty. It had been too much to hope that he might find Alicia asleep, despite the lateness of the hour. The day's events had been too disturbing for sleep to come easily, and she would probably have a lot of questions.

Not only was the room empty, but her clothes were gone. Tiller-Parsons was suddenly uneasy at what that implied.

The housekeeper was still up, busy with numerous duties because of the influx of guests. He caught the gleam of a lamp as she moved along a hallway and hurried to question her.

"Do you know where my wife has gone?" he asked uneasily. "She isn't in our room—"

The normally pleasant face behind the high-held lamp was rigid and unfriendly.

"If you mean Miss Alicia, she moved to the empty room at the far end of the upper hall," was the retort, and lady and lamp receded along the passage in an aura of disapproval.

Shaking his head, Tiller-Parsons stared after her. It looked as though all the ladies were badly ruffled and were taking a stand against him. Yet how could a man have foreseen such events as had come to pass? After all of his contriving, it was incredible.

Alicia opened the door at his knock, but her eyes were cool and unfriendly. He pushed past her and closed the door.

"What is the meaning of this, my dear?" he asked, and realized how inane the question was. "Surely you don't believe those wild accusations? We've been over all of that before—"

"I thought, under the circumstances, that it would be better if I was off here by myself," Alicia returned. "Better for everyone."

"But that's ridiculous," he protested. "You're my wife. *They* married my twin brother—"

Her look checked him. She was smiling, her lips tired and wistful, but edged with scorn.

"Did they?" she countered. "It won't wash, my friend. It was a good try, but too far-fetched."

"Far-fetched?" he repeated, suddenly desperate. "But it's the truth. You've got to believe me—"

"You see," she went on, as though not hearing, "we compared notes, the three of us. It was Jennifer who thought of your scar."

"Scar?" Tiller-Parsons repeated stupidly. "But I have no scar—"

"Oh, but you do, Lothario. I suppose you never get to see it, and perhaps didn't even know about it. But it's on your left shoulder, on your back, just out of sight. A sort of white blotch, as though it had been made by a knife. All three of us have seen it. And it would be odd indeed for you and a twin each to have received a wound which would cause such a scar in exactly the same place."

With final cold deliberation, she shut the door in his face.

14

Tiller-Parsons stared blankly at the closed door, his mind equally shut. Here was disaster, complete and final. As he stumbled out into the night, he had no doubts on that score. He was undone, past all explaining—all on account of a scar which he had never seen or suspected.

The Englishmen, once the truth was known, would be horrified and outraged. His career in their employ would be summarily ended.

The worst of it was that losing his job would be only the start. Their suspicions having been aroused on one point, Mr. Gates, the manager, would be certain to start investigating, to dig into other aspects, such as his expenditures—

The moon was up, the evening still balmy. Tiller-Parsons brought up abruptly as he encountered another stroller. As though his thinking had conjured him up, Horatio Gates hailed him affably, removing a pipe from his mouth to gesture toward the moon.

"Ah there, Tiller-Parsons. A beautiful evening."

"Is it? I hadn't noticed."

"I suppose all this is an old story to you—the grandeur of the scenery, the wide sweep of plain and prairie, the mountains against the skyline. To me, it is all new and entrancing. I am certainly impressed. What you have accomplished here, sir, is outstanding."

"I'm happy that you approve—"

"Oh, I do, sir, I do, though in all honesty, there are certain aspects of the overall picture, certain matters which I do not fully understand. Probably it is on that account, because of an incomplete picture, that I find them disturbing. Perhaps you can enlighten me."

Here it is, Tiller-Parsons thought grimly. Lying would be of no further use, since all three of the women he had married had made up their minds. Turning, Gates climbed with surprising nimbleness to perch on a top pole of the corral, so there was nothing to do but take a seat beside him. Unhurriedly, the general manager knocked out his pipe against the log, then tucked it carefully away in a pouch.

"We were several days on the road, down from the river at Fort Benton," he explained precisely. "A most interesting journey, but that is beside the point. What I have in mind was an encounter, a couple of days ago, with a sick man. Badly injured would perhaps be a more accurate description, since his fever and sickness derived from a festering wound. It had been caused by an arrow—an Indian arrow, he told me. It struck me as little short of a miracle that he had not only survived such a wound, but had traveled a considerable distance on foot before being found by us."

Puzzled, Tiller-Parsons listened.

"I'm afraid I don't grasp your point," he confessed.

"Probably not. We did what we could for the fellow, giving him a horse and other needed supplies, after which he went on, being quite insistent on that point. He seemed very anxious to get away from that country once and for all. That became understandable, once he recounted the harrowing experiences he had undergone."

And I'm in about the same boat, Tiller-Parsons reflected, his apprehensions increasing.

"He poured a strange and, at times, unbelievable tale into my ears," Gates went on. "It seems that he had been taking a wagonload of liquor to the Indians—an undertaking which I understand is forbidden, as well as hazardous. I presume he hoped to sell or trade the goods for a fancy price, but matters didn't work out. The Indians helped themselves, without pay, and he was lucky to escape with his life, though receiving a wound from an arrow. Understandably, he wanted nothing more to do with them."

"I shouldn't think he would."

"Indeed he did not." Gates peered placidly at the moon, which gave the appearance of wearing a halo. Tiller-Parsons guessed that the ring was a portent of bad weather on the way, putting an end to the fine fall, and he viewed it with distaste. It was uncomfortably like an omen.

"The background to this trader's activities was what most interested me," Gates went on. "Perhaps he was imagining certain matters, or it may have been the effect of the fever. On the whole, however, he seemed rational, as well as very much in earnest. He claimed to have been one of a crew of cattle drovers—cowboys, I presume is the correct term—escorting a trail herd up from Texas. Somewhere in the Wind River country, wherever that is, he described how they were set upon—not by red men but by white.

"Apparently it was rather awful, a bloody butchery. Massacre was the word he used, he being one of the few to escape alive. And the cattle were stolen—rustled was his term."

A light wind had sprung up, bringing a sudden chill, but Tiller-Parsons found himself sweating. He waited grimly.

"It was this man's contention that the herd was thus obtained by its new owners not alone by fraud but by murder and treachery. He insisted further—and this I find the next unbelievable part of his tale—that the Powder River Ranch received this herd

His own subsequent activities, as he explained them, were prompted by a desire to see justice done, to avenge his fallen comrades."

Gates' voice was calm and without expression, but he had stated his case and posed a question. Tiller-Parsons' earlier guess, that he had deliberately chosen some subject far afield, thus tactfully avoiding reference to Tiller-Parsons' domestic troubles, had been wide of the mark. To the manager's mind, this was connected, but far more serious. And he was a man who would insist on a full and believable answer.

"I had heard of the man you mention and his suspicions," Hank acknowledged. "I've tried to verify them—so far without much success. The crew who delivered the herd here carried the proper papers regarding the stock, so the transaction was concluded according to arrangements already made. If they were the wrong crew, and guilty of such an act, I had no reason to suspect them at the time. Tomorrow I'll show you the records, and we'll go into this in greater detail."

"Of course, of course," Gates agreed. "I'm sure that you're as anxious to get at the truth of this as I am. Meanwhile, we'll say nothing to the others, to spoil their pleasure in this journey. And I'm afraid I'm keeping you from your rest."

With a cheerful good night, he climbed down and disappeared within the big house. Tiller-Parsons remained seated, staring unseeingly at the moon. He had already given all the explanation he could, and all at once, nothing that he said was being accepted.

What should be his next move? A woman scorned was bad enough—but three of them, now leagued together—

He might steal away in the night, fleeing ignominiously. That would mean ruin, and even the frontier would not be wide enough. Still worse, to run would be a highly dangerous undertaking. If he blundered into Indians, any Indians, they would kill him. If he was lucky enough to evade them, there would still be pursuit, for many potent causes. A tracker as skilled as Montana Abbott would probably run him to earth within a matter of hours, certainly of days.

The earlier solution was suddenly impelling, insistent. He stared into the darkness, appalled. Whatever he had intended, when setting out on this planned trail to success, he had not contemplated murder or massacre—

But there had been robbery, bigamy, wife desertion, along with a host of lesser offenses. And traceable to him, the accusations almost leveled, were murder and massacre—

Dropping to the ground, he began a restless pacing, sweating, rejecting notions as they flocked. Only one of them appeared to be workable, to be certain in its effect. His mind kept reverting to it as would a gopher to its burrow. As with the rodent, when a fox prowled in the brush and a hawk sailed overhead, there was nowhere else to go.

And after all, why not? These others, all of them, were already thirsting for *his* blood, not literally but in ways almost equally unpleasant. It had become either him or them. With events driving him on, he was left no other choice.

The scheme, as he pondered it, seemed almost flawless. This was the frontier, remote and beyond the law. The Indians were restless, friendly on the surface, yet guilty of isolated outrages. The guilt for what occurred would fall, as it should, upon them—and there would be no one to contradict, nor even to dispute what had happened.

Spotted Pony would prove a ready and willing instrument, for a number of reasons. He could sack the ranch, and it would yield a huge booty, just as a massacre would jibe with his desires.

It would be days, or more likely weeks, before anyone would know what had happened. With the land buried under winter snows, some might suspect where the guilt lay, but there would be no proof, nothing to connect any single band with the outrage.

There would be no survivors. That was regrettable, but again the necessities of his own survival dictated how it must be. The Indians would see it the same way.

He would be counted as one of the dead. Not alone this chapter, but the book would be closed. Somewhere else, under a new name and identity, he would start anew. And with a little luck, he would be able to salvage enough for an excellent start.

Tiller-Parsons sighed, but the sharpness of his regret was already dulled. This had been forced upon him, and it was the only possible decision. A man could do no less.

The immediate problem was how to get word to Spotted Pony, to arrange a meeting. It would have to be secret, and whoever carried word had to be reasonably trustworthy, as well as skilled enough in the ways of the country to manage, without losing his own hair in the doing.

Being short-handed as far as trustworthy members of the ranch crew were concerned posed a problem. When he had sent those others off with Montana and the herd, he had not foreseen such a contingency.

In his mind he reviewed everyone who might be available. He fixed on one of the men who had come in that day with the new arrivals. Dutch Cassidy should do very well.

Tiller-Parsons did not know a great deal about him, but enough. Cassidy belonged to that drifting army of homeless men who prowled the land like lost souls. He had known Bannack and Virginia City in the heyday of the Innocents. He had run the rivers, trapping, prospecting, scouting, freighting. He was passable at most tasks, not very good at any.

One thing he had in common with most of that faceless legion. For a price, usually not a very high one, he would do anything.

Returning to the house, moving with stealthy quietness, Tiller-Parsons found paper, a quill and ink. Not risking a candle, he wrote by the light of the moon. Only a few words were necessary, to whet the chief's curiosity and arrange a meeting. Spotted Pony could read English writing as well as he spoke the language.

In the meanwhile, Tiller-Parsons decided, while the details were being worked out, he would ignore the unpleasantries of the day and arrange some sort of entertainment for the newcomers. It was essential to preserve at least a surface amity, to keep them happy. And as manager for the ranch, that was his job.

15

Because Tiller-Parsons was at some pains to make it sound like an innocent, routine job, Dutch Cassidy knew that it must be something other than that. But the ranch foreman—Cassidy did not distinguish between the two managers—was paying him well for the task, and in advance. What his particular business might be, Cassidy accounted as none of his affair.

He had second thoughts upon learning that the message was to be delivered to an Indian.

"That makes no danger for you," Tiller-Parsons reassured him. "I know that some of the redskins are restless, but you will wear a white hat. That will assure you safe conduct with Spotted Pony and his band."

"I don't have any white hat," Cassidy reminded him dubiously, but Tiller-Parsons provided one. Clearly all this means for communication had been planned in advance.

Simply to deliver a message had sounded reasonable enough as he rode out from the ranch buildings. Out of sight of them and alone in the night, Cassidy's doubts flooded back. Removing the hat and holding it close in front of his eyes, now that the moon had dipped below the horizon, he could barely make out a vague blur. If some trigger-happy warrior should choose to shoot, instead of waiting to get a close look—

But trouble, when it came, was from a source he had not expected. Another rider loomed in the night, offering a challenge. Cassidy was both relieved and disturbed as he recognized Montana's voice.

"You'll have some reason for riding abroad at such an hour, I'm sure," Montana suggested. "I'm curious as to what it is."

Unable to think of a convincing lie, Cassidy fell back on the truth. After all, he had been given no directions to the contrary. Montana listened and nodded agreeably.

"You're to deliver a note to Chief Spotted Pony himself," he repeated. "All right. There's just one thing. Let me know what he says or does after you've delivered it."

"I'll do that," Cassidy agreed, reflecting that he would let circumstances decide. Riding on, and having been mindful on the journey to the ranch where the Indians almost certainly lurked, he was able to deliver the letter to Spotted Pony. The braves who intercepted him had noted the hat and been not unfriendly.

The chief read the missive and grunted. His next reaction, Cassidy found less to his liking.

"I will meet him tomorrow night," Spotted Pony agreed. "But to make sure that there is no double-cross, you will remain here, at this camp, until I ride to meet him. When I go, you can go also."

It occurred to Cassidy, considering all that he had heard at the ranch and here, that there was no love lost between a lot of different people; certainly there was no trust. But he was treated well enough, spending most of the day sleeping. The difficulty was that both Tiller-Parsons and Montana might be put out at his failure to report back, but that could not be helped.

One thing he could do, he decided, once he was permitted to set out, along with Spotted Pony. At the moment, sided by shadows, the darkness was heavy. Cassidy allowed his horse to drop back; then he was alone.

He was faced with a choice, one of three possibilities. He might return straight to the ranch, or make the most of the opportunity to get out of the country. Or he could spy on the meeting between Spotted Pony and Tiller-Parsons. He had learned where the rendezvous was to take place.

That might be a chancy business, but he swung and headed for the spot. By now, their meeting appeared far less casual and innocent than he had first supposed.

Almost certainly it was none of his business, a fact he'd do well to keep in mind. The trouble, Dutch decided with a resigned sigh, was that he was just lacking in good sense. Or perhaps he was overly curious.

He almost blundered. Tiller-Parsons had named Bald Rock as the place for the meeting, and Cassidy, misjudging landmarks in the darkness, assumed that he had some distance yet to go. Voices just ahead brought him up short; then he leaned forward in the saddle, ears attuned to listen.

The two men were arguing, not amicably. Tiller-Parsons' nerves had been worn raw by recent events, and he felt that he was offering a favor, but the chief seemed to believe that it was the other way around. Both had grown angry. Cassidy's blood chilled at the chief's words.

"You said, let us understand each other," Spotted Pony said in measured tones. "I understand you very well. There are certain ones on your ranch who are in your way, and you want them out of the way. But instead of doing your own killing, you want me to do the dirty work. Very well. I will do so. But when my braves attack, we will make a clean sweep, killing everyone. Doing it that way will be much better for both of us. No one will remain alive to ask questions or to answer them."

"But I don't want a massacre," Tiller-Parsons protested. His qualms still bothered him. "If you can take some scalps and loot the place—"

Spotted Pony checked him impatiently. Along with hatred for the white man in general, he had acquired an overriding contempt for this one in particular.

"It will be done my way," he declared. "That is the only safe method for both of us. Now as to the time—"

Tiller-Parsons gave in, not too reluctantly. It dawned on him that the chief was not only ready to cooperate and enthusiastic, but that he had exhibited no surprise at the proposition. *He's been planning such an attack. I'm only making it easier for him.*

The certainty that Spotted Pony would have struck in any case eased his scruples. He could hardly be counted as responsible.

He might, of course, return and warn the others, in a new twist to the double-cross, but that would be as foolish as it would be useless. They could not escape by running, nor were they in sufficient force to make a successful stand against attack.

The only result would be to get himself killed without helping the others. As it was, he and Spotted Pony were each doing the other a favor.

That was the comfortable as well as the sensible way to look at matters; still, he was a bit staggered to find himself not merely a party to so murderous a scheme, but a prime mover in it. He was most shaken at the realization that he was relieved rather than otherwise, because the chief insisted on doing a complete job.

Where the visiting Englishmen were concerned, it was most regrettable. But it was their misfortune to have arrived at so inopportune a time, without consulting him in advance. He could have warned them that the natives were restless.

Riding, absorbed in his thoughts, Tiller-Parsons heard nothing of the commotion behind.

Having pulled up at a convenient vantage point, Dutch Cassidy listened to the argument with increasing shock and disbelief. The two chiefs, who differed only in the color of their skins, were discussing details of a massacre as casually as though it were no more than a hunt for buffalo. Having heard of Spotted Pony, Cassidy could understand the Indians' point of view. His was an implacable hatred for all whites, and he was being offered a perfect chance for revenge. It was hardly to be expected that he would do otherwise than accept.

But Tiller-Parsons was supposedly of a different ilk. Occupying a responsible position, and accepted on terms of equality by the Englishmen, he was callously betraying them, merely because he faced ruin if they remained on the scene. Dutch Cassidy made no pretensions to idealism, but he was appalled at the deal.

It was a deal in which he, along with all the others, was scheduled to die.

Having been used as a go-between or messenger made it worse. Some of the responsibility was being foisted on him.

There was no time to think or plan, but in Dutch's case there was no need to do either. He knew what he must do, what he would do. He would get back and reveal the plot to Montana, as he had been asked to; after that, it would be Montana's responsibility.

What they might do then, beyond putting up a fight and going down honorably instead of being murdered without warning, Cassidy could not imagine. He was forced to an acceptance of the conclusion which he had just heard advanced: that the odds against them would be overwhelming. But it was better to fight.

Also, he'd heard that Montana Abbott had been an army officer, a leader of forlorn causes. He might come up with something—

Automatically, with a reflex action, he jerked his horse to a stop. Why leave it to Montana, the whole matter to an increasingly uncertain future, when he could handle it himself, quickly and easily?

More bewildered than astonished at the inspiration, Dutch shook his head at the audacity of the idea. Out of nowhere, it had popped into his head. He could kill the chief!

If he did that, with no one around to hear or know, it would certainly have some effect on events and their outcome. It would be some hours before the dead man was found, and once the warriors discovered him, there would be confusion. They would, of course, be out for revenge, but leaderless, lacking any particular plan. That would give Montana a better chance to counter the attack. In any case, the situation could hardly be worsened.

Cassidy swung his horse, then spurred. He was accustomed to obeying orders, not initiating action, but this was simple and direct enough for anyone, and there was no time to lose.

Spotted Pony was a dim blur in the night, a receding splotch in the darkness. He'd have to get closer, to make sure—

Cassidy was leaning forward, leveling his gun, his horse at a run. Half-consciously he was aware that this was rougher country than he'd been traversing before, when suddenly the other horseman swung about. Spotted Pony had heard the pursuit, of course, and he was ready to fight—

The two guns blasted almost as one, small crimson blossoms against the vastness of the dark. It came to Dutch Cassidy that he had been a trifle slow, not capitalizing on the advantage or the initial surprise that had been his.

Whether his own bullet sped wild or was accurate, he had no idea, but the Indian was either lucky or a marksman; confusedly, Cassidy remembered having heard that Spotted Pony had been trained in the white man's ways.

His horse was hit; the slogging, staggering impact of the heavy-caliber bullet seemed to rock Cassidy as well as the animal. It almost halted the running cayuse in mid-stride. Then, with a frantic leap of re-action, the pony was off the trail, soaring into space, falling, tumbling—taking him with it to oblivion.

There was no time to think, no chance to help himself. If it was true that in such a critical instant one remembered the events of a lifetime, apparently he did not fit the pattern. He had time for a single thought: this particular section of country was a lot rougher than he'd supposed, and he had no doubt that the drop he was taking, along with his horse, would finish what the bullet had begun.

A solid, heavy crunch, remorseless as a grinding boot, testified that they had hit, but the jarring im-pact was not final. The dead horse was still tumbling, but he and the cayuse had parted company, both going down, with even blacker depths below.

He hit again, and this time it was a springing yet savage thing, a lashing of tree branches as they yielded to the impact, bending, tossing him off again. Far from gentle though it was, the bounce broke his straight fall. He hit again, shockingly, the breath driven from his body. Other sounds, still drifting up-ward, no longer troubled his ears.

16

A trifle belatedly, Tiller-Parsons was making dis-
coveries about women in general and the trio he
had led to the altar in particular. Courted and
cherished, they could be as lovely as a dream.
Tricked and deserted, they could reveal steel beneath the softness.

Jennifer Jones, as Tiller-Parsons had discovered
during the period of their courtship, was of a saucy
disposition, as pert as a jay-bird. At first this trait
had delighted him. Had it been profitable really to
love a woman, he felt that she might easily have
been the one.

Accosting him brightly, she surveyed him, head
tilted to one side, much as she might consider the
good points of a horse. Under the scrutiny, Tiller-
Parsons refrained with difficulty from squirming.

"It's a strange coincidence," she murmured. "On
the day that I met you, I had been reading a novel
dealing with ancient Chinese customs. The heroine
of the tale was the number two wife."

Tiller-Parsons' somewhat desperate search for an apt rejoinder failed. Jennifer went on with a laugh, as though all this were vastly amusing.

"I never dreamed that I was slated for the same role." She smiled. "But I suppose you were following the old adage: that there is safety in numbers. Isn't it a pity that it doesn't hold good? Almost as much as that so many of us should have been so deceived by your passionate protestations! But at least we have each of us learned *our* lesson. So we intend, all for your own good of course, dear sir, to make sure that *you* learn your lesson!"

Tiller-Parsons' career had hinged on a glib tongue. Now it failed him.

"The three of us have talked things over, Henry, and have decided to give you a reprieve," Jennifer went on; "not because you deserve it, or even because we have any inclination to show you mercy. It's simply a matter of courtesy, of hospitality. Our hosts have invested a lot of money in this ranching enterprise. You have made sure of that. They have come a long way to see the country and enjoy a vacation, so on our part, it seems only fair to make their stay as enjoyable as possible.

"Because of them, Henry, we're declaring a truce for an indefinite time. Its duration will depend on your behavior. We are ready to do our best to make it an enjoyable occasion for everyone."

"That—that's very considerate of you," Tiller

Parsons stammered.

"We think so," Jennifer assured him sweetly.

Relieved, Tiller-Parsons was glibly voluble. Jennifer listened to his promises with a smile; still, he was certain that his charm was as potent as in the past. Men might dislike and distrust him, but that seemed only to enhance his appeal to the ladies.

"This is very good of you," he added. "And I'll do my best. As soon as I learned that our guests were on the way, I started to plan for their entertainment. Alicia and I discussed the possibilities and hit upon something in the nature of a housewarming. Some of the cowboys are musically inclined with such instruments as banjo and fiddle. We can invite the neighbors and have a dance. I'm afraid it won't quite equal an old-fashioned English ball, but it should be enjoyable."

Jennifer eyed him in amazement.

"A ball?" she repeated. "Here? But where are these neighbors of whom you speak so lightly?"

He waved a vague hand.

"A couple of ranches are within riding distance, and they'll be glad to come. Entertainments are all too rare here on the frontier. I'm going to leave the details up to you and the others. If you will take charge, I'm sure it will prove a memorable occasion."

Jennifer eyed him suspiciously. He was almost too agreeable. But she had made the suggestion, and it would give everyone a part, all working together. The ball was discussed with their hosts, who were also the guests; then everyone set to work making preparations.

Tiller-Parsons watched, hiding a sardonic smile. This dance or housewarming would be a climax to the visit, and it should prove a memorable one, even if not quite what they expected. Having been reasonably certain that everyone would cooperate, purely as a matter of good breeding, he had anticipated the event, conditioning his planning and Spotted Pony's upon it.

Watching the preparations, he knew a qualm of regret. The thing was rather less than sportsmanlike, to say the least, and Spotted Pony's warriors would be merciless. But the intentions of all these others, over the long run and in regard to him, left him no choice. And if the climax did not come at the ball, it would be just as savage and final, wherever it was played out. Spotted Pony had waited a long while for such a chance, and he could not be deterred or swayed from it, even if Tiller-Parsons should be so foolish as to beg him on his knees.

Self-interest demanded that he work with the Indians. Everyone, from Jennifer to Horatio Gates, had made it plain that this interlude would be followed by an accounting. That would spell ruin, and it had to be forestalled, no matter what the cost.

On the surface, a light-hearted gaiety prevailed, but to Montana, aware of the undercurrents and all that was held in abeyance, it was like the lull in the eye of a hurricane. To find himself in the hurricane's eye was not a new experience. He had known it literally during the war, caught with his command on the coast and far to the south, when a storm had swept up from the gulf with devastating effect. The momentary lull near the middle of the onslaught had been less a reprieve than a warning of worse to come.

He had the same feeling now. Contests were temporarily in abeyance, as the oil of civilization was interposed between abrasive forces. But this surface politeness only meant a delay, though he hoped that amicable solutions might be reached because of the breathing space.

As he worked with the others, to decorate the house and grounds, there was almost a festive air. Everyone took part. Paper chains were strung, after the manner which Montana remembered as a small boy at Christmas, but more elaborately. A myriad of ornaments came magically into being. There was a breathless quality to the excitement, the anticipation of women, which communicated itself, along with their loveliness.

They almost managed to make-believe, to cover the hurt each had received. The trouble was that he had felt the power of the hurricane and worked with a grim awareness that the lull would be temporary.

Horatio Gates came to him with an innocent-sounding question.

"Have you seen Dutch Cassidy?" he asked. "He's a cowboy, who made the journey here with us from the river. I can't seem to find him anywhere."

It might be that Tiller-Parsons had sent him with an invitation to one of the other ranches. Montana sought him out to inquire. From the vantage point of a ladder, as he held a paper chain near the ceiling of the big parlor, Tiller-Parsons shook his head.

"I'm sure I wouldn't know about him," he denied. "I've scarcely met him, actually."

That seemed reasonable, so Montana was inclined to accept the assertion at face value. But Timothy O'Donnell, whom he questioned next, was more helpful, while at the same time stirring doubt.

"Yeah, he's gone," he confirmed. "I don't know where or what he had in mind, but I saw him take off last night. Likely Tiller-Parsons can tell you."

"I just talked with him, and he claims not to know anything about Cassidy."

"Then he's lying. Cassidy had been powwowin' with him, so I figured Tiller-Parsons had given him some orders. Ain't seen Cassidy since."

"You're sure it was Cassidy that you saw? It couldn't have been someone else?"

"It could have been, only it wasn't. The two of us had been chewin' the fat earlier in the evenin'.

Turned out, when he got to comparin' notes, that my folks and his had both come from the same part of Ireland, on the Shannon. Both of them sailed the same year. We kind of hit it off together, Dutch and me. We was aimin' to visit some more today."

Montana's nod was grim. Here it was again, and the unreasonable quality of Tiller-Parsons' denial was like a stone in a shoe. Why should he lie about such a matter, when there seemed no reason for it? But Montana was certain that Tiller-Parsons never did anything without a reason.

As ranch manager, he had worked hard today, entering in the spirit of the occasion, laughing and joking, managing to provide almost everything that the ladies required. He had made himself so agreeable that almost everyone seemed inclined to be more lenient, if not forgiving. . . .

"I think I'll take a look around for Cassidy," Montana decided. "Keep an eye on things till I get back."

O'Donnell nodded.

"That I will," he agreed. "But it's not me that needs to be observant. If you'll pardon my saying so, Captain, somebody's mighty busy tryin' to pull the wool over our eyes. All this stuff that we're doing keeps everybody busy, not leavin' too much time to think about other matters. But I don't like none of it. Be careful as you ride, man!"

17

Dutch Cassidy was slow in returning to consciousness, a circumstance to be wondered at only in that he might not have been expected to regain it at all. He endured a dark period of transition, which lasted through the remaining hours of the night. During that time he hovered like a startled bird between life and death, the possibility of sudden flight uncomfortably balanced.

When finally his eyes opened, to stare at first on vacancy, his mind was as slow and clogged as the hoofs of a horse plodding through deep, clinging mud. To shake off the feeling of lethargy which held him and rouse himself was a weary process.

But gradually the unending drum of pain, hammering against the roof of his skull, became bearable. His eyes focused, and individual aches and pains began to sort themselves out into an intolerable list. They seemed everywhere, through all his body, and it was only as he was able to remember that he understood.

There had been the plunging fall of his stricken horse, dropping into black depths at the side. He had been bounced from the saddle as the horse struck and bounced also in the descent. That might account for the effects which he was now feeling. What really surprised him was being able to feel, to be alive.

That had happened during the night. Now it was daylight; the sun was shifting to shine against his face. Moving to avoid it, stiffly and painfully, he shrank in sudden terror, striving to draw back, finding himself staring over the side into those black depths which he had almost supposed to be part of a nightmare.

Pulling back, gasping, he took stock. He was sprawled on solid rock, and a ledge of smooth, dark rock rose up behind him. On the other side, an equally sheer wall fell away to the depths. The ledge on which he lay was less than half a dozen feet in width, and to already bruised bones and flesh it was intolerably unyielding.

How far the ledge might run, in either direction, he had no idea.

Risking another look, he saw that the canyon at the side was deep, though not very wide. The opposite wall was almost within jumping distance, had he been in shape to leap or had any reason to do so. Both walls of the canyon reared upward. On the opposite side, only a little higher up, a pine tree had found a precarious hold.

Existence for the tree had proved less than easy. It had a ragged, broken look—

Then he understood why he was still alive. After being thrown from the saddle, he apparently had hit the tree. Its branches had bent under the impact, but its resiliency had bounced him to the side, onto his present spot on the ledge.

Rough as that treatment had been, it had saved him from falling at least another hundred feet. Whether such a reprieve might prove a mercy or a more cruel hoax, he was not at all certain.

Moving experimentally, he could find no broken bones, but such luck was a matter of degree. More than once, in cow camps, he had assisted the cook, pounding a tough beefsteak to a point where, after cooking, it was at least chewable. His body felt like the steak, after its working-over.

The diversity of pains seemed to have consolidated, to have settled into one encompassing, solid ache. The warm beat of the sun, reflected back from the cliff side and rock on which he lay, scarcely eased the stiffness and soreness, but it was aggravating a raging thirst.

His mind was ready to accept this, knowing that injury or sickness brought an increased craving for water. But instinct did not accept so tamely that it must be inevitable. It stirred him to do something however hard. But what?

To climb was out of the question. Reason and experience warned him that the shelf on which he lay was unlikely to lead anywhere, but at least there was a possibility. He could see it for half a hundred feet in either direction, before it seemed to turn or pinch out.

He was in no condition to walk, and even crawling was a slow task, which meant inching, dragging himself. His confusion made a mountain out of deciding which way he should go, but he decided that one way was as good as the other.

A hawk hung like a speck against the blue. Nothing else moved. Such breeze as roamed the heights was shut away by the walls, leaving only the concentrated heat of the sun.

Motion shocked fresh pain into being. Gasping, he lay while it subsided, then tried again, taking frequent pauses to rest. Time held no meaning.

He had reached something, but he had a sick sense he was being cheated. Without realizing, he had rounded the bend, but this was the end of the shelf—a dead end to the trail. It narrowed and pinched out, the wall above as sheer as ever, the drop at the side even less inviting.

Even the hawk had disappeared when he looked up. He was alone in an empty world.

Exactly when he turned and started back was hazy in his mind, but there was dry blood on the rock, and it roused him to realization. This was where he had lain during the hours of unconsciousness. He had made it back to his starting point.

To keep trying seemed futile, a hopeless effort, but thirst and the will to live combined to keep him at it. He reached the other turn, knowing a dragged-out moment of eagerness until he could see what lay beyond. Despair was like a kick in the face. It too, ended in a blank wall, just a few feet farther along.

He was trapped on the ledge, with nowhere to go.

He roused from a stupor, and realized that he had been crying, sobbing like a small boy, lost and fearful. There was no sense of shame, only a vast weariness.

But the sun had moved, and there was a small patch of shade which brought partial relief. The pain had eased, or grown more bearable. For the first time, he was able to think coherently, to fix his mind on something other than himself.

But, remembering what he had overheard the night before, he found that hardly an improvement. At the time, he had been too enraged against both Tiller-Parsons and Spotted Pony to think beyond the immediate aspects. The solution, it had seemed, was to deal with the chief. Had he succeeded, the problem would have been at least partly solved.

But he had failed, and now the vengeance-hungry chief would go on with his plan, attacking and killing. As with a weasel, the taste of blood would merely whet his appetite.

And the time, arranged between the two of them, was tonight!

The attack was planned as a total surprise, with no warning. He might have carried such a warning, had he used better judgment.

Forewarned, the ranch crew, implemented by the visitors, would still be heavily outnumbered, but they could at least put up a good fight. They deserved that much of a chance.

Even then, the outcome would be almost a certainty. Cut off from help, or any chance at escape, the odds would be too great, especially with a traitor in their midst!

But if he lacked any warning, the massacre would be as swift as it was ruthless.

He would be no better off, even if he could escape from this ledge and get word back, and neither would the others. Still, Montana Abbott was a soldier, with a reputation for leading hopeless causes. Given the chance, he might come up with a workable plan.

But the ability to think again was only another sort of torment. Even if uninjured, there was no chance either to climb or descend. The wall was too sheer, too tall. Though not as high here as back where he had lain, it was still a score of feet to the top.

Montana found sign pretty much where he had expected. Given the fact of Cassidy's absence, along with his being seen with Tiller-Parsons prior to his disappearance—which Tiller-Parsons had strangely seen fit to deny—the answer was so sharply narrowed that little guesswork was involved.

There was nowhere else to go, no one else to send a message to, aside from Spotted Pony.

What such a message portended was chilling to think about. Yet again, considering all the circumstances, the humiliation which Tiller-Parsons had suffered, the answer was only too easy to guess.

The surface friendliness which prevailed at the moment between all the factions at the ranch, the careful courtesy on both sides, was after all no more than a veneer—especially with Tiller-Parsons under attack from many points.

He had been more than eager to call a truce, to extend every courtesy to their guests, who were also his employers. But once the Englishmen's visit was over and they were ready to start back, changes would be made. At the least, Tiller-Parsons would be out of a job. Almost as surely, he would be taken East to stand trial for bigamy, and very possibly other crimes. His career, which had promised so much, would be finished.

You judged a race horse on its past performances, a fighter on his record. On that basis, Tiller-Parsons' reaction was completely predictable. For him it had suddenly become a matter of all or nothing. With much less involved, he had betrayed women, used men as pawns, and not boggled at murder as a weapon.

That women were again involved could hardly be expected to deter him. His record showed him to be a monster. However jauntily he wore the cloak of respectability, tailored garments instead of buckskin, such clothes did not change the man.

Even without the confirmation which Cassidy might be able to give, Montana could pretty well envision what was in the wind, like a winter storm blowing down from the arctic. Having found sign, where Cassidy had come, he'd risk a little more in the hope of finding Cassidy. There seemed little doubt that Cassidy had stumbled into trouble.

If he had carried a message to Spotted Pony, the meeting place would more than likely be in that vicinity. Under the sun of high noon, the land looked peaceful, empty. But the sign was here, the trail made by a single horseman, spoor less than a day old.

That other eyes might be watching was so likely a possibility that his skin prickled. Now it had become like reading the pages of a book. One more turn of page or trail could bring a climax.

Here a second horseman had entered the picture. His pony had been unshod, so in all possibility it was an Indian cayuse. At this point its run had been suddenly checked; it had pivoted sharply, dancing impatiently while its rider took stock, before going on.

Back-tracking, Montana found a spatter of red, splashed like raindrops across the grass. There the trail ended, but the sudden deep gorge at one side was an explanation. Horse and rider had gone off together. Cassidy had acted, or perhaps reacted. His failure to return was easy to understand.

18

The voice roused Cassidy from his stupor. It was persistent, insistent, disturbing. At first it seemed to be part of a dream which was more like a nightmare. Then, opening his eyes, he placed the sound. Montana was kneeling on the rim above, looking down, calling his name.

"Dutch!" he said urgently, as the latter stirred. "I'll lower a rope, Dutch. Get the noose over your head and under your arms, and I'll soon have you up here."

The end of a lariat plopped beside Cassidy's hand. Mechanically, Cassidy tried to obey, but the effort was too great. The last reserves of energy had been drained from him in crawling this far along the rocky shelf. His hand seemed to make a gesture of weary negation.

Montana was disappointed, but not very surprised. That a man could have gone off the trail and survived, even though caught on the ledge below, was more than he had expected. Now the impact of the fall, added to the long exposure, was taking it toll.

Had Cassidy been able to help himself, even t grasping the rope, it would have saved time an rendered his task immeasurably simpler. Since h could not, Montana considered the alternative. Ther was nothing, here at the top of the ledge, to whic he might tie an end of the lariat, anchoring it whil descending to Cassidy. The nearest object was tree, half a hundred feet farther back, hopelessl out of reach.

There was just one chance, which he disliked But it was either that, or ride away and leav Cassidy. If he did that, the injured man would b dead before he could return with help. He wa clearly at the last extremity.

Even if he could hold out, there was not tha much time to waste. The unfolding story was s clear as to be unmistakable. Like the storm, troubl was on the way. For whatever he might be wortl they would need him back at the ranch.

Montana chanced it, taking such insurance as wa possible. A well-trained horse would stand groun hitched with the bridle reins dropped. But at th brink of a canyon, and under circumstances such : faced them, that would be expecting too much, eve of a dependable animal. Never having ridden th horse before, he could not judge it. And the liv of both of them, his own as well as Cassidy's, d pended on the result.

He found a good-sized stone not far back along the trail, lugged it, then tied the reins to it. Terror, a snorting plunge, could send the cayuse hurtling back, or cause the stone to slide over the brink. Either alternative might spoil the situation past retrieving. Yet it was the best he could do.

With the rope tied to the saddle-horn, Montana slid down it, onto the ledge beside Cassidy. Cassidy lay with eyes closed, his breathing so faint that Montana was not sure if he still lived. He unscrewed his canteen, placing it at Cassidy's lips. Water dribbled into his mouth, and after a moment, Cassidy choked, then roused to drink thirstily. His eyes opened on a note of wonder.

"'Tis nectar from heaven," he breathed. "I didn't know till now that you wore wings—Montana."

"Let's get you out of this," Montana returned practically. "The sooner the better."

Somewhat revived by the water, Cassidy surveyed the rope, seeing the outline of the horse at the top of the cliff. His head shake was short but positive.

"A waste of time," he breathed. "I'm finished. And belike neither of us would make it."

"I can't leave you here."

"A dead man rests as easy one place as another. And I won't be keeping you long. Another sip of the water."

He drank again, then spoke urgently, though his voice was weakening, so that Montana had to bend close to hear.

"Tiller-Parsons sent me with a message to Spotted Pony. Then they met, and I heard what they said. The Indians plan a massacre at the height of the—"

His voice ended in a sigh. Montana's breath echoed it. The need for helping him up from here was past. As he had said, one resting place was as good as another.

The pony shied and tried to pull back as Montana ascended, but with nothing to hinder him, he retained control. Had he been carrying an inert burden and trying to climb, it might have been a ticklish business.

Cassidy's meaning was clear. Montana had heard that one of the girls had suggested a ball, but apparently the same thought had already been in Tiller-Parsons' mind. His purpose, then, was to use the dance as a diversion. It would keep everyone occupied, and by the end of a long night they would be worn out, and then the attack would come.

From the point of view of the Indian, that was merely good generalship. But that a man of another race would lend himself to such duplicity, destroy his own people, was all but unbelievable.

At least, it would have been with most men. In this case, Cassidy had heard the plot.

Montana pondered as he headed back. Foreknowledge should help, so that Dutch Cassidy's death might not be in vain. Even so, the prospects were bleak.

There were two alternatives. They could load up and set out at once, heading for the nearest settlement. Where days or weeks would be required, they would have only hours. If they were overtaken and surrounded, the chance for survival would be far less than within the shelter of the stout walls of the ranch house.

In it, they could stand off attacks for a while, since Spotted Pony would be denied the vital element of surprise. From there, they could make things more costly for the renegade band of braves.

But only for a while. Cut off from retreat, with no help possible and winter on the way, at best it would be only a matter of time.

Montana had more than once led forlorn causes, so finding himself in such a situation was nothing new. But to hit upon a plan, a scheme which offered a fighting chance for survival, was not easy. Between them, Spotted Pony and Tiller-Parsons had planned well.

The dance, or ball, was scheduled for that evening; so the attack would probably come at dawn. Ready, they could probably repel it, but that would be the beginning of a siege which they could have no hope of outlasting.

Even if a messenger could get out, there was nowhere to go for help; none that could or would be sent.

The attack was intended to come as a surprise, so if they were to have a chance, it had to be turned into a counter-surprise. Everything would hinge on that. Otherwise, the odds against them would lengthen with each hour, and the end would be as inevitable as it would be hopeless.

The alternative would hardly bear thinking about. Death in battle was one thing, and bad enough at best. But an Indian massacre was another matter entirely. With Spotted Pony cherishing an implacable hatred, his warriors would be ruthless. Survival, for any who escaped the initial assault, would be even worse.

He rode mechanically, leaving it to his horse to pick its own trail. Its sudden floundering plunge caught him by surprise. It was instinct, a natural reaction of muscles as well as mind, which enabled him to jump clear as the cayuse went down.

The pony was struggling to its feet again almost as quickly, eyes rolling in pain and terror. Montana needed only a glance to see what had happened, the cause as well as the effect. A front hoof had broken through and into a gopher hole, catching the limb, throwing the horse heavily. One look at the hanging leg, as the pony favored it, standing on three limbs, confirmed the bad news. The leg was broken.

There was nothing to do but to put the horse out of its misery, then plod on foot for the remaining distance. An already bad situation was compounded. For a while he was apprehensive that the gunshot might have been heard and would be investigated, but nothing happened. Even so, the delay was bad.

Darkness was falling when he came in sight of the ranch buildings. Tonight there would be a heavy darkness, for the long-threatening storm was beginning to move in, and clouds were obscuring the stars. But that was perhaps a small break in their favor.

Indians were as complex in nature as white men, a prey to superstitions and fears in about equal degrees; it was mostly in type or character that their apprehensions differed. They liked to prowl by night, though at times they feared the dark, particularly in those hours just short of dawn. Having experienced those same hours many times, when sleep and the low bodily ebb slowed and confused the senses, Montana had no difficulty understanding such inhibitions.

Had the moon been riding high, they might have come loping in for an early attack, ranging like wolves. But in heavy, cloud-hung blackness, they would prefer to await the dawn, to strike as sleep followed exhaustion. It was a brief reprieve.

Lights were springing up all through the house, some with colored shades, the result of the decorators' ingenuity, lending a fairyland effect when viewed from a distance. Near the barn he made out extra wagons and buggies, showing that the invited guests from other ranches had arrived.

In the long run, with the raiders sweeping the country like a scythe, it might make little difference; but to receive special invitations to come to their deaths was as chilling as it was grim. It was a yard-stick of the man who spun his web as a spider does.

An air of excitement, tinged with gaiety, could almost be felt. They were making a special effort to put all unpleasantness into the background, at least for the night. This party was in the nature of a house-warming, and they were determined to behave like civilized beings. With the exception of Tim O'Donnell, none suspected that peril might threaten.

As a tough ex-sergeant, O'Donnell would remain tight-lipped for as long as he dared. No one knew better the devastating effects of panic, so he would do his worrying in silence.

A shadowy figure was advancing to meet him. O'Donnell had been watching, his anxiety mounting as time dragged. Relief and apprehension mingled in his voice.

"Ah, Captain, it's happy I am to see you! I was beginning—" He broke off, suddenly realizing that Montana was on foot. "You've had difficulties?"

"Some. My horse put his foot in a gopher hole.

I've had to walk."

O'Donnell expelled his breath in relief that it had been no worse. But Montana was alone.

"Cassidy—?"

"I found him dying. It seems he dueled with Spotted Pony last night. He intended to stop the Indian, but it worked the other way. He was able to tell me what had happened—and what they plan."

O'Donnell had heard enough already to guess at the rest. The manner in which verbs and pronouns were linked was starkly revealing.

"I take it that Spotted Pony thinks his hour has come?"

"His plan is to wipe us out—probably at daylight."

"I had thought it was the storm I felt in my bones. The unholy devils!"

Knowing his meaning, Montana nodded. "Tiller-Parsons made the arrangements with Spotted Pony. Where is he?"

"Inside." O'Donnell's voice took on a quality of eagerness. "Let's go find him!"

19

The transformation had a quality of magic. The warmth of human companionship, the ingenuity of the workers, all combined against the background of loneliness to bring a lump to the throat, a mist before even the eyes of Henry Tiller-Parsons. Looking about, he knew a moment of doubt, a sense of regret. This was the sort of thing he had aimed for from the beginning, the kind of company he had hoped to attain. Ivòry shoulders flashed above evening gowns, and laughter rippled like music.

His imagination was too active for his own enjoyment. He could think only of a flower garden in bloom, a field at harvest time—and the sudden total devastation of hail striking without warning, of red death at dawn—

It was worse than foolish to feel regret, particularly since the matter was now beyond his control. He had taken the realistic course, the only way possible. But it really was too bad.

A door opened, and he swung, starting at sight of Montana. O'Donnell was a step behind as they halted, gazing around. They were looking for somebody, and instinct assured Tiller-Parsons that he was the man. He had taken note of Abbott's absence, and as it grew prolonged, had decided that Montana would not be returning. He had ridden to look for Cassidy, and he had probably encountered some of Spotted Pony's band.

Panic replaced his sense of mild regret. Whatever Montana wanted, it would not be to his liking. There was no telling what Montana might have discovered, or at least been led to suspect.

Crowded as the big room was, they had not yet located him. Tiller-Parsons slipped quickly through a door into an adjoining room, then on out into the night.

Looking back, he drew a long breath. He had not been seen, but it would be better to keep out of sight for a while. In any case, he needed the fresh air to clear his head—

A scream rose in his throat, choked short of utterance, as a shadowy figure leaped, knocking him backward. An elbow crooked about his neck as he sprawled; then bony knees were upon his chest, and a painted, savage face was leering above. A heavy, greasy stench, compounded of all those things which he found most distasteful, was in Tiller-Parsons' nostrils. Clutching fingers loosened from his throat to tangle in his hair. A long blade was lifted, poised. . . .

"He was here," O'Donnell said worriedly. "But he must have seen you first!"

"It doesn't really matter," Montana decided. "Our first job is to alert everybody to the danger, to be as ready as we can for the attack when it comes."

Since he had not been bothered on his way back, he doubted if Spotted Pony's warriors would be along, at least in force, until later in the night. But they might already be on the watch. A break in the tempo of the party might warn them and bring a speedy assault, before they could ready themselves for it.

"We'll mingle with the others and pass the word— one person at a time," Montana decided. "Make sure that everybody keeps on as though nothing were happening."

Montana noted with satisfaction but no particular surprise that the news was taken in stride. Cheeks paled, feet faltered in the dance, then regained their tempo. There was no panic, not even unnecessary questions. Montana gave his news first to Sir John and Mr. Gates.

"Please don't let on, gentlemen, but I have some unpleasant news," he said. "I believe you've heard of Chief Spotted Pony and his band—some renegade braves who have long been trouble-makers. They are getting ready to attack us. They may strike during the night, but probably will hit at about daylight. Should our actions betray to them that we suspect an attack, that might hurry them before we could ready a defense. Yet we must be prepared to defend ourselves at any moment."

Gates' calm did not desert him. Sir John looked thoughtfully at his half-emptied glass.

"I've rather had the feeling that something was amiss," he acknowledeged. "Cave-man instinct, perhaps. You're taking charge?"

"Unless you have other preferences," Montana agreed. "It's a nasty situation, but not hopeless."

"As bad as that, eh? Well, carry on. We're with you."

O'Donnell explained to Rose. Her eyes grew large as she listened, but she confirmed the opinion he had already formed. In the face of trouble, she would be as steady as any man.

"It's going to be bad, isn't it?" she asked.

O'Donnell was grimly honest.

"Without Montana to handle things, it would be. But he has a reputation for doing the impossible. Tell the other women—but don't let on that anything is amiss. I'll be passing out guns."

Rose seemed to take reassurance from what she saw in his face.

"Of course. And I have confidence in you as well. So, Timothy—should the worst happen—"

O'Donnell's eyes betrayed his anguish, but his nod was casual.

"In such an eventuality, I will save a couple of bullets," he promised. "Be sure of that, girl."

The house was a strange contradiction, in some aspects approaching a mansion, in others as primitive as its surroundings. The walls were mostly of logs, solid enough to stop bullets or turn arrows, but the doors were flimsy, and there were no loopholes for rifles, which would have seemed an obvious precaution. Many of the windows were covered with oiled deerhide, scraped thin, the frontier's substitute for glass. These had no shutters.

A few of the windows were glass, and with the interior brilliantly lighted, their movements could be watched from the outer darkness; since a sudden volley could take them by surprise, they covered those windows on the inside with blankets. But at best it would be a flimsy shelter in which to withstand attack.

Something with which to counter the attack, in addition to guns, was imperative. But a more thorough ransacking of the supplies was discouraging. Montana had hoped that an ample supply of powder might have been included with the most recent arrival, but there was none. Whether this oversight was deliberate or due merely to carelessness on the part of Tiller-Parsons, the effect was the same.

A considerable excess of small hardware, nails, nuts and bolts, remained from the carpenters' supplies. These, mixed in buckets of powder, could be used to make bombs which, exploded by gunfire, would be devastating in their effect. A score, or only a dozen, buried at ground level and strategically scattered outside, might reverse the odds when the warriors came crowding.

That was what Montana had hoped for. Instead, finding barely enough powder for a single bomb, he eyed it in dismay. Incongruously enough, there was a handful of caps to insure an explosion when a bullet struck, but so heavy and clumsy a bucketful could hardly be tossed out with much chance of proving effective. Concealed in advance, the odds of it being in the right place at the right time were a hundred to one.

Should it prove a dud, their enemies would only be further enraged that nothing remained to use against them.

Coming to stand beside Montana, O'Donnell shook his head. As a former sergeant, he understood what Montana had intended and how paltry a single bomb could be. From an adjoining room, the wail of a fiddle and the scrape of boots lent a further note of mockery.

"I'd had the same notion, Cap'n," he observed dejectedly. "This could be a help—used when and where needed. But once they start, they'll do the picking, not us."

"Maybe," Montana conceded. "On the other hand—" he was thinking aloud—"Spotted Pony was educated in the white man's ways. He hates them, but still they influence him. There just might be a chance—"

He picked up the laden bucket, then a shovel in his other hand.

"The fix we're in, we make the most of any sort of a chance. Pull that long face into something a little less discouraged and go dance with the ladies— all of them. I've a trap to set."

He slipped out into the night, quickly moving away from the door. For a long moment he stood as patiently as a cat, ears and eyes strained, testing the dark. Nothing moved, and the only sounds came from inside the house.

Choosing a spot at some distance, he dug, easing the shovel in and out of the soil as though the bomb were already in place and might be set off at a touch. The night held an eerie quality. The clash of steel against a stone might bring an attack.

When a small pit was excavated, he lowered the pail into it, then replaced the dirt around it, so that the ground remained level. A torn piece of sacking, thrown carelessly, concealed the operation.

The essence of setting a trap was either to hide it completely, or to leave sign so obvious that it would not be associated with a trap.

Candlelight and soft music contrasted strangely with rifles and revolvers, placed handily, the barrels reflecting back the light. Every man, including the English, wore a cartridge belt and holstered revolver, and was accordingly hampered in the more intricate movements of the dance. Beyond these preparations, they made a courageous pretense that there was nothing unusual about the night.

One of the visiting ranchers had suggested the possibility of posting men in the barn and other outbuildings, but Montana had vetoed that. Their forces were too small to be scattered, then cut off. It had to be the house or nothing.

Whether the enemy were already outside, or in those buildings, they could only speculate. Montana's guess was that, aside from a few scouts who would keep watch, Spotted Pony would hold his warriors well back until the time for attack. In any event, they gave no sign.

Neither did his own party, who gallantly maintained the pretense of enjoying themselves. If cheeks appeared paler under the candlelight, voices remained steady, the glances from feminine eyes challenging as well as sparkling. There was nothing to do but wait out the night. The initiative rested with Spotted Pony.

Tiller-Parsons had not returned. His continued absence went unremarked but not unnoticed.

That the enemy was almost certainly close at

hand, yet waiting out the night, stretched nerves almost to the breaking point. But Spotted Pony, in addition to following custom, knew the value of patience. If their victims had been forewarned and were expecting an attack, the strain was in his favor. Should the attack come as the surprise which it was intended to be, weariness and a general let-down would follow so long a night. Dawn would be the hour.

Even the pretense ran heavily as a faint grayness became visible at the edges of the blankets. Montana gave them credit; a disciplined regiment could have done no better. Bravery was not a lack of fear; it was holding steady when apprehension choked like dust in the mouth, poured with the heaviness of lead in the veins.

Daylight was slow in coming, held back by a heavy pall of cloud. To anyone inclined to give way to superstition, the omens were unchancy. But that could apply equally well to the other side.

Attack came, predictably, with a sudden wild screeching, punctuated by the blasting of guns, of arrows making sudden tears in the taut deerskins. A pane of glass shattered. But everyone was prompt to take a pre-assigned position, making use of the scanty light to pick targets and return a devastating fire.

A war axe slit the hide at a window, warriors piling through. Their own eager rush choked them, and axes at direct range, in addition to guns, cleared the space as suddenly. The surging wave of men hesitated, broke and drew back. One of the visiting ranchers was jubilant.

"They got more'n they bargained for," he observed. "And it'll be raining pretty soon, a real storm from the look of things. That's all to the good, for us."

Montana did not delude himself. They could probably hold, but a siege would go against them. If they were to survive, this must be decided quickly. By now, it was almost light enough to make his move.

A second wave of warriors swept at them, but by now the light was against them. The interior of the house would soon become a shambles, but its walls afforded good shelter from which to pick and choose when firing. Even frenzied enthusiasm could not stand so raking a fire, while there were no targets in return.

Again they pulled back. This would be his chance, if there was any hope. Opening a door a crack, Montana thrust a white flag ahead.

The neighboring rancher scowled. "What's the idea?" he demanded. "You ain't aimin' to surrender?"

"Just to parley, if they will," Montana explained. "Spotted Pony knows the meaning of such a signal. Let's hope he'll respond."

Among the milling warriors, there was hesitation. Then, in a gesture which emphasized his contempt,

Spotted Pony stepped into the open. It was a gesture of courage if not of trust.

Montana opened the door wide in turn. "Are you willing to parley, Spotted Pony?"

The chief shrugged. "*We* have nothing to lose," he said.

20

Even the scream in Tiller-Parsons' throat seemed, like the hand on his neck, to be strangling him. Above him, shadowy but savage, a merciless face wavered, the eyes glaring like those of a cat. Tiller-Parsons could do no more then thresh wildly with feet and legs.

Then a voice grunted sharply, a powerful hand plucked his antagonist from him, and the chief was looking from one to the other with his usual mixture of disgusted contempt. Tiller-Parsons swallowed painfully, sucking in a gasping breath.

"Thanks, Chief," he stammered. "I was coming to find you. Your man made a mistake."

Spotted Pony did not deign to ask what he wanted or what sort of a message he might bring. Tonight, he was the unbendingly hostile savage who had seized him several days before, on the way to the ranch. That time, Tiller-Parsons had been able to talk him out of it, but on that occasion he had had something to offer. Now Spotted Pony was in control, and he enjoyed showing his contempt.

"No mistake," he grunted. "You fool—all white men fools." He gave an order in his own tongue, the words unintelligible to Tiller-Parsons. Obeying, ignoring the white man's struggles and protests, the warrior who had been on the point of scalping him, assisted by another brave, hustled him to a small, remote shed. The full measure of their disregard was that they did not try to stop him from screaming or calling out, but he remained silent from very hopelessness.

The closing door was the beginning of a long night. The shed was windowless, the darkness almost total. Two truths became apparent to Tiller-Parsons as the hours wore on and he was left alone. The first was the implacable nature of the man he had thought to use, the unrelenting hatred of Spotted Pony for all whites. And his own conduct, he realized belatedly, had only served to reinforce the contempt and rage.

He was being left alive, at least for a while, but despite the blackness he saw clearly for the first time. Holding him so was only another measure of the Indian's contempt, an additional expression of hate. Knowing what was to come at daylight, they were hours of torment. Tiller-Parsons had no slightest doubt that he was slated to die with the rest.

Exhaustion overcame him, and he slept fitfully. When he finally roused and fumbled uncertainly at the door, he was bewildered to find that it had not been locked.

Perhaps it was his training among the whites. Spotted Pony stood an instant, his stare baleful. Then them their ability. He did not doubt the threat. Whatever might be said of this particular white man, even his enemies admitted that he did not speak with a forked tongue.

He had consented to parley because of his certainty that he was in complete control of the situation. Now he hesitated. Triumph was like dust on his tongue. To back down, even to save his life, was unthinkable. He was Spotted Pony, and not as other men.

For Spotted Pony was a renegade, even in the eyes of most of his tribe. He had disdained the council fires, riding wide, leading his lawless group, boasting of his hate and what he was going to do.

Better now to die than to back down, to live a legend than to die at long last in shame. And yet—

Uncertainty gnawed, like a rat at a wheat stalk. His shamed glance strayed; then his eyes widened at sight of the man who was advancing, moving like a sleepwalker. Fury surged up from Spotted Pony's throat, stinging like heartburn. Even Tiller-Parsons was in on this, having lured him to a trap—

Wild fury erupted from his throat in a gobbling shriek. He drove his pony at Abbott, snatching for his tomahawk as the cayuse jumped.

He was calling the bluff, but Montana had not been bluffing. As the gun muzzle swung, the chamber was emptying in a roaring fusillade, lost and swallowed in the overwhelming thunder of the blast.

21

To lift first one arm and then the other, coming upright as slowly and awkwardly as a half-frozen cow, was mechanical, an instinctive reaction. The blast itself had subsided, but its roaring still pounded in his head. Montana looked about dazedly, his mind as fuzzy as the flakes of snow which were drifting from the leaden sky.

He was torn and bloody, but alive. The latter was the astonishing part, for he'd had no expectation of surviving at such close range to the blast. Then he understood that the confusion was not all in his mind. There was moaning and yelping, on a sub-dued and frantic note, with scant resemblance to the gobble of the war whoop. Then came the di-minishing pounding of hoofs.

The buildings were intact, but a gaping crater yawned where he had sunk the bucket of powder. Dirt and debris filled the open spaces, even the nearer roofs.

Further movement disclosed no broken bones, despite burns and bruises. The blood was on the outside, and not his own.

Tim O'Donnell was the first to reach him, though others were close behind. The ex-sergeant set an arm about Montana's shoulders as he staggered.

"Glory be, you're alive!" he breathed. "Which I'd never have bet good money on!"

"I guess I am," Montana admitted, but his mind still boggled at the results.

"The chief was right on top of that charge of powder when it went off," O'Donnell said soberly. "He was trying to come at you, though it seemed to be the sight of Tiller-Parsons that set him crazy. His horse took the full force of the blast, and sort of smothered or contained it, I guess. On that account, it didn't do nearly the damage that it might have. It killed a couple of the Indians, along with Tiller-Parsons, and scared the daylights out of the rest of them. I reckon they'll run till their horses drop."

Montana was beginning to understand. The result had been freakish, but even better than he had hoped. Though neither Tiller-Parsons nor Spotted Pony had intended it that way, they had played decisive roles.

O'Donnell summed it up sardonically.

"To give credit where it's due, I guess we could say that pair went out in a blaze of glory!"

The storm had dumped a couple of feet of snow, but it had been no blizzard. The white blanket had covered all signs of strife, as though in promise of a new era.

"Sure and I'm as lucky a man as you," O'Donnell confided jubilantly to Montana. "You are alive and in good shape, and I have won a woman like Rose! She's agreed to marry me—and this time it will *be* a marriage! Seems she likes this country, which is sort of surprising, everything considered."

"She found you here, didn't she?" Montana countered. "That works both ways, you know. I'd say you both deserve it."

Horatio Gates came up as O'Donnell moved away. He had been checking the books and papers left behind by Tiller-Parsons.

"It's rather too bad that the old boy got off on the wrong trail, then rode it so hard," he observed. "He had an amazing amount of talent. What he accomplished here is outstanding. Well, at least his luck didn't all desert him at the last. Considering all the circumstances, I can't think of a better ending to his problems."

"Will you all be staying for a big game hunt?" Montana asked.

"I think not. We were hoping for a bit of adventure, and that has been provided. They are all agreed that we'd best be heading back before the snows get too deep. I'm sure we'll all remember our stay here."

His tone became brisk.

"Another excellent choice on Tiller-Parsons' part—perhaps better than he intended—was to hire you, Montana. But you're not the sort who requires two or three men to do a job. So, in addition to being ranch foreman, I'm hoping that you will act as our manager over here as well. We're all agreed that you've done an excellent job."

Montana had foreseen the offer and had toyed with the idea of accepting it. But now—

"I appreciate your good opinion," he said. "But I guess I'm what is called fiddle-footed."

"You mean you will be moving on?"

Abbott nodded, watching where O'Donnell and Rose were laughing together. She would walk proudly beside her man under any circumstances, but a gentlewoman of her quality deserved something more than a sod hut or a homestead shack. This big house would be a fitting setting—

"Well, we're too deeply in your debt to try to persuade you against your will." Gates sighed. "But your decision leaves me with a problem. Men with the ability to manage an outfit such as this are not easy to come by. As one of the cowboys remarked, they don't exactly clutter up the landscape."

"But luck is where you find it," Montana suggested. "Why not offer the job to O'Donnell? Since he's to be married, he'll have need of a good job.

And from what I have seen of him, I'm sure he'll handle it competently."

"An excellent suggestion." Horatio Gates was too much of a gentleman to betray his sudden insight into Montana's motives. But all at once he was forced to blow his nose with unnecessary loudness.

DOUBLE-BARREL WESTERNS
Twice the Action—
Twice the Adventure—
Only a Fraction of the Price!

Two Complete and unabridged novels in each book!

The Sure-Fire Kid and **Wildcats of Tonto Basin**
by Nelson Nye.

_____2474-8 $3.95 US/$4.95 CAN

Gunslick Mountain and **Born to Trouble**
by Nelson Nye.

_____2497-7 $3.95 US/$4.95 CAN

The Bushwackers and **Ride the Wild Country**
by Lee Floren.

_____2610-4 $3.95 US/$4.95 CAN

The hard-riding, hard-bitten Adult Western series that's hotter'n a blazing pistol and as tough as the men who tamed the frontier.

The hard-riding, hard-bitten Adult Western series that's hotter'n a blazing pistol and as tough as the men who tamed the frontier.

#26: LARAMIE SHOWDOWN by Kit Dalton
——2806-9
$2.95

#25: POWDER CHARGE by Kit Dalton
——2754-2
$2.95

#24: COLT CROSSING by Kit Dalton
——2728-3
$2.95US/$3.95CAN

#23: CALIFORNIA CROSSFIRE by Kit Dalton
——2674-0
$2.95US/$3.95CAN

#22: SILVER CITY CARBINE by Kit Dalton
——2649-X
$2.95US/$3.95CAN

#21: PEACEMAKER PASS by Kit Dalton
——2619-8
$2.95US/$3.95CAN

#20: PISTOL GRIP by Kit Dalton
——2551-5
$2.95US/$3.95CAN

#19: SHOTGUN STATION by Kit Dalton
——2529-9
$2.95US/$3.95CAN

LEISURE BOOKS
ATTN: Customer Service Dept.
276 5th Avenue, New York, NY 10001

Please send me the book(s) checked above. I have enclosed $ _____
Add $1.25 for shipping and handling for the first book; $ .30 for each book thereafter. No cash, stamps, or C.O.D.s. All orders shipped within 6 weeks. Canadian orders please add $1.00 extra postage.

Name _____

Address _____

City _____ State _____ Zip _____
Canadian orders must be paid in U.S. dollars payable through a New York banking facility. ☐ Please send a free catalogue.